THE
BOOK
ARTIST

ALSO BY MARK PRYOR

The Bookseller
The Crypt Thief
The Blood Promise
The Button Man
The Reluctant Matador
The Paris Librarian
The Sorbonne Affair

Hollow Man
Dominic

A Hugo Marston Novel

THE
BOOK
ARTIST

MARK PRYOR

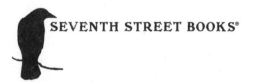
SEVENTH STREET BOOKS®

Published 2019 by Seventh Street Books®

Cover photo © Alamy Stock Photo
Cover design by Nicole Sommer-Lecht
Cover design © Start Science Fiction
Map by James W. Ziskin

This is a work of fiction. Characters, organizations, products, locales, and events portrayed in this novel are either products of the author's imagination or used fictitiously.

Trademarked names appear throughout this book. Start Science Fiction recognizes all registered trademarks, trademarks, and service marks mentioned in the text.

Inquiries should be addressed to
Start Science Fiction
101 Hudson Street, 37th Floor, Suite 3705
Jersey City, New Jersey 07302
PHONE: 212-620-5700
WWW.SEVENTHSTREETBOOKS.COM

23 22 21 20 19   5 4 3 2 1

Library of Congress Cataloging-in-Publication Data

Names: Pryor, Mark, 1967- author.
Title: The book artist : a Hugo Marston novel / Mark Pryor.
Description: Amherst, NY : Seventh Street Books, an imprint of Prometheus Books, 2019. | Identifiers: LCCN 2018037151 (print) | LCCN 2018039219 (ebook) | ISBN 9781633884892 (ebook) | ISBN 9781633884885 (paperback)
Subjects: | BISAC: FICTION / Suspense. | GSAFD: Mystery fiction. | Suspense fiction.
Classification: LCC PS3616.R976 (ebook) | LCC PS3616.R976 B65 2019 (print) | DDC 813/.6—dc23
LC record available at https://lccn.loc.gov/2018037151

Printed in the United States of America

To the booksellers and librarians
who spend their days providing us with mystery and intrigue,
with love and loathing, with delight, horror, hilarity, and learning.
For all you do, for readers and writers, thank you.

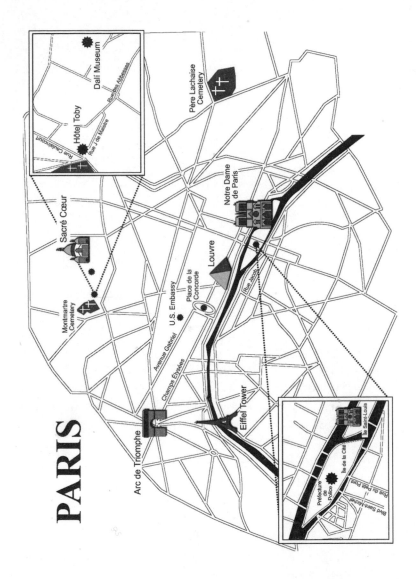

CHAPTER ONE

Hugo Marston held the door open for the young woman as she came into the foyer of the apartment building, bundled up as she was against the rain and cold. A shopping bag dangled from one of her wrists, and she held a small, white dog in the crook of her other arm.

"*Bonsoir*, Mademoiselle Errico," he said, standing aside so she could get out of the cold and all the way into the lobby of their apartment building.

"Oh, Monsieur Marston," she blushed. "And good evening to you, too."

Hugo gave her a smile and ducked out onto Rue Jacob. He was normally the friendly sort, especially with people in his building, but Miss Errico was new there and had delayed Hugo with her chatter on too many occasions for him to misread the signals. As pretty as she was, chatty, dog-carrying twenty-five-year-olds were not on his radar.

He pulled his coat around him as the chill seeped in, and his fedora kept the light rain out of his eyes as he made his way toward the River Seine. His path was illuminated by the glow from the store fronts, and occasional streetlamps overhead.

Perfect weather for reading by the fire, he thought, as he turned onto Rue des Saints-Pères.

No chance. Tonight was the US Embassy's Christmas party, and senior staff were required to be on hand no matter what. Hugo had asked if the flu might exempt him from attending, and he'd been told by a frowning Ambassador J. Bradford Taylor, "Death *might* exempt you. Absolutely nothing short of that."

Truthfully, it was one of those events that Hugo loved to hate. For a people-watcher like him, a former FBI profiler no less, it was like a biologist watching a herd's annual migration or, in quite a few instances, a yearly and elaborate mating ritual.

At such events, Hugo played a game with himself, guessing who was who by how they behaved. Some were employees of the embassy; those he didn't know personally, he identified by the way they sipped carefully at their drinks so as not to imbibe too much, by how attentive they were to their spouses, and how jovial they were with their colleagues. But mostly he recognized them by the way they kept one eye on outside guests. Hugo saw it in their expressions and knew that the diplomatic DNA in their blood mandated it.

At least Claudia would be there. Journalist, French nobility, beautiful, funny, and sexy. Also harder to pin down than a black belt in judo, at least when it came to dating. It was as if she were from another generation, one so much younger, where relationships were flexible and uncategorized. He was hoping to talk to her tonight in a quiet corner, to try and gauge a little bit better where they stood. He'd told her so over the phone that morning, and she'd laughed her gentle, sexy laugh, that was made all the more husky by the cold she was fighting.

"Oh, Hugo, I love the old-fashioned man that lives inside you."

"It's not old-fashioned," he'd protested. "I just want to know where I stand."

"Six foot two and dashingly handsome," she purred back. "And I can't wait to see the most gorgeous man in my life tonight."

That was something at least, quite a compliment from a woman who'd been designated as one of Paris's most eligible women for several years running.

Hugo turned onto Quai Voltaire, where the wind was oddly calmer but the cold more biting, and he pictured his loyal colleagues looking out at the guests who enjoyed the party the most—the expat business community, which was always well-represented and never afraid to cut a little loose. That was one of the reasons Hugo was there. He was head of security and carried a gun everywhere he went, but sometimes his role was more hands-on, literally, like steering the grabby CEO away from the young diplomat's wife, or leading the inebriated heiress to a comfy couch.

He started across Pont du Carrousel but stopped halfway to look down at the waters of the Seine. She was his reason to pause in the middle of any walk, and no matter how many times he gazed at her, she came with a sense of uncertainty because the River Seine always changed. She ran through the heart of Paris, a looping, swirling artery that pulsed into and out of the city day and night, moody and unpredictable.

Tonight she seemed angry, or maybe just impatient. Her waters were brown and churned between the concrete banks, small but furious swells chasing each other down, smothering those in front, hunting farther, dragging down braches and other debris and sweeping them under the bridge, out of view beneath his feet.

Hugo straightened as his phone rang.

"Hello? Tom? Where are you?" he asked.

Tom Green. Former CIA spook, ex-FBI, current womanizer, sometime-drunk, foul-mouthed, but always, *always* disrespectful of authority. Also, Hugo's best friend for the past couple of decades.

"Amsterdam. This place is fucking nuts; you should come out here."

"Again? Why are you in Amsterdam, Tom?"

"You know why."

"I thought we decided that was a false lead."

"No, *you* decided it was a false lead. I decided it might not be."

"So you went without me? Without even telling me?" Hugo was frustrated—partly with himself. Did he really expect Tom to be keeping him informed? *Yes, I do, that much at least*, he thought.

"Sure looks that way, doesn't it?"

"Not smart, my friend."

"I was on my way back from a job," Tom said, explaining not apologizing. "I got a tip from a source, and it made sense to check it out while I was here."

"Like last time. When he wasn't there and you wasted a week."

"I have all the time in the world for that asshole. Plus, like I said, Amsterdam is awesome—I'll come here five times a year if I have to."

"Weren't you in Senegal?"

"Yep." Tom had been gone almost a month, his room in Hugo's apartment empty, and the fridge delightfully full. "But I flew back through Schiphol."

"Uh-huh, right. Because there are no flights from Senegal to Paris."

"Hugo, enough with the nagging. Do you want a progress report or not?"

"I suppose I do."

"He's here."

"He's there." Hugo took a deep breath. "Are you sure, Tom? Have you seen him with your own eyes?"

"Yes and no."

"Then what makes you so sure?" Hugo pressed.

"I went to the hotel where he's staying, and checked it out. Thoroughly."

"Yes, but did you—hang on." Hugo checked his phone's screen to see his boss's name flash up. "Tom, I'm sorry, but I need to go. Can I call you right back?"

"Hugo, this is important. Where the fuck do you have to go while I'm tell—"

"Thanks, I appreciate the understanding." Hugo hung up and clicked over to the man demanding his attention. "Ambassador, good evening."

"Are you avoiding my party?" Ambassador Taylor asked.

"Boss, you have to be kidding," Hugo said. "You know how I love these social events—all that small talk and trying to remember who's who. I wouldn't miss that for the world."

"Right, sure, that's exactly what I thought."

Quite apart from socializing being one of his main roles as US ambassador to France, that sort of thing came naturally to J. Bradford Taylor. The man was as ordinary-looking as anyone you could meet, but he was a true extrovert, and with a steel trap for a memory. Hugo had seen him dredge up the name of someone he'd met just once, two years previously. This was possibly a function of Taylor's previous life with the CIA's clandestine operations, but also a natural gift.

Hugo chuckled. "Never fear; I'll be there. I'm just running a few minutes late. Oh, and then Tom phoned me to slow me down."

"That's one of the reasons I'm calling, actually."

"Tom Green?"

"Yes. But first things first. Can you head to Montmartre and pick up a guest?"

"They have taxis up there, I think."

"Funny. She's a special guest, and she needs a chaperone."

"Let me guess." Hugo groaned. "Politician who can't figure out how to use the metro. Let me send Ryan." Ryan Pierce was Hugo's second-in-command, as reliable as he was brilliant. And he actually liked Montmartre. Every time Hugo had been there, all three times, the narrow, winding streets of old arrondissement had been packed to a standstill with tourists.

"I tried him first. He's sick."

"He didn't tell me that."

"He didn't tell me, either, but I took one look at him and sent him home. Diligence and hard work is commendable, right up until you risk giving me the flu."

"Well, I was walking over to the embassy, but text me the address and I'll take a cab up there."

"Thanks. . . . So, about Tom."

"Right," Hugo said. "What's up?"

"You and I have had a don't-ask-don't-tell policy on our previous lives. At least as far as the details."

"A sound policy. You worked at the CIA; I was at the FBI." Hugo scanned the traffic for a vacant taxi but saw none. He started across the bridge toward the Right Bank. "But if you want some war stories, buy me a drink and I'll tell you a few."

"You know what I'm getting at."

"I'm not sure that I do."

The ambassador cleared his throat. "Would you like to explain what Tom is doing in Amsterdam?"

"Drugs and hookers would be my guess."

"We have those here."

"Yeah, but that place is famous for them. And you know Tom—he likes variety."

"Hugo, he tore up some guy's hotel room."

"Oh, he did?" Hugo said, surprised.

"He did," the ambassador said.

"I just got off the phone with him, and he mentioned . . . finding someone and checking out his room. He didn't describe it the way you did, though."

"Well, he wouldn't, would he?" Taylor said, sounding frustrated.

"How did you hear about this?" Hugo asked.

"Let's just say that when a former CIA operative goes off the reservation, other former CIA operatives are usually the first to find out."

"Then there's probably little I can tell you that you don't already know."

"I know what's in the file. And we both know those things contain what their authors want them to contain."

Hugo paused for a moment. "You know, boss, there's a reason we have this don't-ask-don't-tell policy. It's good for both of us."

"It is until I start getting dragged into your mess," Taylor said. Then his voice softened. "Look, I'm not just your boss; I'm also your friend. Just tell me what I need to know to help you, to help Tom. I don't want something exploding in my backyard and have no idea what it is or what I'm supposed to do. No judgment, I promise, I just want to be able to help if that time comes."

Hugo spotted a break in the traffic, and he trotted across the street. A breath of chilly wind wrapped itself around his throat, then slipped off and away like an icy scarf.

"OK," he said. "We could probably use a little help with this one. Let me find a taxi and I'll get back to you."

CHAPTER TWO

Hugo climbed into the back of a Mercedes taxi and read out the address that Ambassador Taylor had texted him. He buckled up and dialed the one person who was more important to him at that moment than the ambassador.

"Claudia, it's me."

"I know. I actually have you as a contact in my phone."

"Right." He smiled. "So, I'm going to be late tonight. I wanted to let you know."

"But I'm almost there," she protested.

"You'll see plenty of people you know. . . . Just load up on champagne, and I'll be there as soon as possible."

"What's the holdup? Your hair? Makeup?"

"Both. Plus the ambassador wants me to go to Montmartre to pick up a special guest."

"A special guest with no legs?"

"I know, it seems a little unnecessary. But I gather she doesn't know her way around Paris."

"Taxi drivers do," she suggested mildly. "Does Taylor have the hots for her or something? He can be very protective when he falls for a woman." That laugh again. "Like someone else I know."

"I'll take that as a compliment. And you may be right, but I have no idea."

"Well, hurry back. I'm getting sick and halved my run today so I could be on your arm."

"Oh, right. How's the marathon training going?" This was some-

13

thing new for her, but she'd embraced it with total enthusiasm, and Hugo admired her for it.

"I like the gym work better than the running, but it's growing on me."

"Good. Well, find Taylor and hide out until I get there. But don't give him the flu."

She blew a kiss at him down the phone and hung up. He looked out of the window for a moment, at Paris passing him by. He loved this time of year, when the flow of tourists was reduced to a trickle, and the shops and restaurants sparkled with Christmas lights. With a start, he remembered his boss, his promise to call him right back, and dialed his cell. Taylor answered quickly.

"Hey, Hugo. Thanks for calling back just as three American CEOs show up drunk. They're drooling over Emma."

"Do you need to launch a rescue mission? We can talk about this another time."

"Rescue Emma?" The surprise in his voice was real.

"Good heavens, no." Hugo laughed. Emma had been his secretary for as long as he'd been at the embassy and, with the possible exception of Claudia, a stronger and more capable woman Hugo had never met. "I meant rescue those poor bastards."

"They deserve what they get," Taylor said. "But just in case, give me the short version."

"My pleasure." Hugo took a deep breath and started his story. "So, back when Tom and I were still with the bureau there were a string of bank robberies in Houston. Things were quiet in the BAU, and someone figured a profiler could help find the guys responsible. I didn't mind, since Tom was assigned to the Houston office and, if we were successful, I was close enough to swing through Austin and see my folks."

"An innocuous start to an impending disaster?" Taylor said.

"Yep. And I'll cut to the chase. Literally. I figured out which bank they were likely to hit next, and Tom and I staked it out. Sure enough, they hit it right on schedule."

"Nice work."

"You'd think," Hugo said. "Except this time, and for the first time, they shot people. I didn't see that coming."

"People were killed?"

"Not just people," Hugo said, his heart heavy with the memory. "The bank was in the neighborhood where Tom lived. Where he lived with his sister."

There was a brief silence. "Shit, one of the people killed . . ."

"Was Tom's sister." Hugo could picture it like it was yesterday. Her bright-yellow dress stained with blood, and the devastation written on Tom's face as he knelt beside her fallen figure, rage and anger soon overpowering his shock.

Silence sat between them for a moment. Then Taylor asked, "So what happened?"

"We chased them. Followed them to an abandoned house a few miles away. They had no idea we were on their tail. I posted up out front and Tom went round the back. I radioed for backup, for a SWAT team to come get them."

"Protocol."

"Right, protocol. Not something Tom was ever a fan of."

"Even back then?"

"Especially back then."

"So I'm guessing he didn't want to wait."

"One of them tried to get away, came out the back and saw Tom. Drew on him. Tom shot him dead."

"Hugo, it's me. Be honest. Is that the real story or the official one?"

"Ah, your BS detector going off, is it?"

"Loud and clear."

Hugo couldn't help but smile. Taylor's no-nonsense attitude had always been a breath of fresh air in the diplomatic world, where hedging and half-truths were the norm. Hugo himself was prone to inopportune outbursts of truth-telling, so he appreciated his boss's insistence on it now.

"Fine," Hugo said. "Since you insist. I was waiting in front of the house, like I said. I heard a gunshot and ran across the yard, then followed the veranda around to the back." Hugo felt his heart take an uptick at the memory. It was so clear to him, the sound of that shot, the thick Houston air that wrapped itself around the house, and around him, like a wet cloth. And the rising dread that Tom had done something unnecessary. "When I got there, Tom was just inside the doorway, and one of the two men inside was dead."

"Just to be clear, Tom shot him? It wasn't suicide."

"It wasn't suicide, no."

"And what happened then?"

"Well," Hugo took a breath. "I made sure the second guy was secure, and we waited outside the house for backup to arrive."

"All four of you were outside when they got there."

"Correct."

"I see."

Yes, what you see is that Tom moved the body to make it look like the guy was escaping. And I didn't stop him.

Ambassador Taylor continued with his questions. "So one of them was dead, and the other?"

"Rick Cofer is his name. He was taken into custody and went to prison, eventually. And then parole."

"After robbing a bunch of banks and killing people?"

Hugo grimaced. "Well, we only had proof of that one robbery. And let's just say that as a result of that afternoon, with Tom going off the reservation, the US Attorney's Office wasn't wild about taking the cases to trial. Cofer got a great deal, but waived all appeals and also any civil suit against the government."

"Against you."

"I'd like to think it'd be against Tom, but yeah."

"I'm missing something here." Taylor frowned, and Hugo could hear the wheels turning in his mind. "One bad guy dead, the other in prison and now paroled. Are you telling me that this Cofer guy is in Amsterdam and Tom is chasing him?"

"It's kind of the other way around—Tom thinks Cofer came over here to do *us* harm."

"But why? He robbed the banks, he killed Tom's sister. You were just doing your jobs—why would this be so important to him after all this time? Why take it so personally?"

"Yeah, you *are* missing something. Cofer is taking it personally because he saw Tom execute his partner in crime in that house. . . . That partner in crime happened to be his twin brother."

"Ah. I see now," Taylor said quietly. "That explains things a little better."

"I had Tom on the phone earlier. He mentioned the hotel room you heard about. He said it was Rick Cofer's."

"Look, Cofer might be there, but that wasn't his hotel room."

"How do you know?"

"The US federal government has started to use that hotel, just in the last year. The room Tom broke into was being used by . . . let's just say, an American on a diplomatic mission."

"One of your spook types, you mean."

"Normal security captured a man going through the room, and it took another ten seconds to ID Tom."

"He's convinced Cofer is there."

"And he may be. But that wasn't his room."

"I can try to summon Tom back, boss, if that's what you're asking me to do."

"Good lord, no," Taylor guffawed. "Tom doesn't listen to his superior officers at the best of times; I can't imagine he'd listen to you ordering him back to Paris. Not when he has the bit between the teeth."

"So, what do you want me to do?"

"About Tom? Not a damn thing. Go out there and help him if you want, but other than that I don't expect anything of you. I just wanted to know what the hell was going on."

"And now you do."

"Thank you for that. I also want to know the minute you think Cofer is in Paris, should that happen."

"Fair enough," Hugo said.

"Good." Hugo could hear Taylor stand up and take a deep breath. "Now, then, you're on your way to get my guest?"

"Yeah, and I'm thrilled to be chaperoning a blowhard politician too incompetent to find her way to her own embassy."

Taylor laughed. "Then you'll be delighted to hear that you're actually meeting a young artist visiting from the United States. She had an art exhibition in DC, and the Dalí Paris museum has sponsored her to bring it here."

"An artist? I'm not much into painting, but it's definitely an improvement on politics."

"Sculpture, actually, it's very modern, very good. Opening night for her show is tomorrow. I'll be going and so will you."

"Thanks for thinking of me, but I do books, not art. Especially sculpture. And doubly especially not modern sculpture."

"Yes, I thought you might say that, but that's why I wanted you to meet her. I mean, apart from the fact that she's indescribably beautiful. I thought you'd make an exception from your narrow-mindedness about art because her sculptures are all made out of books. Really, it's very clever."

Hugo wasn't sure he'd heard right. "Made out of books?"

"Yep, books."

"Interesting. And indescribably beautiful, you say?"

"I do."

CHAPTER THREE

lia Alsaffar was staying at l'Hôtel Toby on Rue Joseph de Maistre, right beside the Montmartre Cemetery. Hugo asked the taxi driver to wait, then stepped out into the cold and through the sliding glass doors of the hotel into a modern, surprisingly spacious lobby. Most hotels in Paris were small, somewhat cramped, but this lobby area was bright and open, with couches and what looked like a small library to his right. He saw no obvious reception desk, just two well-dressed employees, a man and a woman, right ahead of him, perched atop stools on either side of a grand piano. They both looked up from their electronic notebooks.

"*Bon soir, monsieur,*" the young man said. "Are you checking in?"

"*Non,*" Hugo said, taking off his hat. "I'm here to pick someone up, a guest. Alia Alsaffar."

The two clerks exchanged quick glances, then the young man spoke. "Mademoiselle Alsaffar just left. Two minutes ago."

"She left?" Hugo was surprised—Taylor had told him she was expecting him.

"*Oui, monsieur.*"

"Do you know where she went? I'm from the US Embassy, and I am supposed to be driving her there."

The young woman pointed to the front doors. "She went left, along Rue Joseph de Maistre. Her . . . friend left, too."

Friend? Hugo thought. *Taylor never mentioned a friend.* He read the clerk's expressions, and made a deduction from the fact that not only had Alsaffar left, but she and . . . *whoever* it was, had gone in opposite directions.

"They were arguing?" he asked.

That glance again, wondering this time whether they were violating a guest's privacy. The young woman looked down, and her colleague just shrugged.

"Can you tell me what she's wearing?" Hugo pressed. "I'm responsible for her safety."

"Black boots, jeans, and a red jacket. And a red hat," the young man said, a little too quickly for his colleague's liking, apparently.

That's a yes, then, Hugo thought. "*Merci*," was all he said, though. He put his hat back on and braced himself for the cold, then exited the automatic doors and hurried back to the cab. He directed the taxi driver to take him up the street Alsaffar had gone. They drove slowly, but after a hundred yards or so Rue Joseph de Maistre arrowed into Rue des Abbesses.

"It's one-way, monsieur," the cabbie said. "I have to turn left, but the restaurants, and probably your friend, are to the right."

"*Merci*," Hugo said, and he hurriedly paid the man. He climbed back out into the cold and looked along the street. This was one of the major arteries that kept the area of Montmartre alive and ticking. A narrow street, yes, but normally pulsing with activity, throbbing with tourists and vendors, all competing for each other's attention, and money. It was one of the streets that took visitors toward the Sacré-Coeur Basilica at the summit of the butte Montmartre, the most prominent landmark in that part of Paris, and probably the best view of the city from anywhere except the top of the Eiffel Tower. Here, in spring, summer, and autumn, the three times Hugo had visited, he'd been irritated at the crush of people, and the garbage they bought as mementos.

But that was the wonderful thing about the cold, the rain, and the weeks before Christmas. With the tourists all but gone, Paris lapsed into her old habits, shrank into the assortment of villages she'd once been. This was especially true of Montmartre, because it was normally one of the busiest parts of the city. The crêpe vendors still plied their trade, but they looked unhurried, had time to nod *bonjour* to the locals and enjoy the rich aromas of their own delicacies as they sizzled on the hotplates in front of them. In this rain and cold, it struck Hugo as he walked, that Montmartre had had returned to its people, with the gleaming, cobbled streets uncrowded, more homely and welcoming.

And tonight Rue des Abbesses was quiet, almost empty. The sidewalks were wide and the road narrow, and on either side shops and restaurants snuggled cozily against each other. The small, tightly packed cobbles glistened with the rain, giving off a warm glow from the soft lights of the buildings overlooking the street.

He saw not a woman in red but just a few couples wandering along, arm-in-arm, and a handful of others who lingered at the glass storefronts. He set off, his breath steaming in front of him. He had no idea where she was going, but Ambassador Taylor had mentioned the Dalí museum, which was in the direction he was headed. He checked his phone to make sure of that, and his stomach growled as he passed the entrance to a bistro called Le Sancerre, where the rich aroma of garlic hovered like a siren tempting him inside. He settled for a glance at the menu as he passed by, and the words *escargots* and *canard* caught his well-trained eye—snails in garlic butter and duck, two of his favorites on the same menu.

Duly noted, he thought as he kept going.

A flash of red fifty yards ahead caught his eye, someone coming out of a store. He quickened his step and was soon close behind her.

"Excuse me, Ms. Alsaffar?"

She stopped and turned, her large, and very beautiful, eyes wide with surprise. The ambassador had not exaggerated. Alia Alsaffar was gorgeous, even wrapped up against the cold. Thick, wavy, black hair flowed out from the wool hat she wore, and in the low light her olive skin seemed to shimmer. And Hugo couldn't tear his gaze away from those hazel eyes.

"My name is Hugo Marston. The ambassador sent me."

"Sent you?"

"To bring you to the party. At the embassy." He smiled. "Right now."

A hand flew to her mouth. "That's tonight? Oh, sh— . . . damn it. I totally forgot."

"That's OK, we can still make it."

"I'm sorry, what was your name again?"

"Hugo Marston. I'm the RSO at the embassy."

"What's an RSO?"

"Regional Security Officer. In plain English, I'm head of security there."

He offered his hand and when she slipped off a glove and took it, Hugo forgot what he was about to say, at a complete loss for words. It was a sensation he'd not experienced in years. Not since he'd met Claudia in a random encounter at a café near his apartment.

"Well, Mr. Marston, I'm not exactly dressed for an embassy Christmas party, now am I?"

"I can wait while you change, if you like. And, please, call me Hugo."

"Hugo. I like that name."

He was glad to be in the dark because he felt himself blushing, just a little. Also something he'd not experienced in years.

"Thanks, so did my parents. They were fans of Victor Hugo."

"And you?"

"A big reader, yes."

She snapped her fingers. "You're the one who collects rare books."

"That's me."

"The ambassador told me about you."

"Why would he do that?"

She laughed. "I don't recall, to be honest."

"Probably for the best." Hugo gestured back the way they'd come. "Shall we?"

"You know, Hugo," she said slowly. "I'm not really in the mood for a party."

"Is there something wrong?"

"A bit of a . . . disagreement with a friend."

"I'm sorry to hear that."

"What can you do? It happens." She sighed. "More and more, it seems."

"Where were you headed, if you don't mind me asking?"

She smiled. "You're very formal, aren't you?"

He returned the smile. "I've been called that before. And worse."

"Well, originally I was going to just wander through Montmartre, but it's cold and rainy, so now I'm less excited about that idea." She looked around, then wiped a drop of rain off the end of her nose. "But it still sounds better than going to a stuffy Christmas party at the embassy. No offense."

"None taken," Hugo assured her.

"What about you?" she asked.

"What do you mean?"

"You're missing the party because of me. Shouldn't you head back?"

"If I miss it because of you, Ms. Alsaffar, I will be very grateful indeed. Not my kind of thing."

She laughed. "OK, Mr. Polite, I know you're on the clock, but call me Alia. And if you're quite sure about missing the party, I don't want to get you in trouble."

"You won't. The ambassador knows how much I want to be there."

"Well, good." She cocked her head and looked at him. "Are you hungry?"

"Actually, I am."

"Then let me buy you dinner." She waved her arms in both directions. "We have a plethora of choices, what do you fancy?"

"I did see one place that serves *escargots*, my particular favorite."

She wrinkled her nose. "Eww. Snails, right?"

"Right. But it's all about the fresh bread dipped in garlic butter."

"I'll take your word for it."

"Fair enough. Right this way." Hugo and Alsaffar started toward the bistro. "I should let my boss know we're not coming," he said. "Would you mind finding us a table? I'll be right in."

"Of course, take your time," she said. Then she winked. "As long as they have a fully stocked bar, I'll be just fine."

Hugo watched her enter and be welcomed by a waiter, then he dialed Ambassador Taylor. "Everything all right?" the ambassador asked.

"Well, she's not dressed, and not in the mood. Seems like she had an argument with a friend."

"So, no special guest for my party?"

"I'm sure some CEO or celebrity will step up."

"No, it's fine, I don't need one. Are you at the hotel?"

"At a restaurant. Why?"

"I don't know. Do me a favor . . . stay with her until she's back at her room, will you?"

Something in Taylor's voice struck Hugo. "Sounds like there's something you're not telling me."

"Yes and no. There was an incident before she left the States. Close call with a car in Washington, DC, that might have been an accident, and probably was. Call it a feeling, but I'd be happier if she wasn't wandering the streets of Paris by herself. She's on my turf, and I'll go the extra mile to make sure she stays safe."

"If she's in danger, and I'm with her, I'd kinda like to know, boss."

"Do this, buy her dinner. Expense it, then escort her back to the hotel. And, hey, you don't have to come back to the party."

"Sounds like a good deal for me," Hugo said.

"Good man."

Hugo kept the phone in his hand after they'd disconnected; he had another call to make. He took a deep breath and dialed Claudia.

"So, don't be mad," he said.

"Hugo, are you serious? You're not coming."

"I need to babysit his guest, an artist, I'm sorry. She doesn't want to come to the party, and I need to stay with her until she's back at her hotel."

"What does *need to* mean?"

"The ambassador asked me to. And you know me, a good soldier who always follows orders."

"So she's pretty, huh?"

"That's your assumption?" Hugo asked, amused.

"Either you or Taylor is playing the protective card pretty hard." He heard the humor in her voice. "Maybe both of you."

"He did say she was, and I quote, 'indescribably beautiful,'" Hugo said.

"And do you agree?"

"She is pretty, yes, and seems very nice. Young, maybe early thirties, but nice."

"Is that too young or just-right young?"

"Honestly, this is probably a bad time for that discussion," Hugo said, serious for a moment.

"I know, Hugo. We were supposed to have it here. Tonight."

"Yes. I'm sorry." He felt deflated, and now he regretted accepting the dinner invitation. "Really, I'm sorry."

"And I dragged myself here despite being sick." He rarely heard annoyance in her voice, but it was there now.

"Go home. To bed. I'll bring you soup later, if you like."

"I know how to heat soup, Hugo."

"Right, of course. Look, it's not entirely my fault; Taylor told me to keep an eye on her."

There was a moment of silence between them. Then she said: "Look, it's all right. Really." And there she was, his Claudia, full of compassion and understanding. And logic. "And let me just say this. I know you've been chasing harder than I have, that I have no claim to you and no right to . . . you know. Go and have fun tonight. Dinner with a pretty woman . . . it's fine."

"Dinner," he said. "How did you know?"

"Please, my love. I can almost smell the *escargots* from here."

"Oh, you're good," he said.

"You're not the only one who can profile people."

"Me and garlic," Hugo said, laughing. "That's a little obvious, a little too easy."

"Maybe, but I'm right, aren't I?"

"You are."

"Well, have fun and let's talk tomorrow."

"Thanks, and that's a deal," Hugo said. "You should go home and get some rest."

"I will. And I meant what I said, you have fun tonight, Hugo, OK? Please don't worry about me or chivalry, or doing the right thing. Have some fun."

They hung up, but immediately Hugo's phone buzzed, and he considered throwing it in the nearest trash can so people would leave him alone for the rest of the night. He felt even more that way when he checked the screen.

"Tom, hey, sorry—"

"Fuckface, you were supposed to call me back."

"Yeah, I know. Something came up. Look, is there anything happening right this moment that I need to know about?"

"This moment I'm standing in front of a window and underneath a red light."

"I'll take that as a no. Let me call you in the morning."

"The morning? Why?"

"Because I'm busy tonight."

There was silence for a second, then Tom laughed. "A glass of pinot noir and a book do not constitute busy, Hugo."

"Very funny. I mean *actually* busy."

"That so?" Tom sounded skeptical. "Do tell."

"I have to go. I'll fill you in tomorrow." Hugo looked through the bistro's front window and saw Alia Alsaffar at a table for two, looking at a menu in her hands. "But I think I might be on a date."

CHAPTER FOUR

The small restaurant was not even half-full, but it felt cozy thanks to the Christmas decorations, the green-and-red lights over the bar, and sprigs of holly on each table. Silver tinsel framed the large mirror at the back of the restaurant, and the large wooden coat racks were laden with jackets, hats, and scarfs. Waiters glided back and forth from the kitchen to the occupied tables, trays either loaded with plates and glasses, or tucked under their arms. Hugo ordered one of the better bottles of Bordeaux, silently thanking Ambassador Taylor, and then they turned their attention to the food menu, although Hugo had decided on his meal long ago. Alsaffar eventually concurred on the duck confit and ordered the same dish for herself, but she decided just to watch Hugo eat his appetizer of a half dozen snails.

"It's kind of funny that you like those so much," she said.

"Why?"

"No reason. I just don't think of snails as food."

"I'm happy with just five of them," he said. "You should really try one."

"I probably should, this being my one and only ever trip to Paris," she said. "But I think I'll pass."

"Try the sauce at least."

She took a piece of bread from the basket, tore it into four smaller pieces, and dipped one into the garlic-butter sauce on Hugo's plate. She popped it into her mouth and chewed slowly, and her eyes widened with pleasure.

"That is good," she said. "So very good. Can't they find something other than slugs to serve with garlic butter, though?"

27

"Snails," he corrected. "And special ones, not just any old snail will do."

"I'm sure they're honored to be chosen." She looked up suddenly, over Hugo's shoulder and out the front window. "Uh-oh, this could be trouble."

"What's up?" Hugo turned and saw a man in his midtwenties walking into the restaurant. He was handsome, with a thick head of swept-back brown hair, but his face was like thunder, and he marched up to the table and glared down at Alia.

"What are you doing?" he demanded, not even looking at Hugo.

"Eating dinner." She gestured toward Hugo. "Hugo Marston, meet my friend Josh Reno."

Reno continued to ignore Hugo. "'Friend,' now, is it? Not 'apprentice,' 'assistant,' 'acolyte' even?"

"We've had this discussion, Josh. I'm not having it again. Certainly not here and now."

"Right, because you get to decide when and where we talk, and what we say. You get to decide everything because now you're a fucking star, right?"

Hugo stood, and when he spoke his voice was gentle. "Hey, Mr. Reno, I don't mean to get in the middle of anything, but I'd love to finish my dinner without any unnecessary drama. Would you mind continuing this later?"

Reno finally looked at Hugo with bloodshot eyes. "Would I mind? Yes, I'd fucking mind."

Hugo didn't flinch, but there was no mistaking the alcohol sweetness on Reno's breath. Their waiter, an older man with a shock of white hair that stood almost straight up, approached.

"Is everything all right?" he asked in French.

"*Oui*, monsieur," Hugo replied. "Or if not, it soon will be."

The waiter moved away, eyes uncertain, but he gave them their space.

Reno was an inch or two shorter than Hugo's six-two, and probably thirty pounds lighter, but he didn't back down. "Who the hell are you, anyway? Did she seriously just pick you up?" He looked past Hugo at Alsaffar. "Or is this someone you've had on tap for a while and just not mentioned to me?"

"My name is Hugo Marston. I work for the embassy and was here to give Alia a ride to the embassy's Christmas party."

Reno rolled his eyes, and when he spoke his words were slurred. "Jesus, now she's too important to take the metro?"

"She decided she didn't want to go to the event after all, and, since I don't like parties either, we're having something to eat instead."

"Well, that sounds more like her, changing her mind last-second and leaving people in the lurch. Yeah, that part I can believe."

Alsaffar spoke up, her voice firm. "Josh, this is not helping. We'll talk later."

"How dare you do this to me? You're basically ruining my career— you know that, right?"

"No, I'm not," she said.

"Destroying everything I've worked for."

"That's a little dramatic, Josh."

"No, it's not!" He was red in the face. "I've given up my life to help you, and now you're the star, it's *bye-bye, Josh, thanks for all the help, now get lost.*"

"None of this was my call," she insisted, "I told you that."

"Yeah, you did. And all that tells me is you won't even take responsibility for your own actions."

"Josh, please," she pleaded. "Go back to the hotel and we'll talk later. This is not the time or place."

"You don't get to tell me what to do any more," Reno said, eyes blazing. "I'll go where I want, and it's not back to the hotel."

Hugo was about to intervene again, but Reno spun on his heel and stormed out of the bistro, and just about everyone inside watched him go.

"I'm so sorry about that," Alsaffar said. "Long story."

"Not your fault," Hugo said, retaking his seat. "And if the service here is as slow as I hope, we have plenty of time."

"OK then," she smiled. "I guess I can fill you in. He's an artist, Josh.

A great painter, a good sculptor. Better with execution than ideas, but he has talent."

"As well as a temper." Hugo refilled their wine glasses.

"Honestly, I'm afraid he does. He's not violent or anything, but he can shout and scream occasionally. Usually at some inanimate project that isn't going the way he wants it to." She took a sip of wine. "Anyway. He and I worked together on a project about three years ago, and we became friends. Then, when my work started to get attention, he traveled with me as kind of an assistant, setting things up, helping with travel logistics. Especially, with this book installation, it's taken us all over the country."

"Driving the U-Haul, that kind of thing?"

"Exactly. I was invited lots of places to show my work, but, since I'm not famous, it was up to me to get it there."

"Sounds like a lot of work," Hugo said.

"It was. Exhausting at times. So it was good to have Josh around. He's strong, hardworking, and because he's also an artist he understands how important it is to accept when you're offered space in a gallery, even if it's on the other side of the continent. And he's been amazing in terms of setting up, too, because when I display my pieces, he just puts them where I want and doesn't quibble with me."

"And what does Josh get out of this arrangement, if I may ask?"

"There you go, Mr. Polite again." She smiled to show she was kidding. "It's not the pay, I can tell you that much." She suddenly sat upright, almost blushing, Hugo thought. "And not ... *that* either. Completely platonic, I promise you."

Hugo held his hands up. "Hey, none of my business."

"Well, if we *had* been, it'd explain why he interrupted our date with such drama."

So it is a date. "True enough."

She smiled. "Not that this is really a date, but you know what I mean."

Ah well. "Absolutely."

"No, he's upset with me because of how this trip is working out.

You asked what he got out of it . . . Well, in exchange for his help, I always arrange for some of his work to be on display too. Half a dozen pieces and a poster with his picture and information about him, some quotations from me about how awesome he is."

"So he gets to sell his work, too."

"Right. And get some exposure, which is incredibly hard in the art world if you're not already well known." She sighed and ran a finger around the top of her wine glass. "He thought he was going to get some exposure here, maybe sell some stuff, because this exhibition was organized by the same people who did the last one, in Washington, DC, and they were fine with it over there. But we heard today that they didn't ship any of his work over. Neither of us read the fine print, or double-checked. It's both our fault, but he's the one left out in the cold."

"Literally."

"He wanted me to pull some strings, have his work delivered anyway and hope it gets here in time for the last few days." She shrugged. "I tried. I called the man who is sponsoring everything, but he refused. Nicely, for the most part."

"Why?"

"He doesn't like Josh's work that much. He didn't say that, but I know, I can tell. He said that because we have the honor of having the exhibition at the Dalí museum, we shouldn't dilute my work with his. Plus, he said that the museum itself hasn't agreed, and wouldn't."

"But why does Josh blame you?" Hugo asked. "None of this sounds like your fault at all. Certainly not any more than it is his."

"I know. But he's a little paranoid." She laughed gently. "All artists are, to some extent. We all feel like frauds, like we don't know what we're doing and are about to be exposed as shysters."

"I met the author James Ziskin last year," Hugo said. "He said the same about writers."

"There you go, then. All artists feel that way. But we also tend toward envy, I'm afraid."

"A natural human emotion."

"But not always a pleasant one. When someone starts to rise out of the depths of anonymity, the artists around them are happy, of course, but also envious. Sometimes actively jealous."

"Josh Reno's jealous of your success?"

"He'd admit to slight envy, not to being jealous. But, yes, I think he is. And this trip isn't helping, in more ways than I just told you."

They sat back as the waiter arrived with their food, large plates of duck confit served atop a pile of mashed potatoes, and surrounded by colorful vegetables.

They both thanks the waiter, and Hugo said, "Go on."

"Well, he's not been very useful here. My sponsors, Rachel and JD Rollo, paid for everything to be shipped over and set up." She looked down. "They didn't even want to pay for his airline ticket and hotel."

"Do sponsors usually pay for that?"

She nodded. "Usually it's just gas money, though. Maybe a cheap motel room in Kansas."

"Let me guess. You paid for his ticket."

"And hotel room. He's been good to me. Good *for* me. It's the least I could do, but . . ." Her voice trailed off.

"He found out today?"

"We had a talk, yes, about all of it. Including that."

"And he didn't take it well," Hugo prompted.

"He saw it as the end of our association. Not just me moving up and away, but him, as a result, moving down. I was his outlet." She took a bite of duck and closed her eyes in appreciation for a moment. "Good choice. This is delicious."

Hugo was chewing his own mouthful and nodded in agreement.

Alsaffar continued. "So, Josh thinks I'm leaving him behind. Abandoning him."

"You kind of are," Hugo pointed out. "Except that it's not your fault."

"That's true, but now he has to go back to America and try and make it by himself. It doesn't much matter whose fault it is, or isn't, he's on his own now."

"That's how the world works. He doesn't have a right to ride your coattails to fame. You made it on your own merit; almost all artists and writers do."

"Well, I had benefactors of a sort," she said.

"But in terms of talent and hard work, you got yourself here."

"You're right, I know. And he'll see it that way. Just not tonight, apparently." She brightened suddenly. "But, hey, we're in a bistro in Paris. Enough of my problems, we need to be enjoying ourselves."

"Yes, we do. Why don't you tell me a little more about yourself."

"Well, I'm Alia Michelle Alsaffar. Half Iraqi, which explains the skin, and half Irish, which explains the hair. I trained as a social worker, but have been taking photographs all my life. I had a photography business for a while, weddings and the like. I dabbled with various art forms, painting and sculpture, and found I had a passion for the latter."

"When was this?"

She laughed into her wine glass. "That's your polite way of asking how old I am, right?"

"No, I'd never do such a thing," he protested.

"I'm thirty-two. I've been pursuing my art career full-time for about the last five years."

"And now you're the talk of the town."

"We'll see after tomorrow, I guess."

"Ah, yes. Opening night of the exhibition. Are you nervous?"

She threw him a look that said, *Duh, of course.* But she said, "I'll be fine once it's open and a few people show up. And once someone opens the champagne."

"A lot of people will show up—just you watch."

"I'll hold you to that," she laughed. "After all, this is the biggest launch of my career. . . . People have to show up, right?"

"Quite right. . . . So you have family to share this journey with?"

"Not really. My father died when I was young, I never knew him, and my mother and stepfather died more recently."

"Oh, I'm sorry," Hugo said.

"Don't be. I've accepted and dealt with my mother's death, and my stepfather . . . well, he wasn't the supportive daddy I'd have chosen."

"No?"

"I don't want to talk about him, Hugo, but I will say he did more for me in death than he did in life."

"I'm scared to ask what that means."

"He didn't care for any art, let alone mine. But when he died, I inherited an apartment in London that I didn't even know existed. Probably used it for his mistresses. I also inherited a ne'er-do-well stepbrother who got my step-dad's cash, and who'll be at the event tomorrow." She flashed white teeth at Hugo. "And that's all I have to say about family."

"Understood, then let's move on from that. Do you have plans for after the exhibition?"

"Do you mean next week or next year?"

"Either," Hugo said. "Or both."

"I have that apartment in London. There's a guy renting it from me, but he agreed to terminate the lease early to accommodate me."

"That's nice. Or did he do it because you're famous and beautiful?" Hugo blushed. "Sorry, that was painfully corny."

Alsaffar laughed. "That's OK, I'm happy for the compliment. But to answer your question, I've never met my tenant, John Smith. And, yes, that's really his name. He's some hermit who has no idea how beautiful, or not, I am, since we've done everything by email. He wouldn't even talk to me on the phone."

"I imagine there are photos of you on the internet."

"Oh, yeah, good point. If hermits use the internet. Anyway, my plan is to live in London and do another show in Mayfair in about three weeks. Assuming all goes well here, of course." She leaned back and looked at him for a moment. "Now tell me about you. Who's this Hugo Marston I'm having dinner with?"

"Not as exotic as Alia Alsaffar, I can promise you that," he said with a smile. "I grew up in Texas, Austin to be specific. Joined the FBI like I'd always wanted to, then joined the diplomatic corps so I could see the world."

"What did you do for the FBI? Sounds exciting."

"Sometimes it was, sometimes not so much. I was in the Behavioral Analysis Unit, the BAU."

"Ooh, a profiler? That's pretty sexy. You know, Hugo, next time you're having dinner with a strange woman, you should lead with that."

"Duly noted." *And why do I care so much that you find it sexy?* "That's basically my story."

"No wife and kids?"

"Correct, no wife and kids. A needy friend named Tom, if that counts."

"We all have one of those. Oh, I remember now." She snapped her fingers. "Why the ambassador was telling me about you, that is."

"And why was that? How did you two connect, even?"

"Ambassador Taylor is friends with JD and Rachel, or knows them at least. They're at your Christmas party, I expect. Anyway, because of my medium, books, the ambassador got to talking about you." She gave him a small smile. "He suggested that you might be slightly less interested in sculpture."

"Well, it's not my strong suit, a little bit like poetry." Hugo heard the defensiveness in his own voice. "I'm sure it's my fault, and I'm probably missing out on a lot."

"You are. How about you come to the opening tomorrow? I'll explain some of my work in person."

"My boss already told me I was going, actually."

"Under duress, eh?"

"No, I'm looking forward to it, really. I'm a big fan of the Dalí museum."

"Good." She gave him a mischievous smile. "I should probably have a date for my own opening, don't you think?"

"I hadn't thought about it, but sure."

"OK to call it a date?"

Hugo's mind went to Claudia, who had been the last person to give him butterflies in his stomach. The smartest, sexiest, and most independent woman he'd ever met. But, as he'd discovered, he was never quite sure where that independence left them, which is why he'd wanted to talk to her about it. They certainly weren't in a steady relationship, but they were also ... some kind of item, at least when they found time for each other. And as he gazed at the smiling Alia Alsaffar, he realized he had no idea what the rules were anymore, not between Claudia and him, anyway. Was she seeing other people? Hugo hadn't so much as had dinner with another woman until tonight, let alone shared any intimacy with anyone. But he felt something with this young woman, a chemistry that set his blood fizzing and fogged his mind.

And he was suddenly very glad the ambassador had offered his services as a driver.

"Sure, a date. I'd like that," he said. "So, I'm curious, why books?"

"I was an addict growing up—couldn't read enough. Even after lights-out, I had my nose in a book under the covers. And when it came time to clean out my bedroom, I'd throw out clothes and toys before books."

"So why not become a writer?"

She laughed gently. "Writing is hard. I mean, I tried it for sure, even took creative-writing classes, but I never produced anything very good, certainly nothing I wanted other people to read." She shrugged. "But I was good with my hands. And making things, fixing things. I used to help my neighbor with his car. So it seemed natural for my interests to turn toward painting and sculpture, and even more natural to incorporate books."

"Now I'm curious to see your work," Hugo said.

"Oh, you don't have to say that." Her eyes twinkled with amusement. "But since you've already committed, there's definitely no backing out now."

Hugo held his hands up in surrender. "I'm already there, I promise."

"Good. And thank you. All artists have this fear that no one will show up to their exhibitions. I gather authors have the same terror when it comes to their signings."

"I can imagine."

She took another sip of wine and smiled at him. "But now I know there'll be two of us there, at least."

CHAPTER FIVE

The next evening, Hugo and the ambassador took a taxi from the embassy north into Montmartre, and the driver let them out by the metro stop on Rue des Abbesses. The cold enveloped them immediately, and Hugo handed over too much cash so he could quickly put his gloves back on.

"Lovely evening for a stroll," Taylor said into his scarf. "I think it's about to rain, too."

"Maybe it'll be snow, that'd be beautiful."

"And even colder," Taylor grumbled.

"Stop complaining." Hugo started toward the cobbled square ahead of them. "Here's the market I want to stop at. Claudia said one of the vendors makes incredible fudge."

"Fudge, really?" Taylor hurried after him. "Hugo, are you going to tell me or not?"

"About?"

"Last night. I already asked, and you wouldn't tell me in the car because the driver was listening."

"Right."

"Now he's not listening, you can tell me."

"Nothing happened."

"There's a bounce in your step that tells me something different."

"I'm excited about the fudge," Hugo said.

"Right, and you're rushing to buy Claudia her favorite fudge not out of guilt after something happened, but because you want to carry a packet of fudge with you all evening at an art show."

"Yep."

"Jesus, slow down." Taylor was panting by the time they reached the small square that was filled with colorful stalls. "And that's another thing."

"Here we are." Hugo stopped walking and looked around. "Isn't this neat?"

A dozen parents stood around smiling as their children whirled past on a colorful carousel, waving from their perches atop carriages, planes, and flying squirrels. Around the carousel, street vendors were bundled against the chill, their eyes roaming over the browsers, eager to pounce on an interested party. Two beautiful Indian women, sisters maybe, were selling scarves of every color, and next to them a young man with a thick beard offered samples of his honey. Cheese from the Pyrenees was being sold next to him by a burly older man, who stood back from his wares with a cigarette dangling from his lips.

"This is very cool," Taylor said. "Now tell me what happened last night?"

Hugo gave him a sideways look. "Do you have romantic intentions yourself, boss?"

"If I were twenty years younger, maybe. Scratch that, definitely."

"You just seem real interested in my evening, is all."

Taylor sighed and explained it slowly, like he were talking to a child. "Because I live my safe, boring life vicariously through you."

Hugo laughed. "Well, you'll be disappointed then."

"Seriously? You meant it when you said nothing happened?"

"We had a nice dinner, then I walked her back to the hotel."

"And . . .?"

"We had a drink at the bar. After that, I left." Hugo left out the details he knew Taylor would want. The occasional touches, the laughing at silly jokes, and the lingering looks they'd shared. He wouldn't have minded letting Taylor in on some of this, but not yet. These memories needed to remain as just Hugo's for now, something for him to savor and enjoy all to himself until something more happened. Or until they disappeared into nothingness, if that was how it was to be.

"You didn't walk her to her room?" Taylor suggested.

"She actually knew the way, she's a pretty remarkable woman."

"Funny." Taylor sighed again. "Well, let's go find that fudge. And it damn well better be good."

It was. Both men thanked the seller for their samples and stood there with their eyes closed as the surprisingly light delicacy quite literally dissolved in their mouths.

"Wow," said Hugo. "I'll take a pound of that, please."

"*Oui, monsieur.*"

"And I'll take two pounds," Taylor said. He turned to Hugo. "Claudia, eh? What did you tell her about last night?"

"We haven't spoken today. I left her a message and she left me one, we've not connected."

"She coming tonight?"

"I invited her, but her return message said something about a training run, for that marathon she's doing," Hugo said. "I hope it was all right to invite her, in case she does show up."

"One of the benefits of being the United States ambassador," Taylor said, puffing himself up. "We can get anyone into anything as long as we're there."

"Must be nice."

"The flip side is, we *have* to go to lots of places we don't want to."

"Like art exhibitions?" Hugo asked.

"Which reminds me. You were pretty quick to agree to this one."

"You ordered me to go, I didn't agree to anything."

"Oh, right, I forgot."

"Plus, she asked me nicely last night." Hugo nudged his boss. "In fact, I'm her date for the event."

"You never mentioned that part. Also, I didn't order you, I asked nicely."

"As you always do." Hugo was serious for a moment. "Which reminds me, what was the trouble, something about a car you said?"

"Back in DC? She thought she was being followed, then the car following her almost ran her over when she crossed the street. Probably just some lunatic."

"Why would someone want to hurt her?"

"She was with her assistant, Josh Reno, and he managed to get the car's license plate."

"I met Josh last night," Hugo said.

"You did? I thought he and Alia were on the outs."

"They are. Were. Quite publicly. That's how I met him." Hugo figured he'd go into that later, if need be. "The license plate, you were saying."

"Yeah, it didn't exist."

"A plate with fake numbers?"

"Numbers, letters, maybe both. But, yes, the driver had altered the plate."

"Interesting," Hugo said. "Shows premeditation of some illegal act. Either the driver was following and trying to hurt Alia, or he was up to some other illegal activity and the rest was coincidence."

"But we couldn't really come up with a suspect or a reason why someone would do her harm. She certainly couldn't think of anything. So we're left with that coincidental run-in with someone up to no good."

"And a nagging doubt in the back of your mind."

"Correct." Ambassador Taylor clapped Hugo on the shoulder. "We've been in this business too long, we see ghosts and ghouls around every corner."

"But when you're in the business," Hugo said, thinking of Tom hunting a real or an imaginary Rick Cofer, "it's better to see them when they're not there, as opposed to not seeing them when they are."

Hugo was pleased to see a line of maybe fifteen or twenty people at the entrance to the small Dalí museum, all wrapped up in wool coats and long scarves. He was happy to be seeing Alia again, too, and would have been content getting a personal tour from her, let alone being her date, whatever that meant under the circumstances. He was excited for her, wanted her exhibition to do well, especially the launch.

But someone in the line was less than happy. He stood three people

ahead of Hugo and the ambassador, a frown on his face and his feet
kicking at the ground. His hands were thrust deep into his pockets, and
every now and again he'd shake his head.

Hugo nudged Taylor and gestured forward. His voice was a
whisper when he spoke. "That's Josh Reno."

"Ah," Taylor replied. "Doesn't look happy."

Just then, Reno looked over his shoulder and spotted Hugo, who
gave him a friendly nod. Reno looked down, then straightened himself
up and stepped out of line. He walked up to Hugo, who readied himself
for a confrontation.

"You were with Alia last night," Reno said.

"That's right."

"I . . . I owe you an apology."

Hugo was taken aback, not expecting that from Reno. "Oh, it's
OK, please don't worry about it."

"No, really. I had a few drinks, and I was upset. But I was out of
line, and I'm sorry if I ruined your dinner. I feel like an idiot."

"We all do dumb stuff from time to time," Hugo said. "I appreciate
the apology; it takes a brave man to do that."

"Yeah, well." Reno shrugged. "That's all, I just wanted to say sorry."

Hugo offered his hand and, when Reno took it, Hugo said, "No
hard feelings, Josh. Now go claim your place in line, I think that couple
is holding it for you."

"Thanks, man." He gave Hugo a brief smile, and nodded at Taylor
before sidling up to where he'd been standing. The couple let him back
in, and they all continued the slow shuffle forward toward the doors.

Once inside, Hugo and Taylor swapped their hats and coats for
a ticket with the coat-check clerk, a heavy-set man with thinning
hair and ruddy cheeks. He looked a little old to be doing the job, and
seemed to Hugo more interested in reading his book, *The Paper Trip*,
but he gave them both friendly nods and smiles when handing them
their tickets. Hugo held out a five-euro note as a tip, but the man didn't
take it, instead pointing to the small plastic bucket that sat next to a
bottle of hand sanitizer.

"*Merci*," the man said with an obvious American accent, and then he turned his attention to the couple behind Hugo.

A museum employee checked their names against the list of invitees and then directed them downstairs to the exhibit space. Hugo had visited the museum once before, but not for several years, and when he reached the foot of the stairs he looked around. It was a relatively small space, one large room with several smaller ones at the end of short corridors that led off it. Most of the Dalí sculptures looked to have been moved out, or perhaps shifted to one of the smaller rooms.

"Books, eh?" Taylor said. "This is actually quite impressive."

"It is," Hugo agreed. He was relieved, too, because he didn't want to not like Alia's work, and he didn't want to have to lie and say otherwise.

The main floor was dominated by what looked like a thick tree trunk, ten feet tall with its largest branches chopped down to nubs, and all of the bark flayed off. It was, though, made of books laid flat on top of each other, the spines inward so the pages showed the look of wood. It was textured and real-looking, yet obviously a clever piece of art.

He moved closer to study it, see if it had a name, and suddenly felt a hand on his arm. He turned to see Alia Alsaffar smiling at him.

"What do you think?" she asked.

"It's exceptional, it really is. And if I may be so bold, you look stunning," Hugo said with a smile.

She did. Her eyes sparkled with the excitement of the evening, and her beautiful coffee skin glowed, untouched by makeup as far as he could tell. But it was her dress that took Hugo's breath away. It looked, at first glance, to be made of small strips of leather sewn together, the top one tight around her neck like a collar, connecting to the web-like dress that hugged her body. It was revealing, daring, and very sexy, yet it showed less than it seemed to, and, standing close, Hugo could see that it was, in fact, made from rectangles of leather that had once been the spines of classic books. The faded gold and colored lettering that spelled out the titles of the books and authors glittered subtly as she moved. The look was bondage, but the details were purely literary, a deceit that tickled Hugo's sense of humor greatly.

"I meant the art, silly," she said. "And thank you. You clean up pretty well yourself."

"The dress is genius—did you come up with the idea?"

"I did, and sewed it myself. Is it too revealing?"

"No, it's absolutely perfect." He gestured to the tree made of books. "And I like this a lot, too. It's clever but also looks amazing. How did you ever think to create such a piece?"

"I always hated seeing books thrown away, even being sold off for pennies. Not just because it seemed like a waste of literature, but because of the waste of wood. Paper can be recycled, but once a tree has been cut down, well, I guess you can replace it, but that particular tree is gone forever."

"This was your way of returning those used books to their original form," Hugo said.

"Exactly."

"I think it's brilliant, then. Show me something else."

"With pleasure." She looked around. "Hey, have you seen Josh? We didn't talk last night, and I have no idea where he's been all day."

"I saw him outside, in line to come in here. He actually apologized for making a scene last night; I was impressed."

"Really? If he's not mad, I wonder why he's not returning my texts or phone calls."

"There he is," Hugo said.

Reno was at the back of the main room, leaning against the wall with two glasses of champagne in his hands. He was looking around at the thirty or so guests, but Hugo couldn't read his expression. Somewhere between bored and annoyed, if he had to guess.

"I should go talk to him," Alsaffar said. "Make sure he's not angry with me."

"Want me to go with you?"

"No, I don't think he'll cause a scene in here."

"OK. I'll hover close by just in case," Hugo said. He moved away, giving her space to approach Reno, but circled back and placed himself in front of another of her pieces. This one was a bookcase, made of books of course, but each outward-facing cover contained the word *case*. It took him a moment, but when he studied the books on the shelves, all of which had their spines showing, he saw that the titles spelled out a message when read in sequence, telling mini stories. A different story for each shelf, each with its own theme. The top one read:

> What was she thinking? / Embracing danger / While I was gone / As if / Nothing mattered / When / The killer inside me / Once / Out of sight / Beneath the surface / Struck / Forced to kill /

"You have to add in the punctuation yourself," a voice beside him said. "Commas in the top one."

She was tall and slim, and she wore a long-sleeved black dress that had a mock turtleneck, with a keyhole opening in it, and a daring slit up the side. Her long brown hair was down over her shoulders, parted expertly to the side and framing her fine, and very beautiful, features. Large, blue-gray eyes held Hugo's for a second, appraising him.

"It's very clever," he said.

"Each shelf is a different genre of literature. Crime fiction on top, then romance . . . you get the idea." She smiled and held out her hand. "I'm Rachel Rollo."

"Hugo Marston." He shook her hand. "Nice to meet you. Alia told me about you and your husband, supporting her work. This trip. She had glowing things to say."

"She's a sweetheart. And a talent, for sure. In fact, we didn't need to financially support her for this exhibit, the Dalí museum did that."

"You're just here for moral support?" Hugo asked.

"Any excuse for a trip to Paris." She winked conspiratorially. "My favorite city in the world."

"Mine too. Where are you staying?"

"The Crillon. It's expensive, but the service is amazing. So are the beds."

Expensive would be an understatement, Hugo thought. "Alia mentioned you're also an art critic."

"I do that for the *New York Times* on occasion, yes."

"You're covering this show?"

"No. I offered, but, given my connection to her, they thought it might be a conflict of interest. Which makes sense; we've been with her from the beginning."

"Of her art career?"

"Even before, I suppose. She took some anniversary photographs for us and we liked them so much we had her create a portfolio of her work. That was several years ago. Anyway, she wanted to branch out into other things and we encouraged her. Supported her."

"That's very kind of you," Hugo said. "And it has obviously led to great things."

"She's very good." Rollo looked around. "So do you like it?"

"In all honestly, I've never been a huge fan of sculpture, but since books are my thing, this is a nice compromise."

"You should see this piece," Rollo said. She put a hand on his arm and steered him away from Alsaffar and past several groups of chatting visitors. That included the ambassador, who raised an inquisitive eyebrow. Hugo ignored him. They wound up in front of a television screen showing what looked like a blank page on a computer.

"What is it?" Hugo asked after a moment.

"Have you heard of the concept of slow television?"

"No, I haven't."

"I think it started in Scandinavia somewhere. Australia, maybe. Anyway, they put cameras on the front of a train, and a ferry, and just record what happens."

"Not much, it sounds like."

"That's the point. Fifteen, eighteen, twenty-four hours of continuous television, with the landscape changing and nothing else."

"Sounds a little boring," Hugo said.

"It can be. It can also be mesmerizing. The idea is that with all other kinds of television, be it fiction or documentary, there is always something edited out. The finished product is manicured and refined. With slow television, you get to see everything."

"So you just play it in the background or something?"

"You can. You get to choose when you watch."

Hugo pointed to the television screen in front of them. "So what's this?"

"Alia's taking slow TV to the max with this piece. She recorded an author every time he sat down to write, put the camera not on him but on his computer screen."

"Wait, so she recorded the writing of an entire novel?"

"From the title to *The End*," Rollo said. "If you watched it, you could read the book as he's writing it."

"That's actually pretty cool. How long is the recording?"

"I think it's a little more than a hundred hours."

Hugo laughed. "If only I had that much time to sit in front of a screen."

"Good point. So what do you do, Mr. Marston?"

"Please, call me Hugo. I'm head of security at the US Embassy. Regional Security Officer, they call it."

She leaned in, and Hugo caught a whiff of expensive perfume. "Do you carry your gun at all times, Hugo?"

"Not at all times, no. I find Paris's museums to be pretty safe, for example."

"Glad to hear that. And, if you're unarmed, you can have a drink, yes?"

"I suppose so."

"Then let me prove to you how captivating this piece is." She gestured to the television screen, where the title of the book had appeared letter by letter: *When I Was Old in the Mountains*. "I'll be back in a moment. Champagne suit you?"

"Very well indeed," Hugo said. "Thank you."

He looked around for Alia but didn't see her, or Josh Reno. *Talking privately and settling their differences*, he thought. Hoped. He turned his attention to the screen and watched the cursor blink at the start of the story, found himself waiting with bated breath for the opening lines. They came slowly but surely, and Hugo hung on each one, his mind seeming to help the author, making mental suggestions for the next word or phrase, punctuation even. After a while, he felt a hand on his arm.

"Champagne," Rachel Rollo said, handing him a glass. "How long have you been watching?" She had a twinkle in her eye.

"Oh, I don't know, maybe three . . ." He checked his watch and almost gasped with surprise. "Good grief, it's been fifteen minutes. How is that even possible?"

"I told you," Rollo said. "It's captivating. Enthralling."

"It really is," Hugo said. He raised his glass. "Thank you for this, cheers."

"Cheers." They clinked glasses. "I should drag you away before you spend the entire evening watching this screen," she said.

"Apparently that's exactly right," Hugo laughed. His phone buzzed in his pocket, and he pulled it half out and glanced at the screen. "Would you excuse me a moment, Ms. Rollo? I need to take this call, I'm sorry."

"It's Rachel. And, please, go ahead."

"Thanks." Hugo stepped away and answered his phone. "Claudia, what's up?"

"*Monsieur Marston?*" It was a male voice, not what Hugo was expecting.

"Yes, who is this, please?"

"My name is Michel Prost. I am an emergency medical technician."

Hugo's heart skipped a beat. "Has something happened to Claudia?"

"*Oui, monsieur.* Can you come to her?"

"Where are you? What's happened? Is she all right?"

"We're on Rue Norvins, *monsieur.*"

"Rue . . . that's right here. You're outside the Dalí museum?"

"That's correct. Can you come now?"

CHAPTER SIX

Hugo raced up the stairs, not bothering to get his hat and coat, and ran out onto Rue Poulbot, following the bricked street around to the right. It had grown dark, and lights flashed ahead of him, bouncing off the walls and the road itself, telling him exactly where to go.

The ambulance was parked to one side of the narrow Rue Poulbot, with its nose toward Hugo and two wheels parked on the sidewalk, so other traffic could get past. But as Hugo rounded the corner, he saw no other cars, just an elderly couple standing behind the ambulance, with concerned looks on their faces. Hugo slowed as he reached the vehicle, and a paramedic appeared from the back of it.

"I heard footsteps," the man said. "Are you Monsieur Marston?"

"Yes, where is she?"

"In the back."

Hugo hurried to the open rear doors. Claudia lay on a gurney with an oxygen mask covering her face. He hopped up into the ambulance and nodded to the paramedic monitoring her.

"What happened?" Hugo asked.

"She passed out on the street," the young woman said. "The couple out there found her and called us."

Claudia propped herself up on one elbow and used her other hand to pull down the mask. "Hugo, I'm fine. I'm so sorry to be a pain, really."

"Don't be ridiculous," he said. He took her hand and gave it a squeeze. "What happened?"

"I was attacked by three large men. I managed to kill two, but the other one got away."

"Claudia . . ."

"Oh, fine, you can have the boring, real story. I was running. My ten-mile training run, one of the routes is up to the Sacré-Coeur."

"You're still sick, though," Hugo chided. "You shouldn't be running at all."

"I felt better, I really did. Anyway, I was puffing a bit and suddenly felt light-headed. Next thing I know . . ." She waved a hand. "Here I am."

"Are you going to the hospital?"

"No. That's why I had them call you. I knew you were close, and they don't want to release me to my own devices."

"Quite right." Hugo turned to the paramedic. "Thank you for taking care of her. Is she OK to be released to me?"

"*Oui, monsieur*," the young lady said. She unclipped the oxygen monitor from Claudia's finger and helped her patient sit upright. "She seems fine, heart rate is normal, oxygen levels good, no sign of concussion. She's all yours."

Hugo stepped out of the ambulance and helped Claudia down. "Thanks," she said, "but I promise, I'm totally fine."

"I'll call us a cab," Hugo said. Claudia shivered in the cold, damp air, and he held her close as he reached for his phone.

The male paramedic, Michel Prost, stood a few feet away and was about to light a cigarette when his colleague shouted to him from the back of the ambulance.

"Michel! No time for that, we have another call."

Prost groaned. "Someone else can take it, *non?*"

"*Non*, we're up." She turned to Claudia. "You are quite sure you don't want to go to the hospital?"

"I'm fine," Claudia insisted. "Someone else needs you more than I do."

"I'll see that she gets home safe and sound," Hugo said. "Thanks again for your help."

Hugo helped Claudia to a nearby wooden bench, and they sat. He took her hands and they watched the ambulance leave, its siren and flashing lights reflecting off the stone walls and dark, damp road. When it had rounded the corner, Hugo squeezed Claudia's hands and said, "Some pretty steep hills to try running up when you're not feeling your best."

"I noticed," she said.

"You need to take better care of yourself," he chided. "Get better and then resume training."

"This is my first marathon, Hugo. I can't just skip a week and then pick right back up." She gave him a smile. "Not at my age, anyway."

"I hear you," he said.

"Plus, I thought I was all right. I thought maybe a run would clear out my lungs, get my system back in order."

"Is that what you thought, Doctor Roux?"

She swatted his arm and sat back. "Shut up and call us that cab."

Hugo took out his phone, but before he could dial, the display lit up with Ambassador Taylor's name. Hugo answered.

"Boss, what's up?"

"Someone told me you'd run off suddenly. Is everything OK?"

"Claudia. But she's fine, or will be. Fainted while running; nothing more than a light head in the end. But I'm taking her home just to keep an eye on her. Can you make it back solo?"

"Well, in theory I could, yes."

Something in the ambassador's voice alerted Hugo. "What's wrong?"

"I'm not sure exactly, but if there's any way you can swing back here, I think it'd be a good idea."

"What aren't you telling me?"

"I don't know exactly. But they're saying someone is dead. The cops are all here, and they're saying someone has been . . . murdered."

Hugo told Claudia what the ambassador had said.

"Then you need to go. It's all right, I'm fine." Claudia watched him, obviously sensing his need to return to the museum. "I'll get that cab and go straight home."

"I'm not leaving you out here alone. Are you OK to walk?"

"Of course, Hugo. I just ran six miles."

"And then collapsed."

"I told you, I'm fine now."

"Then walk with me to the museum. We can find somewhere comfortable for you, and when I figure out what the hell's going on, I'll take you home."

"OK, sure. Thank you."

They set off, more slowly than Hugo would have liked, and he dialed Ambassador Taylor as they walked, wanting more details. He tucked his phone away when, two times, he was sent straight to voicemail. Five minutes later, they were at the entrance to the museum.

So were the police. Four cars with their lights flashing, and four men in uniform trying to corral the art show's guests as they came out of the museum, some milling aimlessly around and talking in quiet voices, while others stood there looking shocked. He looked around for the ambassador but didn't see him. He couldn't see Alia Alsaffar or Rachel Rollo, either, but he knew they might be inside talking with the police.

Hugo led Claudia to the front door, but they were stopped by a uniformed officer.

"Sorry, *monsieur*, police only."

"Of course," Hugo said. "Can you please tell me who has been killed?"

"*Non, je m'excuse*, I cannot give any information at this time."

That was the answer Hugo was expecting, but it still left him frustrated. "Then can you tell me who is in charge?"

"*Oui, monsieur*, it will be Lieutenant Intern Adrien Marchand."

"Will be? He's not here yet?"

"Correct, he's *en route*."

Hugo gestured toward Claudia, who was still very pale. "My friend here just fainted in the road while running. Do you think she could sit down inside the reception area?"

The *flic* hesitated, but then waved another officer over and asked him to add Claudia's name to their list of people present, and then escort her inside. The large glass windows of the museum afforded Hugo a view of her settling into a couch and closing her eyes as she relaxed into the soft leather.

"Fine, indeed," he mumbled to himself. Hugo thanked the policeman and stepped back, phone in his hand. He scrolled through his contacts until he found the name he was looking for. She answered quickly.

"Hugo, how're you?"

"A little chilly, but in general I'm good, Camille. You?"

Lieutenant Camille Lerens was a well-respected member of the Brigade Criminelle, the unit of the Paris police whose job it was to investigate the city's most serious crimes, including murder. She also had the distinction of being the highest-ranking black detective in the unit, and she was most certainly the only transgender one. She was also a close friend.

"Enjoying my evening off," she said. "Something going on, or is this a social call?"

"I was hoping you were working."

"Not a social call then."

"There's been a murder in Montmartre," Hugo said. "At an art exhibition that I was attending."

"Wow, Hugo, you really do attract trouble. No one you know, I hope."

"That's the thing. I was here with Ambassador Taylor but had to run outside for a moment. Now they won't let me back in, so I have no idea who the victim is."

"We get like that with crime scenes," Lerens said.

"Yeah, well, I've attended a few myself. I want to make sure my boss is OK. Can you call the lead detective and get me in? I may even be of some use."

"I hate to admit it, but you usually are. Do you know who the lead is?"

"Yeah, Adrien Marchand. You know him?"

"Of course." Lerens was quiet for a moment. "I can try, Hugo. But Marchand is not one of my biggest fans."

"Old guy, is he?"

"Quite the opposite. Only been in the unit a year. Young, very eager, and has a chip on his shoulder."

"About you?"

"I'm not sure whether it's my skin color or gender that bothers him the most. Maybe both."

"What a shame." Hugo thought for a second. "Hang on, the officer who gave me his name said he's a lieutenant intern. You outrank him."

"I do, but I'm not his supervisor, and it's frowned upon to mess with someone else's investigation."

"We're not messing with it, we're offering to help."

"Help, right." Lerens chuckled. "I'm sure he'll see it that way."

"Camille, please. Can you at least try?"

"I'll try, Hugo, but no promises. Call me later, let me know what's going on."

"Thanks, I will."

Hugo shuffled in circles to keep warm but stayed close to the main doors, glancing through the glass to check on Claudia and to see if anyone might be coming to get him. After five long minutes, a burly officer appeared at the top of the stairs and pushed his way out into the cold. He looked around for a moment, then his eyes settled on Hugo.

"Monsieur Hugo Marston?" he asked gruffly.

"Yes, that's me."

"Can I see some form of identification, please?"

Hugo showed him his embassy credentials, noting with pleasure the surprise in the man's eyes as he caught sight of his badge.

"Follow me," the officer said, and he turned to the *flic* with the clipboard. "Add his name. Hugo Marston."

Hugo hurried to keep pace with the large policeman who wasn't going to wait for him. They went into the warmth of the museum's reception area, and Hugo looked over at Claudia.

"I'll be as quick as I can," he said.

"Don't worry about me," she said. "I've called Jean to come get me." She gave him a wan smile. "I kind of figured you'd be stuck here a while."

"Good thinking." Jean had been her father's driver, and a good friend to Claudia since childhood. Hugo gave her a wink and started down the stairs. "And you may be right about me being here a while. Call me later, when you feel up to it?"

"I will." She blew him a kiss and settled back into the couch.

Downstairs, a handful of policemen and women eyed him as he reached the main floor. He could feel the tension down there, the sense of urgency and excitement that always hung around a crime scene like an invisible but ever-present fog. Alsaffar's pieces dotted the floor as if they'd been abandoned, and they seemed like follies in that situation, extravagancies, totally out of place at a murder scene.

Hugo looked around, trying to see where the killing had taken place, but it was impossible to tell. He presumed close to where the gaggle of cops had gathered.

The gruff policeman turned to Hugo. "Wait here, please," he said. "Lieutenant Intern Marchand is two minutes away. And don't touch anything."

CHAPTER SEVEN

As he waited, impatient and unhappy at the lack of information, Hugo decided to reserve judgment on Lieutenant Intern Adrien Marchand despite what Lerens had said. That became somewhat harder when the polished shoes, three-piece suit, and carefully waxed mustache under a turned-up nose arrived and paused on the last step, the detective looking around like a king surveying his realm. His gaze settled on Hugo.

"Who let a civilian into my crime scene?" He looked around, and the gruff *flic* looked at him with surprise on his face.

"You told me to bring him in."

"Upstairs, for God's sake." He pointed back up the stairs. "The reception area." The officer started to mumble an apology, but Marchand waved him into silence and spoke to Hugo directly, and in French. "I have men outside identifying everyone who was in the museum from the moment it opened until the moment the body was found. I have six officers taking statements down here, in a couple of the side rooms. That good enough for the FBI? Do you even understand a word I'm saying?"

"I do, and that sounds good to me." Hugo stepped forward and extended his hand, enjoying the surprise on Marchand's face. Hugo continued in French. "If I can be of help, I'd like to be. Otherwise, I need to make sure my boss is all right, and then I'll stay out of your way."

Marchand took his hand for one brief shake. "I have a lot of respect for Lieutenant Lerens," he said. "I particularly appreciate the way she doesn't interfere in my investigations. Usually."

Hugo smiled, using every ounce of self-control to not joust with the overly tailored man. "She is an excellent detective," he said. "One of the best I've worked with."

Marchand smiled. "And let me guess. Even excellent detectives need help from time to time."

"I'd say so."

"Of course you would." He eyed Hugo for a moment. "Let's go see our victim, shall we?"

"I don't even know who's been killed," Hugo said.

"Well, it's nice to know my men aren't gossiping as well as inviting strangers in."

"Do you mind telling me?"

"Why don't you see for yourself?" Marchand turned and walked toward the back of the museum, letting Hugo trail behind in a wake of expensive *eau de toilette*.

The body was in one of the small side rooms. A crime-scene technician handed Hugo a pair of disposable gloves, and Hugo snapped them on, steeling himself for what he was about to see. The victim was obscured from view; two men in scrubs were blocking Hugo's sight. Then they moved apart and Hugo's heart sank.

She lay on her front, face down on a bench made of books, with one arm falling over the edge, her hand resting on the floor. He couldn't see much of her, or how she'd died, but there was no mistaking who it was with that thick, lustrous hair and the webbed dress that shimmered under the overhead spotlight that was supposed to be highlighting her work, not her. A police photographer snapped pictures, the *click-click* of his camera the only sound in the room.

"Killed at her own exhibition," Marchand said quietly. "That'll hit the headlines."

Hugo fought back the anger and the swell of sadness that surged inside him, that threatened to drown out his objectivity and undermine the investigator in him. He looked away, took a long, slow breath, and consciously refocused his mind.

Access points, he said to himself. *How did the killer come and go?*

He inspected the entrance he'd just come through, a sliding pocket door that looked to be the mirror image of one on the far side of the room. A simple latch could lock it from the inside. He tried it, and the door opened and closed silently on its runners.

"Monsieur Marston," Marchand said. He gestured toward the crime techs, who had finished their work. The photographer, too, turned away from the body and stowed his camera, letting Marchand and Hugo move closer.

Hugo scanned the floor around the bench for anything the killer may have dropped, or for signs of a struggle. Marchand leaned over her and gently moved her hair, and his gloved fingertips came away covered in blood. Hugo pointed to her neck.

"Knocked unconscious and strangled?" Hugo asked quietly.

"Looks like it."

A voice spoke up behind them. "That'll be up to me, *messieurs,* if you don't mind."

Both men straightened and turned. "Dr. Sprengelmeyer, good evening," Hugo said.

"Not for her it's not," Sprengelmeyer said grimly.

Marchand looked back and forth between them. "You two know each other?"

"Monsieur Marston appears at my crime scenes with some regularity," Sprengelmeyer said. "What is this, the third? Fourth?"

"Just the third," Hugo said. "I think."

Sprengelmeyer grunted and gestured for Marchand and Hugo to give him some room, which they did. Hugo took that moment to appraise the rest of the room. The theme, as best he could tell, was seating constructed from books. There was a grand armchair, almost a throne, a foursome of small chairs for children, a *chaise longue,* and the simple bench that Alsaffar lay on now.

"Good guess, Monsieur Marston," Sprengelmeyer said after his brief examination. "At first look, I would have to agree that she was knocked out and then strangled to death. There is significant petechiae in the eyes and behind the ears. Even some on the cheeks. I can be more definitive after the autopsy, but it looks quite straightforward."

Straightforward, Hugo thought. *What a way to describe the end of a life, especially a life as promising as this one.* He had a sudden urge to go to her body, to touch her hair, to say something, anything, to make this better. But neither words nor gestures could change what had happened, could alter her "straightforward" death. Hugo clenched his jaw and, once again, pushed away the sadness and anger that Alia's death was provoking.

"If she was hit in the head, there should be more blood," Marchand said.

"There's plenty of it." Sprengelmeyer pointed to the bench. "The books have soaked it up." He grimaced. "From work of art to biohazard. I suppose you're going to ask me that annoying time-of-death question?"

"No need," Marchand said. "Within the last hour."

"Well, that's just typical." Sprengelmeyer waggled his thermometer. "The one time I can give you a good answer to that question, you already know it."

"Sorry to disappoint, doc," Hugo said grimly, then he walked to the far end of the room, where a tech was dusting the sliding door for prints. "Was it locked when you started?" he asked.

"*Non, monsieur*," she replied.

Hugo turned and looked back across the room. "And no one found any kind of weapon?"

She shook her head no and went back to dusting.

"He or she must have taken it with them." Marchand had joined him at the end of the room, and was looking around. The room was clean and empty but for the art; even the walls were bare.

"I suppose so. Who are they interviewing?" Hugo asked Marchand.

"One of my colleagues will know, why?"

"I need to check on my boss."

Marchand waved a hand at the door they'd come in. "Go see, if there's nothing else you can tell me about this scene."

"Not right now there's not," Hugo said. He took out his phone as it buzzed. Claudia had sent him a text: *All well, am with Jean. Who died?*

He tapped out a quick reply. *Glad you're OK. Will call later.*

He could've answered her, she wouldn't print anything until he gave her the all-clear. But Claudia was a true journalist and, even though he trusted her completely, he knew her brain would go into overdrive and she'd probably bombard him with questions for when she *could* publish that information. But right now, she needed to rest and he had work to do.

Hugo was about to dial Ambassador Taylor when a uniformed officer stepped into the room, breathing heavily.

"Lieutenant Intern Marchand."

Marchand turned. "What is it?"

"We found something outside. It might be the murder weapon."

"What is it?" he asked.

"A snow globe," the officer said. "And it's covered with blood."

They hurried up the stairs to the entrance, and on their way past the coat-check counter, Hugo grabbed his coat. Outside, two *flics* stood over the globe, and Hugo stopped to inspect it. Obviously from the museum itself, the globe was about four inches high, the glass ball maybe three inches in diameter, with silver numbers and glitter that were meant to swirl around the melting clock that was its central feature. A handful of people hovered nearby, trying to be subtle about their macabre interest but fairly obviously taking photographs with their phones. Everyone moved apart to let Marchand through, and Hugo followed him, glad of his warm coat, as the temperature seemed to have dropped even more over the last ten minutes or so.

The globe was intact, having been dropped into a small nest of leaves in the crook of the road, between the cobbles and the sidewalk. The blood was hard to see in the dark, but it was definitely there.

Marchand looked around. "Do you we have pictures of this yet? And if not, why not?"

"I'm right here," the photographer said. He adjusted the settings on his camera and started shooting. Hugo looked away as the flash cut through the dark. After a minute, the photographer stopped and Marchand stooped to pick up the globe.

"Definitely heavy enough to do some damage," he said. He held it up and, with his flashlight shining on it, showed it to Hugo.

"Blood for sure," Hugo said. A crime-scene tech held open a bag, and Marchand put it in carefully.

"Make sure it gets fingerprinted and tested for DNA," the Frenchman said.

Hugo nodded his approval. "You're thinking a crime of passion, where our killer didn't have the time or inclination to wear gloves."

"*Exactement*." Marchand said.

Hugo turned and scanned the dozen or so people still waiting outside the museum, each waiting to give their names and contact information to the uniformed officers. And, Hugo presumed, be asked if they saw anything, heard anything, or knew anything.

"Is that the official exit?" he asked Marchand. He pointed to a set of double doors not more than twenty yards from the entrance, and on the same side of the building.

"It is."

Hugo shook his head. If this was a crime of passion, a murder in the moment, the killer had lucked out. A quiet place out of view, but in the hurly-burly of a busy event, and with two ways to leave the scene of the crime, and two ways to exit the museum. He walked over to the doors and pulled on them. Both opened outward to reveal a staircase leading downward. *Also two ways to get in.* The man who'd taken Hugo's coat stood nearby, so Hugo turned to him and spoke in French.

"These steps. Where do they lead to?"

The man just stared and shrugged. "*Je ne parle . . .*" He shrugged again, and Hugo switched to English, asking the question again.

"Oh, yeah. They take you to a hallway between some of the smaller rooms."

"Is one of them where the murder happened?"

"Yes, I think so. Hey, can you tell me who was killed?"

"I don't think they're releasing that information right now."

"It's just that I'm waiting for someone to come out. I've been watching for her and asking, but I don't speak much French and no one will tell me anything."

"I know they're interviewing people downstairs, or at least collecting contact information." Which reminded Hugo that he still needed to find Taylor. "At this stage they prefer to receive rather than hand out information, I'm afraid."

"What if it's her, though? Can you at least tell me it's *not* her so I can stop worrying?"

"I can probably do that," Hugo said. "What's her name?"

"Thanks, man. This is her event, and she's actually my stepsister. Her name's Alia Alsaffar."

Hugo stood there, not knowing how to respond. Finally, he said, "Wait here for a moment, if you don't mind. Let me find the detective in charge. Can you tell me your name? I know he'll ask."

"Sure." The man nodded. "I'm Rob Drummond."

Hugo spun on his heel and headed back to Marchand, who was handing the now-bagged globe to another officer.

"Do you have someone working on locating family?" Hugo asked.

"*Bien sûr,*" Marchand said. *Of course.*

"The gentleman by the exit doors, large fellow. You might want to start with him."

"Why is that?" Marchand peered past Hugo. "Who is he?"

"He just told me he's the victim's stepbrother."

"Is that so?" The detective started forward, then stopped. "Does he speak French?"

"He told me he didn't, no."

"Of course not," Marchand muttered. "I suppose you better come translate."

"Happy to help," Hugo said.

"And now that I think about it, since an American has been killed, your embassy will want to stay involved, right?"

"As involved as you'll let us be," Hugo said. "Like I said earlier, I'm available to you in whatever capacity you need me."

"Very kind." The corner of Marchand's mouth twitched into a smile, and Hugo wondered if his own passive demeanor had warmed the lieutenant intern toward him a little. *Thawed*, might be a better way to put it. "Let's start with translator."

Hugo introduced the detective to Rob Drummond, who wore a worried look as Marchand and Hugo led him to the upstairs office, commandeered from the museum staff as a temporary, and cramped, headquarters for the police.

"Give us ten minutes, will you?" Marchand said to the half dozen uniformed officers in there. The most senior, a whip-thin man with the single stripe of a brigadier, ushered the others out into the reception area, at the top of the stairs down to the museum proper. Marchand closed the door and turned to Hugo, his voice soft and calm. "Please tell Monsieur Drummond what has happened, and extend my sincere condolences."

Hugo nodded and gestured for Drummond to sit in one of the four blue, plastic chairs. Hugo and Marchand did so, too.

"I'm very sorry to have to tell you this, Rob, but the person killed was your stepsister. Lieutenant Intern Marchand here would like you to know how sorry he is, too."

"Jesus, it's Alia? Really?" Drummond leaned forward, elbows on his knees and his head in his hands, staring down at the floor. "Oh, my god. I don't believe this. I can't believe this."

"I know it's a shock," Hugo said. "And again, I'm very sorry."

"You're sure?"

"I am. I saw her myself."

"Do . . . did you know her?" Drummond asked.

"A little. We had dinner last night, actually." Beside him, Marchand straightened in his chair, and he looked at Hugo with a question in his eyes.

You can ask me your questions later, Hugo thought. *Right now, this man needs some time, space, and attention.*

"So, there's no mistake, no chance . . ." His voice trailed off and he sat there, slowly shaking his head.

"I'm sorry, there's no chance of a mistake. It's definitely Alia."

"But why? She's such an amazing person," Drummond said quietly, not bothering to correct himself this time. "And I don't just mean as an artist, I mean as a human being. Sweet, thoughtful, kind."

"I didn't know her well," Hugo said. "But she sure seemed that way. How close were you two?"

"Not as close as either of us would like," Drummond admitted. "I've been living in London for the past few years and was looking forward to her moving there, seeing her more. I guess we saw each other once a year, maybe even less. It's so easy to keep in touch via social media, you know?"

"Definitely," Hugo said. "That serves me well, being so far from home. What was the age difference between you two?"

"That's why we weren't really close. And have different names. My father met her mother after I'd left the house, what, fifteen years ago? I'm forty-six." He shook his head. "This is all so unbelievable. Who would want to hurt her? Why?"

"I don't know, but I'm sure that's a question Lieutenant Intern Marchand here would want me to ask you. Can you think of anyone she had a run-in with? Even something that seemed minor?"

"No, I really can't. I can't imagine anyone wanting to do her harm. It's insane."

"Let me fill the detective in on what we've said, just a moment." Hugo turned to Marchand and summarized his conversation with Rob Drummond.

"*Merci*," Marchand said. "I understood some of that. Including, I'm quite certain, the part where you had dinner with our victim last night?"

"I did, yes. She was supposed to attend an embassy function and my boss sent me to pick her up, but she decided she didn't want to go."

Marchand raised a skeptical eyebrow. "And you decided that dinner with a beautiful woman was more important than your embassy function?"

"Not a hard decision," Hugo said. "Embassy parties are not my thing."

"And it was just dinner?"

"Yes, we ate and I . . . *merde*, Josh Reno."

"What? Is that a person?" Marchand asked.

Hugo ignored him and spoke to Drummond directly. "What about Josh Reno?"

"What about him?"

"Didn't he and Alia have a falling out?"

"Yeah, kind of, I guess," Drummond said. "But I don't think it was that serious, and there's no way he'd do something . . . like this. No way in the world."

"What makes you so sure?"

"I mean, come on." He spread his hands. "It's Josh. Mister nice guy. Plus, he's been Alia's best friend and greatest admirer for years. He'd do anything for her."

Anything except get left behind, perhaps, Hugo thought. Beside him, Marchand cleared his throat unsubtly, so Hugo took a moment to run through the events at the restaurant, and Drummond's opinion that Reno was incapable of killing Alsaffar.

"But Alia did tell me he had a temper that she'd seen on a few occasions," Hugo added.

"Push him harder," Marchand said. "That Reno character sounds like he just put himself on our radar as suspect number one." He held up a cautionary hand. "Early days, I know, but we need to know more about him." Marchand looked around the small room. "Not here, though. At the prefecture where we can record everything properly. But first . . ." His voice trailed off, and it took Hugo a moment to understand.

"You're going to ask him to identify the body. His stepsister."

"I have to."

"No, I can do it. I knew her well enough to do that, for heaven's sake."

"I'm sorry, no." Marchand shook his head. "Our procedures do not allow for that. If family is available, they must do it."

Hugo looked at him for a moment. "All right. I'll let him know."

"*Merci.*" Marchand's voice softened. "It's going to be a long night for the poor man. I'm sorry for that, too."

CHAPTER EIGHT

I t was midnight by the time they got to the prefecture, a little later by the time they'd settled into an interview room.

Hugo and Marchand had stayed with Rob Drummond throughout his ordeal at the medical examiner's office. They'd had to wait for Alia Alsaffar's body to be wheeled into the viewing area, and then they'd had to hold him up when Dr. Sprengelmeyer pulled back the sheet. Hugo rode with them, too, back to the center of Paris, but Marchand had balked at any further participation.

"I'm sorry, but my driver will take you to your apartment."

"You have a translator standing by?" Hugo asked mildly.

"I'm sure someone will be available, yes."

"And if not? You're all right with waiting until the morning to interview the victim's closest relative here, a man who was at the crime scene, and who knows the person you've identified as your one and only suspect. You're all right with that?"

"My only suspect *so far.*"

"And you won't identify any more tonight if you can't communicate with your only witness so far." Hugo turned to Drummond and switched to English. "You're an American citizen, right?"

"Yes, of course." Drummond already seemed dazed, and the question obviously puzzled him. "Why?"

"Can I assume you'd like a representative from your government present when you're questioned? Assuming the French authorities agree to that, of course."

"Well, yes. I'd like you there. Can you be there? I don't really speak French, and . . . You know."

"I will ask." He turned back to Marchand, who grimaced and waved a hand dismissively.

"I understood enough of that. You invited yourself to his questioning, and he accepted. Is that about right?"

Hugo smiled. "The United States Embassy is grateful for your cooperation and appreciates the accommodations you are willing to show one of its citizens."

Marchand turned away and muttered something that Hugo didn't catch, gesturing for them both to follow him inside the building, but Hugo thought he saw the glimmer of a smile on the lieutenant intern's lips.

Once they'd settled in the interrogation room, a uniformed officer appeared with a tray bearing three disposable cups of coffee, creamer pots, and packets of sugar. Marchand spoke to Drummond in halting, accented English.

"I am sorry. The coffee is not good. *Normalement* we serve good coffee in Paris, but not here."

"Thanks. It's fine, really." Drummond reached half-heartedly for a cup and emptied three packets of sugar into it.

Marchand looked at Hugo, who also helped himself to a cup. "Can you explain that this interview is being recorded? And then maybe ask him about his family history, get him talking about how he's related to our victim."

"Will do." Hugo looked at Drummond. "Are you OK to answer a few questions?"

"Yeah, sure. Whatever I can do to help."

"And, just so you know, there are two cameras in here with microphones, recording everything we say."

"I figured."

"That's important because you need to be careful with your answers. I know you want to help, but if one of us asks a question and you don't know the answer, don't make it up just to be helpful. You can get yourself in serious trouble that way."

"Right, got it."

"Why don't you start by telling me more about your stepsister?" You said you weren't close due to geography and age, right?"

"That's true, yes." Drummond puffed out his sizeable cheeks and blew his breath out slowly. "This is so surreal. I'm in a French police station. Alia's dead. I mean, really dead. That sweet girl gone, and for what? Why?"

"That's what we're trying to find out. And, believe me, you may think you don't know anything, but you know more than anyone in this room. We need your help. Even if you don't know who killed her, you're the first step, our starting place. We'll use what you tell us to properly launch this investigation, which is why we have you here so late. The first few hours are the most important in any investigation, which is why we have to do this now. And why you're here—because at this point only you can help us."

"Sure, whatever you need. Ask me anything."

"Oh, first, can we take your DNA and fingerprints? For elimination purposes."

"Err," Drummond shook his head slowly. "I don't mean to be a jerk, but no. I don't like . . . touching things I don't have to touch, and putting my fingers in some grubby ink that a million criminals have touched . . ." He shuddered. "Sorry, but no. My DNA you can take because you use those sterile swabs, right?"

"We do, yes."

"That's fine, but unless you get a warrant, or whatever they use here, no one touches my hands. Sorry."

Hugo smiled. "I did notice you wouldn't take the tip I offered."

"Cash is the *worst*," Drummond said. "Just disgusting."

"And the bottle of hand sanitizer on the hat-check counter."

"Even that doesn't feel like it helps sometimes," Drummond said. "But thanks for understanding."

"Sure. I'm curious, why were you checking coats? What with you being family."

"Oh, the guy who was supposed to do it, the museum employee, was sick. Alia seemed stressed about it, so I just offered, seemed like a good way to avoid shaking hands with people." He grimaced. "I didn't think about all the cash I'd have to handle."

"Makes sense. So, why don't you tell me about your parents, I guess all three of them."

"Well, OK. My father I never knew growing up, so that's an easy one. My mom went to Germany, she was in the military, met some English guy and they . . . had me. I grew up in America and kept her name, she would never even tell me his, said he didn't deserve to be thought of as a father, just a sperm donor."

"That must have been tough."

"I guess, but it's all I knew. And my mother, she was mom and dad, if you know what I mean. She could arrange flowers and change the oil in the car. She played both roles. Then he showed up, one day. Out of the blue."

"Was that strange?"

"I was in my teens at that point. I was so used to not having a father that he was pretty much a curiosity and nothing more. He had money, I guess was charming, and told me about the English side of my family. But he was more like my mom's friend, not a real father, even though they eventually married. Just before her death."

Hugo translated so far, but Marchand seemed to have understood pretty well. Hugo continued: "So your father met and married Alia's mother at some point?"

"Yeah, her father died about three years after she was born. Cancer."

"That's rough," Hugo said.

"She never showed it, but yes, I'm sure it was hard growing up without her dad, even though I hadn't much minded doing that. Anyway, when she was . . ." He thought for a moment. "Must have been around sixteen or seventeen. Her mother met my father, they married, and we became stepsiblings."

"You were in your twenties?"

"Right." He smiled. "Don't make me do math, please. But yeah, late twenties."

"Are they both still alive?"

"No, they're not. Her mother was killed in a car accident."

"And your father?"

Drummond sat back and looked down at his hands, saying nothing for a moment. Finally, he looked at Hugo, then Marchand, and back to Hugo. "I suppose you'll find out eventually, won't you?"

"Find out what?" Hugo asked.

"About my father."

"What about him?"

"He's dead," Drummond said quietly. "I killed him."

Hugo translated as close to word-for-word as he could remember, and just as Marchand was about to speak, a knock on the door interrupted him. A uniformed policewoman stuck her head into the room.

"Lieutenant Intern Marchand, there's some new information, from the victim's phone. You said to let you know when we got anything at all, so I hope you don't mind me interrupting."

"No, it's fine." He looked at Drummond and spoke in English. "Please, excuse me for a moment." He gestured to Hugo to step outside with him. "I'm only catching half of what he's saying, but it's all recorded and I can have it transcribed if I need to. But if you'll continue with him and take notes, fill me in after, then we can get more done. And more quickly."

"Happy to," Hugo said. He was pleased that Marchand had gone from clear annoyance at his presence to trusting him with this interview. Objectively, this was a simple task and a smart way to divide the labor, but that didn't mean a petty or resentful detective had to let him conduct the interview.

"*Merci*. I'll be back in a few minutes, I'm sure."

Hugo returned to the interview room and sat down. "He said I should continue, since he doesn't speak English too well."

"He's gonna miss the best bit," Drummond said.

"How you killed your dad?"

"Yeah. It was about five years ago. Since my mother's death, and since Alia's mother's death, he'd turned into a drunken asshole. Like, truly mean. Anyway, one of his drinking buddies had a niece living with him. Ten years old, something like that. I went over there one night to talk to my dad. There was no answer when I knocked, but the door was unlocked so I went in. I found the two of them taking photos of her in the basement."

"What kind of photos?"

"The ones adults shouldn't take of kids. Ever."

"Good God, what happened?"

"I lost my mind. I went to call the cops, but they begged me not to, and when I ignored them, they came at me. My dad's buddy, he was so drunk he took one swing and fell over, missed by a mile. But my dad . . . he had a look in his eye, like how dare I question what he's doing? Even though it was . . . sick. He came at me, and I just grabbed him and hit him, over and over. It was like a red mist came over me, I couldn't stop. Didn't want to stop."

"Were you charged with anything?"

"Hell, no. The cops took one look at the digital camera and all but gave me a medal."

"Still, I'm sorry you had to go through that," Hugo said. "Pretty traumatic for you. Did you and Alia talk about it?"

"No. I mean, not really. She knew what kind of person he'd become, she was pretty much estranged from him anyway, at that point. She understood, I think."

No wonder she didn't want to talk about family, Hugo thought.

The interview-room door opened, and Marchand came in and sat down at the small table. "Anything we can use?" he asked Hugo.

"Just getting the family history."

"Oh, yes. He said he killed his father?"

"Yes. I'll fill you in later, an emotional story and the poor man's tired."

"Hugo, he killed his father, are you saying that's not relevant here?"

"Yes," Hugo said, "I am. Trust me, that situation is not this one, even a little bit. A violent and twisted father, basically self-defense . . . not the same."

"Fine, if that's what it was, I agree." Marchand looked at his watch. "Well, we can let him go. Or take him home. We have someone else we need to check out."

"A possible suspect?"

"Too early to tell, but could be," Marchand said. "Someone was nearby, whose number was on the victim's phone, but who wasn't invited to the event."

"Intriguing, who is it?"

"A woman by the name of Claudia Roux. Ever heard of her?"

CHAPTER NINE

Tom sat on a bench, huddled against the cold in his long wool coat, and looked out over Prinsengracht canal to consider his options. The sweet, tempting aroma of the local pancakes drifted to him from a stand twenty yards away, reminding him that it was almost three in the afternoon and he'd not eaten since an early breakfast.

He had half a mind to call off the search for the day and just be a tourist for a few hours, maybe stand in the long, snaking line to get into the Anne Frank House, which was close by. But his feet hurt, and shuffling along for an hour before even getting in did not sound like fun.

Hugo ought to be here helping, he thought. *He'd know what to do next. And he wouldn't have broken into the wrong room at the hotel.*

That had been a mistake. And one he was lucky not to be arrested for. He sat back to think but was interrupted by the gentle ring of his phone. He didn't recognize the number, but answered anyway.

"This is Tom."

"Hi, Tom. Brendon Fowler here."

"Bren, you find something out?"

Fowler had been a colleague of Tom's at the CIA. A tall, muscular redhead with a law degree from Duke, he was a man you could count on in a pinch, even if you no longer worked for the Company. The only odd thing about Fowler was his appetite—he ate pizza and only pizza for every meal of the day. No one had ever seen him eat anything else, and he admitted it was what he consumed on the way into work every morning.

"Bad news, I'm afraid," Fowler was saying.

"Fuck, you drew a blank?"

"Not what I meant," Fowler said. "It's bad news for you."

"How's that?"

"You told me he was a smart guy, if I remember rightly."

"Not that I'd admit it to the bastard's face. But yeah."

"What he's doing isn't smart."

"So you did find something," Tom said.

"Most definitely."

"And you're going to make me beg and plead to get it out of you, I see."

"Nah, you already promised me a pizza coupon, so I'll just tell you. He used his dead brother's passport."

Tom let that process for a moment. "That's actually pretty clever. Obvious, and yet I didn't think of it."

"Right? I thought the same thing at first, but let it sink in," Fowler said. "Think about what it really means."

It dawned on Tom, probably the same way it had on Brendon Fowler. "Shit," Tom said. "It's clever but also obvious. He'd have known that the minute he was suspected of being here, the authorities would flag any passport with the name Cofer on it."

"Right," Fowler said. "Fake passports are almost impossible to get away with these days, but if you do manage to create one, you can stay under the radar. He didn't go that route."

"But using his brother's passport . . . There's no way he can make it back home without being caught, and that'd be a violation of his parole."

"Which, in turn, means . . ." Fowler prompted.

"He has no intention of going back to the States, let alone back to prison. This is a one-way mission for him."

"Right. And, as an aside, we also now know he's not staying at a hotel."

"Because they make a note of guests' passports," Tom said. "He may be on a mission to hell, but he's not ready to be found that easily."

"Right. And this makes him so much more dangerous, Tom.

Seriously, you need to think about getting the authorities involved, officially."

"I can't. We've had barely a glimpse of him, and some lazy cop somewhere will say that just because his dead brother's passport is being used means nothing. Someone else could've purloined it."

"And yet that's not the reason you won't be calling for help, is it?"

"This problem needs to go away permanently," Tom said. "Not back to prison for a few years."

"That's my point. He's already fixing to go away permanently. The thing is he's planning to take you with him."

Tom thought for a moment. "What I don't know is, does he want just me? Or will he go after Hugo as well?"

"Your guess is as good as mine. Either way, he's suicidal."

"If he's also going after Hugo, then he's not suicidal yet. Unless Cofer's planning to haunt him to death."

"Well, let me know if I can help," Fowler said. "Whatever you need, official or unofficial."

"I will. And thanks, Bren, I appreciate it."

"Just do me one favor, will you?"

"Sure," Tom said. "What is it?"

"Stay alive."

Tom gave into his senses and bought a paper plate loaded with Dutch pancakes, juggling with them back to his bench. As he sat facing the canal, a duck flapped onto the bank and ventured toward him, quacking quietly. It fell silent as it got close, but its beak stayed open slightly, and Tom assumed the wee feathered fellow was used to tourists, and maybe locals, sharing their spoils.

"Careful, little man," Tom growled. "This is mine, all of it. And you might want to consider your own place on the food chain. In Paris, Hugo would be eating you alongside a plate of fries."

The duck ignored him, but it flapped its wings and backed away when Tom reached for his buzzing cell phone. Brendon Fowler had sent him a text: *He just checked into the Rijks Hotel on Sint Nicolaasstraat. BE CAREFUL.*

A hotel? Tom thought. *Why would he risk making himself visible like that? Carelessness, or a trap?*

Tom sent Fowler a thumbs-up emoji and looked up the hotel on his phone. It was located in the heart of Amsterdam, and looked to be on a tiny street right where the action was, where the prostitutes and sex shops vied with the smoke shops and marijuana cookie sellers for the attention of the wide-eyed tourists. Tom had spent more than a few hours on those streets and knew what a rabbit warren they could be. An advantage for a local, maybe, but not for Tom. Although he had to assume that as a recent arrival, and recent convict, Rick Cofer knew that area even less well.

Tom looked at the duck, which had turned its attention to a family nearby, and smiled. *Speaking of Hugo . . .* He dialed his friend's number, wanting to update him and ask a question that was bothering him, but the call went straight to voicemail.

"Marston, you ass. You're supposed to have called me back, like five times. I've confirmed that the bastard is here, one hundred percent. He's at a hotel in the red-light district, which I happen to know reasonably well, which will surprise you. I'm gonna check it out. And, yes, I'll be careful. When you get this message, call me, jerk."

He checked how far the hotel was from his location, hoping it'd be far enough away to justify a taxi. He groaned when his phone assured him it was a mere fifteen-minute walk. He got to his feet, found a trash can for his plate and the few crumbs he'd not inhaled, and set off.

The wind seemed to pick up as he walked, blowing into his face and sending angry ripples through the canals that he crossed. He wondered how to approach the hotel, or whether to at all. Cofer, he had to assume, would be looking over both shoulders all day every day, and using the internet as best he could to find out about Tom, and maybe Hugo. Tom had no idea whether Cofer knew of his time in the CIA. It seemed unlikely, since Tom was invisible, non-existent, on the internet, and the Company hardly publicized its employee list. But if Cofer had found out somehow, he'd be even more twitchy. And be more sure that Tom would be looking for him, and able to discover his location.

Shit. I should assume he does know, and is luring me there, Tom thought.

But he went back and forth because he knew that was a stretch. The meathead had just gotten out of prison, and there was no logical way he'd been tracking his and Hugo's careers from behind bars. *And yet he's here, presumably looking for you, pal. Which means he knew you were here, or would come.*

Tom quickened his step, annoyed with himself and the puzzles running in circles inside his head. Around him, people drifted through the chilly afternoon with their heads down, wrapped up in wool coats and scarves, oblivious to anything except getting where they were going. The questions kept poking at him, and he wished Hugo would call him back. As much of a stiff as his best friend was, his mind was unique, and his advice, while frequently annoying and safe, was invaluable. Without slowing, Tom called him again, again going to voicemail.

"One thing I want to know. Just text me if you know the answer, you don't even have to talk to me. Why the fuck did Cofer come here and not Paris?"

That was the biggest question he had. Why Amsterdam?

CHAPTER TEN

"Claudia Roux?" Hugo laughed. "Yes, I do know her, and take my word for it, you can cross her off your suspect list."

"Is that so?" Lieutenant Intern Marchand asked. "Maybe we should talk in my office." He turned to a pale and exhausted Rob Drummond and spoke in slow, deliberate English. "*Monsieur*, I will have an officer drive you to your home. I thank you for your time, and am sorry for your sister."

"Thank you," Rob replied.

"We will be in touch with you again in the next day, maybe two." Marchand gave a small bow and indicated with his head for Hugo to follow him. As they walked down the hallway, Marchand said, "So, Mademoiselle Roux. How do you know her?"

"Assuming there's just one of her, and we're not talking about someone else. I suppose someone else could have the same name."

"But if it's the one you know, you think we can cross her off the suspect list."

"Most definitely."

"This should be interesting." Marchand stopped at an office door and opened it. "After you. Please, take a seat." Hugo sat while Marchand rounded his desk and dropped into his obviously brand-new executive chair. He picked up a piece of paper and showed it to Hugo. "A copy of her driver's license information. It is the same Claudia Roux?"

Hugo glanced at the picture. "It is, yes."

"Tell me about her. How do you know her?"

"She's a journalist. The daughter of a prominent Parisian, Gerard de Roussillon. A count."

"Never heard of him."

"He's dead now," Hugo said. "No reason you should know who he is."

"I don't spend much time with French royalty," Marchand said. "Go on."

"Anything in particular you want to know?"

"Yes. Your relationship with her."

Hugo smiled. "Complicated. But if you're asking if we're romantically entangled, I would say . . . from time to time."

"The details are not my business, but the fact that you are in a relationship most definitely is."

"Fair enough. But I can vouch for her on that night, as well as her character. The idea that she would be a suspect is . . . with respect, ridiculous."

"From where you're sitting perhaps. But how many times have you seen someone shake their head and declare how shocked they are that so-and-so committed murder?"

"I'm just telling you, it'd be a waste of your time to focus on her. What reason in the world would she have to hurt someone she'd never met?"

"Who invited you to the sculpture event?"

"Alia Alsaffar."

"That's right." Marchand nodded. "You had dinner with her the previous night."

"I did."

"Then I have my motive." He said it playfully, but Hugo knew the Frenchman was wondering whether there might be a grain of truth in his statement.

Hugo returned the small smile. "Ah, so your theory would be that Claudia, with whom I have a close friendship and occasionally more, kills Alia Alsaffar because I had dinner with her. Once."

"Did Ms. Roux know you had dinner with her?"

"I should inform you," Hugo said, "that I have dinner virtually every night of the year, frequently with other people. None of them have been murdered, that I am aware of."

"Mademoiselle Alsaffar was," Marchand said matter-of-factly. "Please answer my question. Did Claudia Roux know you were dining with her? Either before or after the fact."

"We spoke on the phone right before, yes. And she didn't mind in the slightest."

"She told you that? That she didn't mind?"

"Yes, she did. Because why would she?"

"Women don't always say what they mean, or what they are thinking."

"As true of men as it is women," Hugo said. "Are you really saying you think she's a suspect?"

"You know how this works. Everyone is a suspect until they are not." Still with that smile on his face and his piercing eyes. "Why did she call Alia Alsaffar?" Hugo said nothing, and Marchand nodded slowly, and said: "Ah, you didn't know."

"I didn't, so why don't you ask her?"

"Because she's not here right now, and you seem to have an answer for everything. I thought you might enlighten me."

"Probably wanted to interview her. She's a journalist, remember."

"Alsaffar never called her back, though. Seems odd."

"Why is that odd?"

"Every artist I've ever met has jumped at the chance for free publicity."

"I imagine Alia was very busy, it being the day of her show."

"Or maybe your friend was calling to warn her off," Marchand suggested mildly.

"If they were both teenage girls and this was all happening at a high school, that might be a possibility."

"She was there, though, Mademoiselle Roux. Wasn't she?"

"At the museum? No, she wasn't." Hugo knew he was splitting hairs, but Marchand's smugness was getting to him.

"Nearby. Did you know she was going to be?"

"She was running. And, no, I didn't know."

"Just happened to be running right past where you and Alia Alsaffar were sipping champagne together. The day after a cozy dinner together. And happened to call Alsaffar's phone a few hours earlier. Why do you think she didn't mention that to you, by the way?"

"She was a little busy collapsing from the run," Hugo said. "We didn't do too much idle chatter."

"Where is she now?"

"Home, I assume."

"A little late for a visit, but I'll go see her tomorrow."

Hugo shifted in his seat. "Look, I know you're going to want to say no to this, but hear me out."

"No. You may not come with me."

Hugo gave a wry smile. "I told you so."

"Think about it." Marchand leaned forward. "If, just if, she becomes a good suspect, then that makes you a witness. And since I don't know whether or not that's going to happen, I would be a poor policeman if I let you interview a suspect with me."

"Fine. But when all this is over, I'll be saying I told you so."

"I hope that is true," Marchand said. "But in the meantime, I have another . . . request."

"Request or instruction?"

"As long as you abide by it, call it whichever you want."

"What is it?"

"I would ask that until I have spoken with Claudia Roux, you do not. Not in person, not by phone, not by text, not even email."

"You're asking a lot, considering that she's innocent, and not even a viable suspect at this point."

"Then think about this. If she becomes one, depending on what else I find out, a phone call from you might be viewed as obstruction of justice. And if she's no more than a witness, then you might be tampering with a witness."

"And if she's done nothing wrong?"

"Then there is no harm in you not communicating with her for a few hours."

He held Marchand's eye for a moment but saw he was deadly

serious. The guy was being a jerk, but Hugo couldn't fault his logic. "Fine. I understand why you'd ask that. But do me a favor. Talk to her tomorrow. Cross her off your list and start looking for the person who *actually* killed Alia Alsaffar."

Hugo was woken at seven the next morning by a clap of thunder that seemed to rattle the windows. He checked his phone and was reminded that he had messages he'd not even listened to from Tom. It'd been too cold to check his phone on the walk home the previous night, and he'd been too exhausted once he got there to do anything but brush his teeth and fall into bed.

The phone buzzed as he was looking at it. His boss.

"Ambassador, how're you?"

"I'm fine, how the hell are you?"

"Too early to tell. Up late last night."

"You helping the police with their inquiries?" Taylor asked. "In a good way, I mean."

"I was until they decided Claudia was a suspect."

Ambassador Taylor was silent for a moment. "You're kidding, right?"

"Nope. Wish I was." Hugo yawned. "To borrow a phrase from Tom, it's fucking ridiculous."

"Why the hell would they think that?"

"Because she was nearby, she'd called Alia's phone, and I had dinner with Alia the night before."

"Oh, right," Taylor said, his voice dripping with sarcasm. "That ugly jealous streak that Claudia shows so often."

"It's OK, it's so ridiculous that it'll take about twenty minutes for them to figure out they're wasting their time."

"Why was she close by? Had she decided to attend?"

"No. That damn marathon she's training for, one of the runs took her up to Montmartre."

"That's funny," Taylor said. "That it just happened to take her up there that night, and at that time."

"Jeez, boss, don't you start." Hugo stretched and climbed out of bed. "I kept trying to find you last night. What did they do with you?"

"Stuck me in a closet. Rather sweet if you think about it. Once they found out I was present, they wanted to make sure I was safe. Kept me out of sight."

"Well, good. I like my job and don't mind my boss; I'd hate to lose you and have to train up someone new."

"Thanks. I think. What's on tap for you today?"

"Well," Hugo said. "If it's all right with you, I'd like to poke around a little. Alia was an American citizen, so I have reason to be asking questions."

"You do. Is Camille on this one?"

"No. If she was, they wouldn't be bothering with Claudia."

"Good point."

"It's some captain called Marchand. You know him?"

"No, but no reason why I would. What does Camille say about him?"

"I gather there's some tension between the two," Hugo said. "She claims it's on his part, and, knowing her, I'm guessing that's true. And to begin with, he was a little buttoned up with me, resisted my charm for a while."

"He must be uptight, then." Taylor was quiet for a moment. "Well, dang, Hugo. I thought it was Camille in charge; but if it's not, maybe you better stand down until Claudia's in the clear and he invites you in to help."

"Which could be lunchtime today or weeks from now. And you know as well as I do, every minute counts in a murder case."

"In *his* murder case," Taylor reminded him. "Hugo, I mean it. My job is to maintain good relationships with the French authorities, not screw up their homicide investigations."

"That's OK then," Hugo said. "*You* won't be screwing anything up."

"Nor will you," Taylor said sternly. "Any inquiries you make will be subtle and outside any official sphere. And sure as hell outside his line of sight."

"But you'll back me up if Marchand finds out and loses his cool."

"Hell, no, I won't. He has every right to exclude you from the investigation, especially when Claudia is a suspect. No matter how nonsensical that might be."

"Right, which is precisely why I need to get involved," Hugo said. "It's completely nonsensical."

"Keep your head down, Hugo. Speaking of that, what news from Tom?"

"Shoot," Hugo said. "I owe him a call. Several, now that I think of it. Let me do that now, and I'll fill you in later." He hung up and dialed Tom, but it went straight to voicemail. "Hey, it's me. Sorry I keep missing you, caught a new murder case here. Someone I knew, too, so I'm a little busy. Anyway, I don't know the answer to your question, but I'll think about it. There must be some reason he'd go there; we just have to figure out what it is. We can talk when you call me back." A surge of fear rose in Hugo, maybe because Alia had been killed and Claudia was in the police crosshairs but, whatever the reason, he was suddenly afraid for Tom. "Call me back, even if it's just to let me know you're OK. OK?"

He stood in front of his bedroom window and watched the heavy raindrops fall, listened to the hiss of the rain as it went past him, and looked at the people in the street below as they scurried out of its way, into doorways and nearby stores. He felt very far away from his friend at that moment.

"Damned weather," he muttered, and put the heavy feeling that sat in his chest down to just that—the low clouds, the incessant rain, and a Texan's need for a little more sun than he'd been getting recently.

CHAPTER ELEVEN

In recent weeks Hugo had shied away from working on weekends. It was a good time to catch up with paperwork and duty rosters, or to do some advance planning ahead of the next dignitary's visit. But a few months ago he'd noticed himself breathing a little heavier after his walk to work, and again on the way home. And a couple of his favorite pairs of pants seemed to have shrunk in the wash, which they'd never done before.

So, since that unhappy revelation, weekends had been about taking long walks through Paris, and even the occasional jog when he could persuade someone, usually Camille Lerens, to join him. He'd seriously considered Claudia's offer to run that marathon with her, but he knew himself too well, knew he couldn't realistically commit to the training sessions. Not just because work at the embassy kept him so busy, but also because he detested running and would find every excuse to back out of the training. And that would've been unfair to Claudia.

Today was different, though, a Saturday that he needed to work. Today Claudia was being eyed as a murder suspect, ludicrous as that was, and whether Lieutenant Intern Marchand liked it or not, Hugo would be looking for the real killer. And not just for Claudia's sake, but for Alia's, too.

He went to his desk, turned his back to the rain, and dialed the Hôtel de Crillon, asking for Rachel Rollo's room. A man answered, sounding surprised, or maybe suspicious.

"Mr. Rollo, my name is Hugo Marston. I work at the US Embassy, head of security. I'm helping the Paris police with the inquiry into Alia Alsaffar's death."

"Not death. Murder. Call it what it was."

"Her murder, yes. I was hoping I could come over and speak to you and your wife this morning."

"When exactly?" His tone remained curt. "We've not even had breakfast yet."

"I'm available all day. What time suits you?"

"I suppose nine thirty would be fine."

"Thank you," Hugo said. "Would you mind if I speak to you one at a time?"

"Why is that necessary?"

"Normal procedure—it's how we conduct every interview."

"I suppose so, then," he said, but he sounded dubious. "Meet me in the lobby; we'll find a quiet place to talk."

Hugo kept his phone in his hand, the desire to call Claudia almost overpowering. But he'd promised Marchand he'd wait until the police had talked to her, and by venturing to the hotel to interview the Rollos, he was about to step onto thin ice as it was. The French detective could cut him out of this investigation with a snap of his fingers if he wanted to, and Ambassador Taylor had made it clear that he wasn't going to burn political capital on keeping Hugo in the loop.

Hugo still had more than an hour until the meeting, and it was a thirty-minute walk, but he was restless, couldn't just sit there. Until now, he'd not let himself dwell on Alia's death, putting it instead into the "investigation" compartment in his head. But images of her crowded in, the sparkling eyes and bright smile. He could almost feel the excited energy of their evening at the restaurant, see the wrinkle of her nose as he popped an escargot into his mouth. And it was unhealthy to fight those memories, the sadness; he knew that and, for what felt like an age, he let the dark cloud of her death envelope him. When the fog had lifted a little, he roused himself, pulled on a raincoat, and retrieved an umbrella from the back of his closet.

Outside the rain had become more of a drizzle, so he used the umbrella as a walking stick and set off along Rue Jacob, then angled down Rue de Beaune. He exchanged muted *bonjour*s with a Christmas-tree vendor who was nailing an X-shaped base onto one of his trees, and Hugo enjoyed the sweet scent of pine for the rest of that block.

When he got to Quai Voltaire, he waited for the light to change and, when it did, he was overtaken by a group of schoolchildren and their teachers, the latter stationing themselves strategically across the road like traffic cops. Hugo smiled at the flow of bobbing, colorful umbrellas and the excited voices of kids who were escaping school for a few hours, rain or not. Their tidy uniforms told Hugo they were at a private institution, which explained why they were in school on a Saturday.

He started across the Pont Royal and looked down at the water, still brown and angry as it churned through the city. He didn't linger this time, though, and shrugged himself deeper into his raincoat when a gust of wind buffeted him. He quickened his step, not minding that he'd get to the hotel early; it'd be warm and dry, at least, and he wondered how the coffee would be. Other than expensive, of course.

When he got to the hotel's lobby, Hugo recognized JD Rollo from the evening of the murder. He was already there, talking to a receptionist. Rollo was a tall man, maybe an inch shorter than Hugo, with close-cropped gray hair and a solid build. He wore an expensive-looking tweed suit over a white shirt open at the neck. Hugo lingered until he'd finished his conversation, then approached.

"Mr. Rollo? Hugo Marston, we didn't get a chance to meet at Alia's event."

"No, but I saw you talking to my wife." Rollo's tone was neutral, and Hugo wasn't sure if there was any meaning in the statement, or if it was just an observation. They shook hands. "I ordered coffee for us and found a cozy spot to sit, I hope you don't mind. Come this way."

"I don't mind at all," Hugo said. "Thanks for the coffee—if you hadn't ordered, I would have."

Rollo grunted an acknowledgement and led Hugo into one of the lounge areas. "They refurbished the place a year or so ago. Did a damned good job, created all these little areas where you can just sit and watch people." He glanced over his shoulder at Hugo. "You're probably a big fan of that, eh?"

Again, Hugo couldn't ascertain the man's meaning, if any. "What makes you say that?"

"You were a profiler in the FBI, no? Isn't that what you guys do, watch people and interpret behavior?"

"Ah, I see. Sure, I guess in some ways. Although it might be more accurate to say that we observe behavior in retrospect."

"Here we are." Rollo gestured to two comfortable, leather chairs separated by a low table. On the table was a silver tray bearing a coffee pot, a creamer jug, and sugar. The aroma of fresh coffee drifted up to Hugo's nose, and suddenly the wind and rain seemed very far away. "How do you take yours?" Rollo asked, reaching for the coffee pot.

"Black, with sugar." He waited while Rollo poured, and then helped himself to the raw brown sugar. "Thank you."

"Welcome." Rollo poured his own, taking it the same way as Hugo. "Now, how can I help?"

"First of all, please accept my condolences for the loss of your friend. I got to spend a little time with Alia, and I can't imagine how difficult this must be."

"Thank you. She was an amazing woman, not just talented but kind, generous, and . . ." He sighed and shook his head. "Like I said, simply an amazing woman. I still can't believe this is happening, to be honest."

"That's a very common sentiment, believe me. When something like this happens, it's not just a tragic loss but an emotional shock that the mind has a hard time processing."

"You've seen this before, obviously."

"I'm afraid so," Hugo said.

Rollo looked at Hugo for a moment, as if appraising him. Then he said, "Well, tell me how I can help find who did this."

"Thank you. I suppose the first question is whether you saw who went into that room with Alia?"

Rollo smiled. "Or, put another way, do I know who killed her."

"If you like," Hugo said.

"No. I don't know who killed her. I wish I did."

"And you didn't see anyone going into that room?"

"I didn't."

"Why wasn't that room open like the main floor?" Hugo asked.

"Why do you think I'd know that?"

"You helped set this up, didn't you?" Hugo asked.

"In some small way, yes." Rollo smiled. "And I do happen to know. There were four rooms down there, closed off. It was Alia's idea, rather cute of her." He paused to sip his coffee. "Each room had its own theme, you see. Throughout the evening, she wanted to open each one up, have a surprise reveal of each room, one by one."

"Why?"

"She thought it would be in keeping with the general theme of the exhibition—each room would be like a new chapter or section of a book."

"Ah, yes," Hugo said. "That makes sense. I like that idea. So, how did you meet her?"

"Several years ago, she took some photographs for us. A family gathering. My parents figured it to be the last before they died, so they wanted someone to record it for posterity. I honestly can't remember how we found Alia's name, why we chose her. But she did a good job, and while she was there she got to talking about art with Rachel. Things kind of snowballed from there."

"Snowballed?"

Rollo shook his head. "Not that way, no. She's . . . *was* a beautiful woman, no question. But we were all good friends, nothing more than that."

"And you guys sponsored her."

"*Sponsored* implies we got something in return, which we didn't." He eyed Hugo as he took another sip. "Which was also poorly worded. We didn't *want* anything in return; it wasn't your usual arrangement whereby one party pays and the other party gives them recognition or some other benefit."

"Pure altruism?"

"I'm not sure there's any such thing, is there?"

"It seems to be what you're describing," Hugo said.

"Well, yes and no. We got great pleasure from seeing her succeed. From helping Alia to get her work out into the world where people could enjoy it. Neither Rachel nor I have any siblings, and our twin boys are off doing their own thing, so I suppose you could say that Alia was somewhere between being a daughter and a sister." He grimaced. "And now I've just made it sound weird."

"No, I get it," Hugo assured him. "I think I know what you mean."

"Point is, there was no romantic involvement from either of us toward her."

"What about from Josh Reno?"

"You'd have to ask him."

"I will. But do you know of any romantic entanglement between them?"

"You sound so old-fashioned, Mr. Marston."

"I've heard that before," Hugo said with a smile.

"But to answer your question, I suspect maybe he had feelings for her, but I never saw anything . . . develop."

"She didn't have them for him?"

"Not that I was aware of. He's actually pretty talented himself, more of a painter than a sculptor. But good."

"Did you support him, too?"

"Indirectly, I suppose. He paid his own way everywhere, and he helped Alia with the logistics and muscle involved with her shows. In return he got some gallery space for his work. I wouldn't say they were a team, but it was a symbiotic relationship. They were friends, respected each other, and both profited from her success."

"You may not be able to answer this question, but I'll ask it anyway." Hugo took a swallow of hot, rich coffee. "It's a given that no one can predict the future, of course, but I'm wondering if he's likely to succeed, make a name for himself, now that she's gone."

Rollo nodded. "You're wondering if he had a disincentive to kill her. I would've said yes to that a few days ago."

"Meaning?"

"Meaning, as of several days ago, his professional and artistic attachments to Alia were intact, which in turn means that as far as he was concerned, when she had a show, so did he. And when she continued her rise to the top, he'd be there with her. That's a huge disincentive to kill her."

"But that changed, as I understand it."

"Right. He wasn't getting space at this event. And with her planning to move to London, I don't think there was going to be space for him in her life. I believe that gives him an actual motive, does it not?"

"Oh, I don't know. If he was angry enough with her, maybe. But in the middle of her own exhibition, that seems a little unlikely."

"And yet," Rollo said, "that's where it happened. Someone killed her there and then."

Hugo nodded and took another sip. "Have you spoken to the police yet?"

"I thought I was right now."

"More of a parallel investigation, you might say."

"Is that so? One the Paris police know about?"

"If they don't, they will," Hugo said. "We're all on the same side, it's just that sometimes people get territorial and focus on that a little too much."

"Get that a lot in the FBI?"

"Not as much as it looks like on TV, but every now and again." Hugo drained his cup. "So you'll have to go over this all again with them, almost certainly."

"Lucky me. You still want to talk to Rachel?"

"If there's nothing more you can think of. Anyone who'd want to hurt Alia, someone she had any kind of dispute with. Anything at all."

"I'm afraid not," Rollo said. He stood, pulled out his phone, and tapped out a message. He waited, staring at his phone for a moment. "Right, she's on her way down. Help yourself to more coffee." Hugo stood, too, and they shook hands. "And find out who killed that beautiful woman, please."

"I plan to," Hugo said. He watched as Rollo walked away, into the lobby and out of sight. More coffee sounded like a good idea, so he poured himself a cup and sat down to wait for Rachel Rollo. Her husband had been a disappointing dead end, had given him nothing to go on at all. That said, Hugo felt like the man had been holding something back, keeping something from him. But Hugo had no idea what it might be, a frustration he put aside as he waited for the man's wife.

Five minutes later, Rachel Rollo appeared in the lobby, and Hugo watched as several heads turned her way. She wore jeans tucked into leather boots, and a fluffy, gray cashmere sweater. Her hair was pulled back into a pony tail, and her makeup was flawless. Hugo stood and shook her hand, catching a whiff of expensive perfume that he couldn't identify.

"Nice to see you again," he said. "Although I would prefer it be under different circumstances."

"Me too. And, Hugo, I'm sorry to do this to you, but can we talk about this another time?"

"Is something wrong?" he asked.

"I got call from the museum. They want to know what to do with the exhibit. The sculptures."

"So soon? Can't they hang on to them for a few days?"

"I'd have thought so, yes, but they're freaking out about what happened. I need to go over there and calm everyone down."

"You're in charge of the exhibit now?"

"Not officially. But they can't find Josh Reno. They tried getting hold of him to take care of this, but they said he's not returning calls or texts."

CHAPTER TWELVE

Hugo walked Rachel Rollo out of the hotel and held open the taxi door as she climbed in. He had half a mind to ride with her since he was now planning on taking a trip to Montmartre himself, but he didn't want to interview her with a taxi driver listening.

Instead, he decided on the metro. The rain had stopped, for now anyway, and the air outside smelled fresh. It was a short walk to the Concorde stop, where he trotted down the stairs and wound his way through the tunnels to his platform. There, a homeless man sat on a blanket with his change cup empty in front of him and his attention not on the commuters passing him by, but on two tiny bunny rabbits that hopped around each other on his blanket. Every few seconds, he'd reach out and pull one back as it hopped too far away. As Hugo watched, the man grinned a gappy smile when one rabbit launched itself at the other in a clumsy, playful attack.

Always a new gimmick, Hugo thought, but he dropped five euros into his cup anyway. As he took his place on the platform, he smiled at what he knew Tom would have said: *At least the old fella has dinner taken care of.*

Hugo took the green line north, and twenty minutes later he climbed the stairs out of the Abbesses station and stepped into the heart of Montmartre. He turned right and walked along Rue des Abbesses, a long, meandering stroll along the cobbled streets and still-empty sidewalks, all the way to the hotel where Alia Alsaffar and Josh Reno had been staying.

Inside, he showed his credentials to the young man stationed by the grand piano, which seemed to serve as their reception desk.

"Excuse me, *monsieur*," the young man said. "But can I get my manager? The police were here already, so I don't understand . . ."

"Of course," Hugo said. "Whatever you need to do."

A moment later, a tall, elegant black woman approached. "*Bonjour monsieur*, how can I help you?"

"*Bonjour*. My name is Hugo Marston, I work at the US Embassy here and I'm part of the investigation into the death of your guest, Alia Alsaffar."

"Ah, yes, such a tragedy. I am so sorry."

"Thank you."

"I am Alouette Tremblay, the day manager. How can I help?"

"I believe the police have been here already, is that right?"

"*Oui*. They spent some time in her room looking through her things. I am not sure, but they may have taken some with them."

"Quite probably," Hugo said. "Would you mind if I look myself?"

"Actually," she said, hesitating. "I wonder if you might be able to help me in that regard."

"Be glad to."

"A man came in earlier. After the police but before you, he left about twenty minutes ago. He wanted to take her things."

"Who was it?"

"I don't know his name, but he said he was her brother . . ."

"You think he was lying?"

"I don't know how to say this tactfully but Mademoiselle Alsaffar was a beautiful woman. Very beautiful . . . exotic. The gentleman who came here . . ." She lowered her voice. "It didn't seem to me they shared many of the same genes."

Hugo refrained from smiling. "Was he a larger gentleman with, shall we say, agricultural cheeks and a slightly thinning hairline?"

"Yes, that is him."

"His name is Rob Drummond, does that sound familiar?"

"No, if he gave me his name I forgot." She shrugged. "And you see, they don't even have the same last name."

"He is . . . was the young lady's stepbrother," Hugo explained. "He really is, so that's why he was asking."

"Ah, *bien*. I didn't know. Perhaps I shouldn't have turned him away."

"He may come back, and if not I can find him so I wouldn't worry. Did the police tell you that you can release her belongings?"

"Monsieur Drummond said so, but I've not heard that from them, no. Which was another reason I declined."

They both looked toward the main door at the sound of raised voices, two men arguing heatedly in English. Hugo recognized both.

"You did the right thing, *madame*, but I think maybe Monsieur Drummond has returned." Drummond and Josh Reno stormed into the hotel, both pulling up short when they saw Hugo.

"What are you doing here?" Reno asked.

"He's part of the investigation, idiot," Drummond said. He turned to Hugo. "Maybe you can tell this woman that I'm Alia's brother. She treated me like a common criminal, trying to steal her stuff."

"Which would be pretty fucking accurate," Reno said.

"Screw you, mooch, you're the one who's done nothing but take, take, take from her."

"All right, boys," Hugo said sternly. "How about we all simmer down and sort this out?" He turned to Tremblay. "Is there somewhere I can talk to these gentlemen? Separately."

"*Bien sûr*," she said. *Of course.* She led them past a self-service coffee and pastry bar, to a space around the corner like a mini library. An armchair and half sofa made the place seem cozy and quiet.

"Josh, can you wait here a moment?" Hugo asked.

"Why can't I wait in my room?"

"As a favor. Please."

"Fine. But not for long, I need to figure out what I'm doing now that . . ." His voice trailed off and he looked at the floor, then sat down on the half sofa.

Tremblay beckoned for Hugo and Drummond to follow her, and the three of them walked back to the main lobby, past the elevators and into a room marked as an office for employees only. "You can use this space," Tremblay said.

"Thank you. Rob, you OK waiting here for a moment?" Hugo asked.

"Why?"

"I'm going to make one quick phone call, and then I'll be in to see you." He left the room and stepped outside the main doors of the hotel, wanting to be sure he wasn't overheard. Light drops of rain spattered his head, so he moved back under the awning and positioned himself so he could both stay dry and not trigger the automatic sliding doors. He dialed the prefecture, irritated with himself for not getting Marchand's cell number on Friday night. He had to wait to be connected, but he hoped that the Frenchman ran his investigations like many American homicide detectives: he'd quarterback the legwork from his office, and remain available to those working under him. Hugo guessed right.

"Marchand, who is this?"

"*Bonjour, Lieutenant Intern,* this is Hugo Marston."

"Ah, working on a Saturday, how very diligent."

"No more so than you," Hugo said.

"How can I help you?"

"I'm at l'Hôtel Toby."

"We've been there already."

And did you find anything of use to the investigation? Hugo wondered. Instead, he said, "I know, the manager told me."

"Why are you there?"

"I found myself between Rob Drummond and Josh Reno," Hugo said, truthfully but also dodging the question. "Monsieur Drummond is asking if he can access Alia's room and take custody of her belongings. He's claiming you gave him permission, but the hotel would like to hear from someone other than him."

"Yes, we've searched, photographed, and taken what we need. The rest is his . . . assuming he's the closest relative here in Paris."

"I'll confirm, but I'm almost certain he is. Her parents are dead and she has no siblings. Other siblings."

"In that case, no problem. Is there anything else you need, Monsieur Marston?"

"Would you mind telling me whether you found anything in her room that might help?"

There was a pause on the line. "I'm not at liberty to reveal any information at this point."

"Because I'm friends with Claudia?"

"Yes, partly. Also, because you are not a member of the Brigade Criminelle."

"I can be of use to you," Hugo said, his voice calmer than he felt inside. "Just as I have been in the past." He desperately wanted to proclaim Claudia's obvious innocence, but he knew it was only obvious to him at this point, and doing so would further alienate Marchand. And that he did not need to be doing.

"I'm well aware that Lieutenant Lerens has broken protocol by allowing you to know details of previous homicide investigations, yes."

"My understanding is that the investigating detective sets protocol for each case," Hugo said mildly.

"*Touché*," Marchand said. "And just as she does in her investigations, so do I in mine. Which means I expect you not to interview, interrogate, or otherwise tamper with *any* of my witnesses. And that includes Mademoiselle Roux, as well as Josh Reno, and the brother of the victim. *Merci et au revoir*, Monsieur Marston." And with that, he hung up.

Hugo tucked his phone away, trying to shake off his irritation. Marchand wasn't being unreasonable, not really. Just not as accommodating as Camille Lerens would have been, and that was frustrating. Especially when Claudia was in his crosshairs. He shivered in the cold and was glad to step back into the warmth of the hotel lobby. He walked over to the grand piano, where Tremblay sat in front of a slim laptop. She looked up and smiled. "*Oui, monsieur?*"

"I just confirmed with the investigating detective that they are finished with Mademoiselle Alsaffar's room, and Monsieur Drummond may take custody of her belongings."

"Very well. Thank you for doing that. And please tell Mr. Drummond he may stay in the room for as long as he needs to handle her affairs, free of charge." She had apparently expected Drummond to be allowed into the room, because she opened a tiny drawer and took out a key card. "Give this to him, if you would."

"Of course. And that's very generous of you." Hugo shook her hand and turned to go.

"While you were outside, Monsieur Reno took the elevator. To his room, I assume."

"Thank you." Hugo paused. "Can you tell me his room number?"

"Oh. Normally we don't do that. For the safety and discretion of our guests." She looked slightly embarrassed at rejecting his request. "If you were a French policeman then, of course, but . . ."

"I understand." Hugo thought for a moment. "Can I ask if his room is adjacent to Mademoiselle Alsaffar's?"

Tremblay smiled. "They asked for that. There is a connecting door, too, but that has been locked from inside Mademoiselle Alsaffar's room since . . . this happened."

"By the police?"

"On their orders, yes," she nodded.

Hugo thanked her and headed to the office to speak to Rob Drummond. "Good news," Hugo said. "Not only are the police fine with you taking custody of Alia's belongings, but the manager says you can stay in her room as long as you like, to take care of whatever needs doing here."

"Oh, OK. That's nice. And a relief. I've been staying at a place about a mile away, a one-star hotel, but I think the star is stolen."

Hugo sat. "Also, we have people at the embassy who can help with the arrangements."

"Arrangements?"

"You're her closest relative, right?"

"Yes. I guess I am."

"It'll be up to you to make the decision about what happens once the police release her."

"Her body, you mean."

"Right," Hugo said, his voice gentle. "I'm sure you've not thought about it, and you don't need to right away. But you're kind of in charge of making that decision."

"I suppose. I just want to go home."

"That's perfectly natural. Did you talk to the police again this morning?"

"No, they called and asked me to come back to the prefecture. I guess I'll go after I get the key for Alia's room."

"Here you go." Hugo handed him the key card. "The manager asked me to give it to you. Do you mind if I come up with you and look around?"

Drummond eyed Hugo for a moment. "Did someone say you used to be an FBI agent?"

"I don't know if they did or not. But yes, I was."

"What did you do for them?"

"Behavioral analysis, for the most part."

"Profiler? Like on TV?"

"Profiler, but nothing like on TV." Hugo smiled. "Nothing's ever like it is on TV."

"I hope some things are." Drummond's head dropped and he shook it slowly. "On cop shows, they always get the bad guy. I'm hoping you can do the same."

"I promise I'll do my best," Hugo said. "It might help if I can look around Alia's room."

"Yeah, of course. Come up with me now." He stood slowly. "But it's not her room you should be looking through."

"Let me guess," Hugo said with a small smile. "The guy staying next door to her."

"Josh Reno?" Drummond shook his head again. "Nah. He's a total mooching asshole, like I said earlier. But I can't imagine he'd hurt Alia."

"Then who?"

"I couldn't sleep last night, so I got to thinking, wondering about who might want to hurt her. The only people I could come up with are that Rollo couple. Something's not right about either of them." They stopped outside the door to Alsaffar's room. "Plus, as I'm sure you've discovered, he was madly in love with her. He'd probably even admit that, if you ask him when his wife's not around. When you add unrequited love to Alia cutting ties to their sponsorship, that gives them both a motive, if you ask me."

Hugo straightened with surprise. "Wait, she cut them out of her life, too?"

"Yeah, they didn't mention that?"

"No," Hugo said, almost to himself. "They most certainly did not."

Drummond stood in the doorway as Hugo carried out a quick but methodical search of her room and belongings. Every time he saw something personal, he had to push back the sadness and anger that threatened to bubble up and spill over. He used his experience to keep those emotions in the right compartment, the one that let him do his job effectively and objectively. For now, anyway.

When he'd finished his search, he surveyed the room, and he did let his mind linger on what Drummond had said about JD Rollo. Unrequited love, as he well knew, could most certainly be a motive for murder.

CHAPTER THIRTEEN

On Sunday morning, Hugo was woken by a knocking on his apartment door. He rolled over and looked at his phone to see that it was already nine o'clock. He dressed quickly in jeans and a sweat-shirt and walked to the door in bare feet. He checked the peephole and was surprised at his visitor but immediately opened the door.

"Hey, what are you doing here? You should've called or texted, I could've made coffee."

"I've had your coffee plenty of times," said Claudia as she kissed him on each cheek. "I can live without it."

"That's what everyone says."

"For a reason. Sit and I'll make some, maybe we'll live."

"Fine." Hugo collapsed into an armchair and watched as Claudia got busy in the kitchen. "How're you feeling?"

"How do I look?"

"A little pale maybe. But otherwise as beautiful as ever."

She looked back and rolled her eyes at him. "You're starting to sound like Tom."

"God forbid. But you really are feeling better?"

"Yes, I am, thank you. I hope that was a one-off event."

"So do I," Hugo said. "So really, why didn't you let me know you were coming?"

"I was told we couldn't be in contact, which means I'm not allowed to phone you."

"Claudia, it also means . . ."

"I know, I know." She waved away his protests with one hand. "My surprise visit is a forensic counter-measure, I believe you'd call it."

"Oh, would I?"

"Look, if I push my way into your apartment unannounced, then you can't get in trouble with that awful detective."

"Maybe not, but you sure as hell can."

"Yes, but we need to figure this out," she said, pouring water into the machine.

"Figure what out? You're innocent."

"There, should be ready in a few minutes." She flipped the switched on the coffee machine, then walked over to Hugo and sat on the arm of the sofa nearest hm. She took a breath, looked him in the eye, and said, "I know I am. So this is some kind of joke that I'm a suspect, right?"

"To me it is, yes. Of course, it's ridiculous."

"That detective, what's his name again?"

"Marchand."

"It sure as hell isn't Maigret," she said with a pained smile.

"I know, he'd have cleared you by now." Hugo took her hand.

"You told him this is insane, right, that there's no way I could or would do something like that?"

"Of course. In the strongest way possible."

"Good. I mean, I knew you would, but . . . thanks anyway."

"Of course. So, did you give them an interview?"

"Yes, at the house." Behind her in the kitchen, the coffee started to brew with a satisfying gurgle. "I should probably have been more polite."

"What did you tell them?" Hugo asked.

"That I was thinking about doing a piece on her exhibit later in the week, which is why I'd called her."

"When did you call?"

"Friday morning. After you'd told me about her, I did some research, and she looked pretty interesting. The world loves a beautiful artist. You know that." She sighed. "That Marchand said her beauty was a possible motive, her messing with my man."

"So you ran up there and strangled her?"

"Right." Claudia rolled her eyes. "He suggested that the phone call was a warning, that we'd argued, and I . . . yeah, killed her."

"Because I ate dinner with her one time, as part of my job."

"That's what I said, but he doesn't seem big on logic, that one."

"Not to mention you were unconscious at the time of the murder, which would make for quite an impressive feat on your part."

"Except he says the timeline allows for me to have slipped into the museum, killed her, and run around the corner to collapse."

The aroma of coffee drifted over them as the maker bubbled to a crescendo, then climaxed with a loud hiss. Hugo got up and went into the kitchen. He poured two mugs, adding sugar to his and Claudia's, but no milk. He stirred them and walked back to his seat, putting both mugs on the table.

"So does he think that was fake?" Hugo asked. "Your fainting spell."

"I assume so. But even if not, perhaps I was so overwhelmed by a mix of adrenaline and emotion after doing it, that I fainted."

"He actually said all that?"

"He didn't need to," Claudia said. "He was very good at implying things without actually saying them."

"Good detectives are."

"Oh, so now he's a good detective?"

Hugo smiled. "He may or may not be. But the truth is, he doesn't know you. He'd be a *bad* detective if he took your or my word for your innocence—I can tell you that much."

"I get that, but given your representations about me, the terrible motive and highly dubious timeline, all that should be enough to move on and find the real killer."

"I'm sure he is," Hugo said. "He'll be following every lead, looking into every suspect, not just you."

She raised an eyebrow. "Hugo, you're defending him."

"Like I said, he has a job to do. And I'm certain he'll eliminate you any moment."

"How will he do that?" She pressed. "If my word, your word, and his stupid theories aren't enough to clear me, what more can he want?"

"He'll look into everything you said, and, when it checks out, then I assume he'll focus elsewhere. With such weak evidence, if it were me, I'd stop completely unless something you said turns out to be wrong or untrue."

"Everything I told him was the truth. I called her about writing an article. I've never met her, or even seen her, in person. I sure as hell didn't hurt her."

Hugo took her hand again. "We both know that. Just ignore Marchand until he knows it, too."

"I'm trying, believe me," she said. "So are you helping with the investigation?"

"I thought I was, but both Marchand and the ambassador have since told me to back off."

"Why does the ambassador care?"

"He doesn't. He just prefers I not piss off the Paris police."

"Well," Claudia said, "I suppose that making nice with the locals does happen to be his job."

"Yeah, I know."

"In that case, I will have to assume," she began, and gave him a conspiratorial smile. "That you're helping unofficially?"

"Well, ma'am." Hugo leaned back, sipped his coffee, and returned the smile. "I'm afraid I'm not at liberty to divulge any case information, especially to a suspect."

"That so?" Claudia waited until he'd put his coffee mug down before she leaned forward with a glint in her eye. Hugo was too slow to see what was coming, but he welcomed the weight of her body, the smell of her hair, and the tight grip of her arms around him when she slid onto his lap.

"Well, screw Marchand and his pointless investigation," she whispered in his ear. "And since I'm here why don't we . . ."

Claudia was in no hurry to leave, and Hugo had no desire to see her go, so they stayed wrapped together in his bed while the rain pounded the window a few feet away. Eventually they decided they were hungry, but they didn't want to risk being spotted together in public, so Hugo concocted a lunch of bits and pieces thrown together from his pantry and fridge: pâté on crackers, pickles, ham on bread that Hugo toasted because it was a day past stale, and several large dollops of hummus each. When they'd eaten, she kissed him on the mouth and left, telling him she had a movie date with a girlfriend.

For his part, Hugo would have liked to share his plans for the afternoon. But with the specter of Marchand hovering over them, he felt it best to say little else about the investigation. When she'd left, he tried Tom again, but the call went straight to voicemail, so he hung up and called the Hôtel de Crillon. He asked to be connected to the Rollos' room, and this time Rachel answered.

"Mr. Marston, so sorry I had to run out on you last time. Are you coming back to visit with me?"

"I'd like to this afternoon, if you don't mind."

"Why not? The police just finished up with us here, so the story is fresh in my mind."

"Story?" Hugo asked.

"Series of events. That evening. Whatever you want to call it." She gave a gentle laugh. "Don't worry, we've not dreamed up some sinister tale to keep each other out of trouble."

"I'm sure not," Hugo said. "Three o'clock work for you? Same place as before?"

"I look forward to it," she said. "They do a nice English tea on Sundays, maybe I'll order one of those for us."

"That's kind, but I'm trying to watch my—" Hugo stopped talking when he realized she'd hung up.

Hugo spent the next two hours trying to read, his phone face-up beside him. He'd picked up a copy of Jim Thompson's classic, *The Killer Inside Me*, at one of the *bouquiniste* stalls beside the Seine, but even that book failed to pin his attention to the pages. He kept checking his phone, just in case he'd missed an incoming call or text from Tom. Hugo was glad when two thirty rolled around, so he could do something proactive, get busy.

When he stepped onto Rue Jacob, he was glad to see that the rained had stopped, bathing the street in weak but bright sunshine. The wind had sharpened, though, and he was relieved to have put on his heavy coat. The familiar journey across the River Seine up toward the Tuileries took him twenty-five minutes, and his face glowed warm when he stepped into the lobby of the Crillon, from the exertion and from escaping the cold.

Rachel Rollo was already there, and as Hugo sat down across from her, a waiter arrived with a cart of food. He unloaded two china tea pots, and two plates of tiny, thin sandwiches. He then set up a tiered tower of pastries, some English, like the fruit cake, and some French, like the *mille-feuille*. The waiter said nothing as he went about his work, like an artist creating a mouth-watering display for its viewers to demolish.

"You do wonder, does anyone ever finish all this?" Rollo said when the waiter had departed. "They say it's for two people, but for heaven's sake, you could feed a nation with this spread."

"I imagine most of the people who stay here are used to having more than they can consume, and aren't too bothered about the waste." Hugo smiled. "Present company excepted, apparently."

Rollo looked around. "We do get pretty comfortable, but this place is a bit of a splurge even for us."

Hugo pictured the man with the bunny rabbits in the underground, what he might be able to manage with all this food. "Will they box it up to go, do you think?" he asked.

"Surely they pay you enough to buy groceries, Mr. Marston," she said with a laugh.

"Almost. But I was thinking of someone else."

"We can ask when we're done. Help yourself, in the meantime." She poured herself some tea, and Hugo did the same. Her face seemed to crumple a little and her eyes misted when she looked up at him. "I can't believe this has happened. Especially to Alia, she was such an angel."

"This must be hard for you," Hugo said.

"It is, but I don't even care about that. What kind of person would do that? And to someone as wonderful and kind as Alia?"

"That's what I aim to find out."

"Please do, there's a monster out there right now, and he can't be allowed to get away with it." She stiffened her spine, as if hoping her resolve would fall in line too. "So, ask me whatever it is you need to know."

"Thank you. First off, did you get your issue at the museum sorted out?"

"Oh, yesterday. Thank you, yes. The manager wasn't sure what was happening with Alia's pieces, so for now they're going to move them into just two of the rooms and put Dalí's art back in the main room."

"Makes sense," Hugo said.

"Interestingly, but perhaps not surprisingly, there's a lot of attention on Alia's work since . . . it happened. Ghoulish interest, I would call it."

"Doesn't that always happen when an artist dies?"

"Very often, yes. More so when it happens like this."

Hugo nodded, then he was silent for a moment. Eventually, he said, "You mentioned that the police came by earlier."

"Yes, they'd wanted us to go to them, but honestly. So cold and rainy, and it's not like we know anything."

"So they came here, to you."

"Yes. Just like you did." She smiled and held up a plate of sandwiches. "Look, they even cut the crusts off, like we're little children."

Hugo refrained from making the smart remark on the tip of his tongue, instead taking two of the cucumber sandwiches. He'd thought these laughable when he first had a proper English tea when stationed in London, but he had quickly come to appreciate the lightness. He thought of Tom again and was suddenly glad his friend wasn't there to see him eat cucumber sandwiches. Not Tom's idea of a meal.

"I suppose the first question they and I will always ask is, do you know who killed Alia? Did you see anyone go into that room where she was found?"

"No, and no." She frowned. "Do you know how much I wish I did?"

"I can imagine. Do you have any clue who'd want to hurt her?"

"I know she was feuding with Josh . . ." She shrugged. "Honestly, I can't think of a single other person. Not that I would dream he'd do such a thing, but I guess you never know."

"Your husband thought it laughable to suggest that Josh Reno would hurt Alia. Even her stepbrother, who can't stand Reno, said there's no way."

Rollo shook her head. "I'm not surprised. Men and women look at these things quite differently. I don't know if you know that."

"I'm not sure what you mean."

"It's hard to explain." She took a sip of tea. "When you walk down the street, what are you thinking about?"

"I guess it depends on what's going on in my life. Work, lunch . . ." Hugo shrugged. "What are you getting at?"

"So there's not one thing that's always in the forefront of your mind when you go out in public?"

"No, I don't think so. Like I said, it depends."

"See, for women it doesn't depend. When I . . . when most women, walk down the street, we're wondering how far we're going to get before someone gives us some unwanted attention. Maybe a comment on our figure, or what we're wearing. Maybe they cross the street and end up trying to chat with us, or maybe they just say hi. I can't tell you how many times I've been told, by complete strangers, that I should smile." Rollo gave an exaggerated smile. "People I don't know and don't care about think it makes me look friendlier, prettier. Which, of course, I should do, because as someone who owes them nothing else, I owe them that as a woman."

"That's very rude," Hugo began, "I'm sorry if—"

"Not if, *when*. My point is, of course men look at each other and say, *Oh, him? No way he'd hurt a fly.* They don't see what men are capable of, normal men, executives as well as construction workers. They don't see the daily assaults, I believe they now call them 'microaggressions,' that women are subjected to every day. If men like my husband, Alia's stepbrother, and probably you, are blind to our lifetimes of abuse, do you think it's possible they might also be blind to a man's ability to seriously hurt, even destroy, a woman?" She sat back, teacup in hand. "There, I lectured you on male privilege without using the word *privilege*, how do you like that?"

Hugo bought himself a moment to think by cramming two miniature egg sandwiches into his mouth. He was impressed, unsettled even, by what she'd said. He'd read a lot recently about privilege, gender- and color-related, and had tried to be more aware. But she was right, he didn't see these regular aggressions, and while he'd not taken JD Rollo and Rob Drummond's word for Reno being incapable of violence, he'd not challenged, in person or in his own mind, where those assumptions had come from. He washed the sandwiches down with some tea.

"Your point is very well taken," he said finally.

"Spoken like a true diplomat."

"Well, technically, I'm not one but, yeah, I'm still processing."

"Keep processing, if you don't mind. The more male processors we have running, the better. And don't *ever* tell a woman to smile, whether you know her or not. Especially if not." Rollo picked up a tiny éclair with her delicate fingers. "Now, back to Alia. What else can I tell you?"

"Is it true that she'd decided to cut ties with you and your husband?"

"Good heavens, who told you that?" She popped the éclair into her mouth and chewed slowly, without taking her eyes off Hugo.

"Is it true?"

She shook her head and swallowed. "No. Not at all. Why would she do that?"

"I have no idea. Maybe after this show she figured she'd be well known enough that she wouldn't need your help. Maybe she just wanted her independence."

"I mean, if the show was a massive hit, maybe she could afford to. And in any case, she wouldn't know that until afterward. But it doesn't even really work that way."

"What do you mean by that?"

"It's complicated, but my point is, even if this exhibition had been a world-beating hit, come the end of the week, she's not going to be rolling in money. And even if she was, and on top of that she won the lottery, why would she just cut us out like that?"

"Like I said, I have no idea."

"Someone thinks that's true, though." Her voice was firm. "I'd like to know who."

Hugo shook his head. "I can't tell you, but I will say it wasn't represented to me as a forgone, completed decision on her part. In other words, the person who told me wasn't completely sure they were right about it."

"Very reassuring," Rollo said dryly.

"Yes, well." Hugo gave into temptation and picked up an English-style scone. He went about the business of halving it, slathering on butter, and topping both halves off with thick strawberry jam. "One of my many weaknesses," he said, before taking a bite.

She arched an eyebrow. "Tell me about your others."

"I couldn't possibly," he said when he'd finished chewing. "I'm curious, did the police indicate whether they'd be talking to you again?"

"You mean, whether my husband and I are suspects."

Smart lady, that's exactly what I mean. "I'm sure they wouldn't put it that way."

"Put it this way," Rollo said. "They asked us not to leave Paris just yet."

"I see."

"Mind if I ask you a question?"

"Not at all."

"Who is Claudia Roux?"

Hugo paused, then said, "Why?"

"That detective, he asked me if I'd known you before the opening at the museum. Of course, I said no. He then asked if I knew someone called Claudia Roux. He went on to ask more questions about her, even though I said no. Questions about you and her, to be specific."

"She's a friend."

"Girlfriend?"

"A friend," Hugo said firmly.

"He made it sound like he had something on her. He didn't ask me about anyone else that way, not Josh, or my husband. Just this Claudia Roux person." Rollo plucked a small jam tart from a middle tier. "And that makes me wonder if you're supposed to be here talking to me about this. Does the French cop know?"

"That I'm here? No, I didn't tell him."

"Well, that's OK." Rollo smiled. "When necessary, I can be very discreet indeed."

CHAPTER FOURTEEN

For several minutes, Tom was stumped.

The man he was after, Rick Cofer, had obviously chosen his hotel with care. Amsterdam's Sint Nicolaasstraat, where the hotel was located, was a narrow, cobbled street that, for the most part, was effectively walled in on both sides by the buildings that fronted the busier pedestrian streets either end of it.

From the map on his phone, Tom saw that the Rijks Hotel sat right in the middle, a Tudor-beamed structure that fronted the little street and was almost impossible to surveil. Making Tom's life harder, or at least more frustrating, was the fact that while he could have found somewhere to lurk at either end of Sint Nicolaasstraat, Cofer could easily turn left out of the hotel instead of right, and Tom would never see him.

But he had no other option, and, it being Tom, he decided to make the most of a bad situation. He started in the Amsterdam Cheese Company on the corner of Nieuwendjik and Sint Nicolaasstraat, taking in the rich aromas of its various wares and nibbling at samples offered by staff as he lingered near the large windows. When the store's employees started giving him looks and by-passing him with their samples, he sighed and, after checking that the coast was clear, he stepped outside.

Even on a cold December Sunday there were plenty of people about, and at least one of them was smoking something strong. The skunky odor hung in the air, and Tom silently thanked the passer-by for sharing his stash, before moving across the street to a cramped grocery store. He picked up a basket on the way in and positioned himself with a half-decent view down Sint Nicolaasstraat from the back of the store. He watched shoppers come and go, but he grew increasingly impatient when no one left or even entered that street. After thirty minutes, the owner, a small, thin man with a bushy mustache, approached and spoke to him in Dutch.

"Sorry, I'm American," Tom said, looking over the man's shoulder.

"Ah, yes. You don't speak other languages, of course."

"That's a little harsh," Tom said. "I speak a few, and know how to say *fuck* in half a dozen. Just not yours."

"It's *rot op*. Now, are you planning to buy something or just stand in my shop all day?"

"It's not just me, you know," Tom said. "I mean, lots of Americans speak Spanish. Especially recent immigrants, but then you'd expect that."

"Sir, I asked you a question."

"And my friend Hugo speaks, like, four languages. Some better than others, but it's still pretty impressive, don't you think?"

"Yes, very. Why are you just standing in here?"

"Waiting for a friend. Now, me, I think my accent is better than Hugo's. I was trying not to boast, but since you asked me directly . . ."

"I didn't ask you." The man had gone from haughty to frustrated. "Not about that, anyway. This is a grocery store not a waiting room."

"French, Italian, Spanish, German, some Russian. That's a hard one, Russian, did you know that they have their own alphabet?"

"Yes, I did. I'm sorry, but I'm going to have to ask you to—"

"I mean, who does that? Why not use the normal alphabet like everyone else? Seems like they're just making things harder for themselves."

"Sir." The man's tone was forceful. "Please leave."

"Well, that's not very nice." Tom adopted a hurt expression. "This how you treat all your customers?"

"You're not a customer!" the man said, almost shouting. "You're just standing here, blocking the way."

"I tried not to, I promise. That's one reason I picked up this basket and didn't use one of those big carts. Then I'd have blocked the way for sure."

"We don't even have any of those!"

"Right, that's the other reason I didn't use one." Tom patted the man on the shoulder. "Well, nice chatting with you, but I have to get going. Have to see a man about a horse."

The owner's face crinkled with confusion. "Horse? There aren't any horses here . . ."

But Tom was past him, and at the exit he dropped his empty basket into the rack and strolled out into Nieuwendijk, eyes peeled for Rick Cofer, and another place to linger.

He stationed himself on a bench with a somewhat distant and limited view of the entrance to Sint Nicolaasstraat, and a much closer view of the two grimy feet that belonged to a homeless man who took up three-quarters of the bench. The feet Tom could ignore, it was the putrid stench that arose from the man every time he shifted that made the bile rise in his throat.

But ten long minutes later, a flash of adrenaline surged through him when he spotted Rick Cofer walking directly toward him.

Cofer was unmissable. Already a tall man, he'd lost the bulk he carried a decade or so ago through either age or prison exercise, and his rangy frame was adorned with the bright-orange soccer shirt of the Dutch national team. He looked older, which was not surprising, but Tom was interested to see how relaxed he seemed.

For a man on a suicide mission, you're pretty chill, Tom thought. *But you're here. You really are here.* Tom stared at the figure of one of the men who'd murdered his sister and, as far as Tom was concerned, had gotten away with it.

As Tom watched, Cofer pulled a matching orange baseball cap, also bright enough to be seen from space, out of a rear pocket and pulled it low over his eyes.

Tom tried to sink deeper into his bulky raincoat and wide-brimmed hat, but Cofer didn't even look his way, just turned to his right and sauntered down Nieuwendjik. When he was fifty yards away, Tom peeled himself from the bench and followed.

Cofer acted like he had no mission, no goal other than to window shop in Amsterdam. He lingered in front of clothing stores, art galleries, even the weed shops, but he never went inside any of them. After twenty more minutes of slow going, Cofer stopped at a German-themed restaurant, studied the menu for a minute, and then went inside. Tom spotted a café, just past the restaurant over a small bridge, where he could get off his feet and watch. He hurried past the Ratskeller with his head down and turned away, and took a table inside the café by the window overlooking Nieuwendjik and, more specifically, Cofer's watering hole.

Again, Cofer seemed to be in no hurry, and, after an hour, Tom worried the American might have slipped out the back of the restaurant. But Tom didn't want to abandon his station and risk running into the man, so he sat tight and ordered another coffee and a second apple strudel.

At two o'clock, Cofer reappeared. Tom's bladder was full, and his head buzzed from the sugar-coated pastries he'd eaten to pass the time, but seeing Cofer gave him another surge of adrenaline. Tom signaled for the bill, digging into his wallet for a handful of euros in case Cofer moved too quickly. But the man remained in no hurry, he just stood on the sidewalk, looked around, and stretched, almost like he dared anyone to spot him, to recognize him. Tom stood and watched as Cofer lit a cigarette and started to amble toward him, toward the narrow canal and the bridge that crossed it. He paused in the middle of the bridge, taking drags on his cigarette as he looked down into the water.

"Why the fuck are you here?" Tom muttered. He picked up his phone and used it to take a photo of Cofer, a wide-angle shot then one as zoomed in as he could make it. An elderly couple at the table next to him shot each other looks, either worried about the crazy American talking to himself, or less than pleased with his swearing. Tom ignored them, focusing instead on texting the pictures to Hugo, with the message, *Don't call me, I'll call you. On his tail.*

A moment later, a reply came through. *10-4. PLEASE be careful.*

Tom grinned and typed back, *I'm fine, Dad. Don't worry.* Hugo sent the thumbs-up emoji, and Tom put his phone away and looked through the window. Outside, Cofer straightened up. He set off again. Just to be sure, Tom left more than enough cash to cover his bill and moved away from his table, sank deeper into the café to stay out of sight. A moment later, Cofer drifted past the café's entrance. Tom counted to ten and stepped outside.

Where to now, amigo? he wondered. He set off after Cofer and pulled out his phone to try to guess where he might be going, but a quick glance at the map told him nothing useful, so he focused on keeping the man in sight, and not being seen himself.

Five minutes later, Cofer turned a corner and Tom hurried to keep his eyes on him. Tom rounded the same corner and found himself at the edge of a pedestrian square looking at a busy market, one like so many in Europe, with stalls of bright flowers, fresh vegetables, and vendors selling art, handmade jewelry, and all manner of foods.

"Shit, where did you go?" Tom muttered. He moved slowly through the crowd, eyes scanning for a flash of orange that would tell him where Cofer was. He caught a glimpse of him on the far side of the market. Tom moved closer and saw Cofer take a toothpick handed to him by the owner of a stall selling dried meats. Cofer picked the meat off delicately and chewed slowly. Then he dropped the toothpick into a trash barrel and nodded enthusiastically to the seller, who reached behind him and grabbed a long, dried sausage that was hanging from a hook like a lasso, and put it in a brown paper bag.

Tom shifted to his left, hiding behind a rack of postcards in case Cofer turned his way, but he didn't. He walked away from Tom toward the edge of the market and a stone archway that marked the opening to a picturesque, cobbled alleyway. Tom couldn't tell whether there were more stores down there, but he had no intention of losing sight of the man who, as far as he knew, was looking for a confrontation. As long as he was in Tom's sights, and not the other way around, Tom had the advantage.

So he took a deep breath, crossed the narrow street that bordered the market, and followed Rick Cofer into the alleyway that, even in broad daylight and in the middle of a busy Amsterdam, suddenly felt empty, and very dangerous.

Tom put his hand in his coat pocket and felt the weight of his gun, a .32 caliber Beretta. It was lighter than his favored 9mm Glock 19, but since he wasn't supposed to be carrying a weapon at all in the Netherlands, he'd gone for something easier to conceal. It felt heavy enough, though, reassuring, and he touched it not because he needed it right then, but because the temperature in the narrow and deserted alley seemed to have dropped ten degrees. His own feet were the only sound he could hear for a full minute, until a soft whistling drifted back to him from ahead. Tom knew it was Cofer, and he tried to discern the tune in case it was meant as a warning, or maybe a taunt, a sign that Cofer knew he was there.

Some obscure classical shit, Tom decided. *Plenty of time in prison to listen to music, after all.*

Even so, Tom moved to the inside of the left-curving alleyway, just in case Cofer looked over his shoulder. Better to stumble into the man at close quarters than get in some kind of shoot-out at a distance. He had no idea whether Cofer was armed but had to assume so; to think otherwise was a potentially fatal mistake. Plus, as big as Cofer might be, Tom had scrapped with bigger, meaner sons-of-bitches than him over the years, and had not lost yet.

Tom left his hand on the butt of the gun, just in case, and moved slowly forward, trying to walk as quietly as possible. Somewhere nearby, someone was cooking a meal with a lot of garlic, and it reminded Tom that he'd eaten little except pancakes, handfuls of cheese, and pastries all day. He shook his head to focus himself on the task at hand.

He glanced to his left as the stone wall gave way to a doorway and a courtyard, a tidy space decorated with potted plants and several wooden benches. Tom couldn't tell whether it was a privately owned place or open to the public but, more important, it didn't contain Rick Cofer, who was still ahead of him, whistling as though everything in the world was right.

And then, a quick movement to his left. Tom turned and caught the dark silhouette of a man towering over him, just a split second of an image before a blinding pain raked across the top of his head and sent him into darkness, and straight to the ground.

CHAPTER FIFTEEN

I t came to Hugo on Monday morning. He'd received the two photos from Tom confirming Cofer's presence in Amsterdam on Sunday, and he'd not stopped looking at them since. He'd also been antsy for the rest of the weekend, checking his phone constantly to see whether he'd missed a message from his friend. He hadn't, and that made him more antsy.

He slept fitfully Sunday night, turning up the volume on his phone and setting it on a saucer so there was no way he'd miss it if it rang, or even if Tom texted. Had it been anyone else, Hugo would've felt some sense of comfort that they knew what they were doing, would keep a cool head and not go rushing in. But not only was Tom more likely to crash about than a bull in a china shop was, Hugo was worried that his friend was overconfident. In the picture, Cofer looked lean, relaxed. Tom was not in the greatest shape of his life, and even when he was, that shape was slightly rounded.

He fell asleep around three in the morning and woke at seven to a blank phone, and a clear idea of why Cofer was in Amsterdam. He called Ambassador Taylor, the only one right then he could talk to about this, and told him about the photos Tom had sent.

"Shit," Taylor said. "Cofer is really there?"

"He is. And I know why."

"Tell me."

"He wanted to split us up. Me and Tom."

"You think?"

"I do. There's no earthly reason for him to go to somewhere completely strange to him. To pick a battle in a foreign country. The only reason I can think of is to bring us, and just *one* of us, to a place that we don't know."

"Divide and conquer."

"Exactly," Hugo said.

"But how does he know whether or not you're familiar with Amsterdam?"

"He doesn't. But he *does* know that we live and work here, in Paris. And that means anywhere else is better for him."

"Good point."

"And he'd guess, rightly as it turns out, that only one of us would come. The reckless one who doesn't have a full-time job."

"Makes sense," Taylor agreed.

"Thing is, I've not heard from Tom since he sent those pictures."

"When was that?"

"Yesterday afternoon."

"Have you tried calling?" Taylor asked. "Dumb question, I'm sure . . ."

"No, it's not. He told me not to. Doesn't want the distraction."

"I see. I don't suppose he has any tracking software on his phone."

"Not a chance," Hugo said. "Your people are to thank for that."

"Yeah, CIA habits die hard. Dammit, what can I do to help?"

"Is there any way you know of to figure out what passport Cofer came in on? If we can find that out, hotels still require guests to show them when they check in. I think the Dutch do that, don't they?"

"We can find out, for sure. That's only helpful if he's staying at a hotel, though."

"Tom left a message saying he was, one in the red-light district. I know, there are a million of those, but if hotels do that still, and if we can identify the passport he's using, that'll make figuring out which one a whole lot easier."

"That's a lot of *ifs*, Hugo."

"I know." Hugo frowned as he thought aloud. "But what bothers me is . . . passports are so hard to forge these days, with all the technology involved in making them. How does a recent convict manage that so fast? I wonder if he knows someone who can . . ." A light came on in Hugo's head. "Holy shit."

"Hugo, what is it?"

"His twin brother. He's using his brother's passport. He didn't have to forge a new one, and how would he anyway?"

"Damn. That's smart."

"Thanks."

"Not you, him."

Hugo smiled grimly. "Yeah, but it's also risky. Which tells me he's not here to play games."

"Right," Taylor said. "He'd know we'd bust him sooner or later like that."

Hugo was still deep in thought. "If Rick Cofer's brother did have a passport, it's been long enough that it would have expired. Rick would've had to apply for a new one in his brother's name. I'll get Ryan to check on whether the State Department issued one; that'll be easy to find out."

"That's good, Hugo. Let me know as soon as he gets an answer."

"I will, I promise."

"So, that's a path to finding Cofer, but we also need to find Tom. What else can I do?"

"Nothing, not for now. I don't think there's anything to be done until we hear from him."

"And we will, Hugo. You know that, right? We *will* hear from him."

"We better. Because if Cofer's as serious about this revenge plan as I think he is, silence is very bad news indeed."

Hugo needed to keep busy as the silence from Tom spread through Monday morning, so at lunchtime he called the l'Hôtel Toby and asked for Josh Reno. When Reno picked up, he sounded annoyed, Hugo thought.

"Josh, this is Hugo Marston from the embassy."

"Oh, yeah. How can I help?"

"I was wondering if we could sit down and talk."

"What about?"

"I'm helping the police with their investigation," Hugo said, keeping it vague. "But it's also my job to look out for US citizens."

"I don't need you to look out for me; I'm fine."

"Have you spoken to the French police again?"

"Yes," Reno said. "Of course. They interviewed everyone at the museum. Especially people who knew Alia, I'm sure."

"Well, like I said, I'm helping them and I'd like to talk to you myself. Just in case something was lost in translation."

"The French police just left, actually," Reno said. "Yeah, that Marchand guy, his English is terrible."

"That's what I'm talking about," Hugo said, relieved Reno wasn't pushing back too hard, or asking questions about Hugo's motivations. "You have a few minutes this afternoon?"

"Yeah, sure. I guess with . . . all this, I'm just a tourist now, I got all the time you need. Marchand asked me to stay put for a while, in Paris, but I'd like to get out of this hotel for a bit, so can we meet somewhere?"

"I'll tell you what. Since you're a tourist, take a cab to Les Deux Magots on the boulevard Saint-Germain. I'll pay for your cab, and buy you coffee there."

"OK," Reno said. "Sounds like a good deal to me."

Forty minutes later, they sat across a small but shiny table inside the café, Hugo with his back to the red leather of the banquette, Josh Reno with his back to the inside of the café.

"Fancy place," Reno said. "But what's with the maggot reference?"

"Ah, no," Hugo said with a smile. "Not *maggot*, but *magot*. One *g* and you don't pronounce the *t* at the end."

"And it means?"

"There was a fabric shop near here, in Rue de Buci. It sold silks linens, lingerie. The word *magot* is translated as a stocky, Far East figurine. If I remember rightly, it was named Les Deux Magots after a popular play. Anyway, in 1870-something, the business moved from there to here, and about ten years later was converted into a café."

"Not the obvious transition. Undies to coffee, but OK."

"Agreed," Hugo said. "But what's kind of neat is that the business was sold at the start of the First World War to a Monsieur Boulay, and the current manager is his great-great-granddaughter."

"Keeping it in the family, I like it."

"Me too. And in the years after the Second World War, it was filled with writers like Hemmingway, Sartre, and Camus. And, the reason I thought you'd like it, plenty of artists, too. Surrealist artists and some guy called Pablo Picasso."

"He used to come here?" Reno looked around, awed by not just the café's opulence but its history, too.

"He sure did." A waiter arrived at the table, and Hugo ordered two *grand crème* coffees. "Anything to eat?" he asked Reno.

"No, I'm good."

The waiter nodded his understanding and left them alone.

"So, how're you doing?" Hugo asked. "Losing a friend, being here in a foreign country, having to deal with it all. Must be tough."

"It is." Reno looked down at the table. "I'll be glad to get out of here, to be honest."

"Let me ask you. That night, you seemed in a better mood."

"I'm usually in a good . . . Oh, you mean after my little outburst at you and Alia."

"Right."

"I apologized; she forgave me. I was drunk and angry, but when I sobered up and thought about it all . . ." He looked out of the window and shrugged. "I mean, she can't be expected to carry me forever, can she?"

"I didn't think she was doing that, carrying you."

"You know what I mean. She did more for me than I did her. I was helpful, yes, but it was never going to last forever, like I said."

"Do you have any clue who'd want to hurt her?" Hugo asked.

"Not really, no."

"That doesn't sound very definitive."

"Well, I mean." Reno fell silent and sat back as the waiter arrived with their coffees. "*Merci,*" he said.

"You mean what?" Hugo pressed.

"Look, everyone in the world has people who . . ." Reno glanced to his right as an older gentleman took a seat two tables away. The American lowered his voice but, to Hugo, the old man seemed lost in his own world and paid them no mind. "I mean, there are people who weren't one hundred percent in love with Alia, or at least had possible reasons not to be. But, to me at least, that's a far cry from having a reason to murder her."

"That's very true," Hugo said. "But what looks like a poor motive to you might seem like a strong one to someone else. In other words, if she upset someone, you may not think it's a big deal. But the person who was upset, well, they may see things differently."

"Sure," Reno agreed. "Even so, what I'm telling you is I don't think I know of anyone who has anything close to a reason to kill Alia. Even someone super sensitive, or super angry."

"Got it. So tell me who might have a reason to be faintly annoyed with her."

"Apart from me, you mean?"

"Apart from you," Hugo said with a smile.

CHAPTER SIXTEEN

Hugo watched Reno as the wheels spun in his head. He was a handsome young man, and perhaps brighter than Hugo had initially credited him. Hugo resolved to check out the man's art, even though it was supposed to be quite modern, which wasn't usually his taste. Hugo looked to his right as the old man reached for his tall glass of beer. His fingers trembled a little, and as he raised it, the sweating glass slipped through his fingers and dropped onto the table with a crash, tipping over and spilling beer over the tabletop and sending a cascade onto the floor.

Josh Reno leapt up, grabbing the napkins in front of him, and from the table between them, and hurried to the old man, who just sat there looking stunned. Hugo looked around for a waiter, but there wasn't one close, and the pair of them standing by the door and chatting paid them no heed.

Reno mopped up the beer as best he could and waved to someone behind Hugo. He turned to see a woman, a manager perhaps, hurry between tables with a large white cloth in her hand. She gently hip-checked Reno out of the way, with a smile and a *Merci*, as she took his place cleaning up the mess.

Nice guy, Hugo thought as Reno plopped back into his seat smelling faintly of beer. *Or a nice performance*. Hugo suppressed a smile, chiding himself for being so uncharitable, so suspicious.

"Now, where were we?" Reno asked, taking a sip and then frowning at his now-cold coffee.

"You were about to tell me who might have had issues, even minor ones, with Alia."

"Right." He shifted in his seat and wouldn't meet Hugo's eye. "You know, my mother taught me not to speak ill of people behind their backs, or gossip."

"So did mine. But then my mother never investigated a murder. Did yours?"

"No."

"Josh, look. Alia is dead. And you may not want to gossip, or say bad things about people. You obviously think that whatever it is you know is irrelevant, and that's fine. But right now you don't get to make that decision."

"What decision?"

"That virtue trumps necessity."

"But if the information is irrelev—"

"You don't get to make that decision either," Hugo said more forcefully.

"OK, fine. It's not that big of a deal," Reno said defensively.

"I'm listening."

"It's just that JD has a thing . . . had a thing for Alia. Held a candle for her, you might say."

"She was a beautiful woman."

"And JD was well aware of that," Reno said.

"Did anything ever happen between the two of them?"

"I'm not sure, but . . ." Reno paused, this time looking Hugo in the eye. "Well, something happened. Early on."

"Tell me."

"It was at one of her first shows, or first after she'd met the Rollos."

"They were bankrolling it?"

"Yes, they were. Not to the extent they did later, but yeah."

"What happened?"

"I can only tell you what I saw. It was at an art studio in San Francisco, I don't even remember what she was showing. But at one point she was gone and I went looking for her. I went to the office and was about to knock on the door when it opened, and JD kinda pushed past me. Alia was inside, by herself. She was red in the face." He took a deep breath and shook his head slowly. "I felt super awkward, so when she just said, 'Shut the door and give me a minute,' I was more than happy to."

"What do you think had happened?"

"That's the funny thing," Reno said. "I honestly couldn't tell. JD might have been annoyed or embarrassed as he went by me. And Alia might have been angry or . . . something else."

"You didn't talk to her about it?"

"When I saw her later on, I asked if everything was OK."

"And?"

"She kind of brushed me off. Acted like nothing had happened, like I'd not seen anything. So I opened my mouth, and I remember this distinctly, I literally opened my mouth to ask about JD and she gave me this look, and said, 'Everything's fine, and I don't want to talk about it.'"

"Did you ask her later?"

Reno chuckled. "You didn't know Alia that well. She was a force sometimes. If she told you to leave it, you left it. I did, anyway."

"This happened several years ago?" Reno nodded so Hugo went on. "You know them both pretty well, right? JD and Alia. As well as anyone."

"Yeah, I suppose. Alia, for sure."

"So give me your gut instinct. What happened in there?"

"Oh, man, come on. I have no idea. Really."

"Well, seems to me it was one of two things," Hugo said. "Would you agree with that?"

"I guess so."

"And since you're guessing, which of the two things was it?"

Reno puffed out his cheeks and then exhaled. "This is just a guess, mind you. But I'd say he put the moves on her and she turned him down."

Hugo nodded. "And since then, any incidents like that between them?"

"No. Not that I saw, anyway. Whatever happened, they got over it." Reno gave a wry smile. "Or she did, at least. Like I said, in my opinion he had a thing for her. Why else would he spend his own money to promote her?"

"Rich people do that sometimes," Hugo said. "Patron of the arts and all that."

"Maybe. I just can't help but think that if Alia had been Alan, a hairy, ugly dude, JD might not have been so enamored with the work."

It was Hugo's turn to smile. "Maybe. What about Rachel?"

"What about her?"

"Did she know about that early incident, whatever it was?"

"No idea. I doubt it."

"Does she think her husband had the hots for Alia?"

"You'd have to ask her, but I doubt that, too. I mean, if she did, why would she go along with all this, sponsoring her, spending money and time, traveling?"

"To keep an eye on her husband, maybe."

"She doesn't strike me as the jealous type," Reno said. "She's a pretty tough lady in her own right. Plus, she was close to Alia—they were friends."

They sat quietly for a moment, then Hugo asked, "Another coffee?" When Reno nodded, Hugo signaled to the waiter for two more.

"What about Rob Drummond?" Hugo asked. "How well do you know him?"

"He's an asshole."

"So you know him pretty well?"

"Well enough. I met him for the first time a few days ago, and we got on OK to begin with."

"And then?"

"I think he thinks I'm responsible for his sister's death. Not that I killed her but . . . I don't know. He's just angry at me, and I can't see why."

"He lost his sister."

"Stepsister." Reno snorted. "And he barely knew her."

"Is that so?"

"To my knowledge, he'd been to precisely one show of hers prior to this one."

"Where was that?"

"East coast—Washington, DC, I think." Reno paused as the waiter put two more coffees on the table and cleared the dirty cups. "And if I remember rightly, he was there already on business, so it's not like he made a special trip."

"What business is he in?"

"No clue. Some marketing thing or other, I really don't know or care."

"You sound kind of angry at him," Hugo said, watching carefully for a reaction.

"Look, do you know who her real brother is?"

"I don't understand."

"Her real brother is me. Not in a blood sense, I know that, but I'm the one who's been with her all this time, helping her and supporting her. Making her smile when she's feeling sad, making her laugh, carrying her shit from museum to art space, being thrilled when she does well and feeling like crap when no one shows up. And then he appears out of nowhere and treats me like the fucking help, like her servant. And then, when this happens, he's in a rush to . . ." Reno waved a hand. "I don't know, make sure I don't steal all her stuff, I guess. As if I would *ever* do something like that."

"Why would he think that?"

"Because he doesn't know me. Because he's a materialistic ass who has no clue what I've done for Alia these past few years."

"I get the feeling there's something specific, though."

"Then I guess there is," Reno said, nodding. "Yesterday, last night, I wanted to go into her room to get some things."

"What things?"

"A book she'd borrowed. And two paintings that she liked, two of *my* paintings."

"Ones you gave to her, as a present?"

"Yes and no. She liked them, I let her keep them in her room."

"And you wanted them back."

"They're not worth anything," Reno said. "Sentimental value only."

"I see. So what happened?"

"I knocked on her door; I know Drummond is staying there now. He wouldn't even open it, and when I asked about the paintings, he said they were hers and I couldn't have them. Like I said, he wouldn't even open the door to talk about it. The big jerk."

"That sounds like something you might be able to resolve in a day or two," Hugo said, trying to sound conciliatory. "So let me ask you this, how did you feel about not being able to show your work here?"

"You know how I felt."

"Angry, yes, I remember," Hugo said. "The kind of angry that the French police might want to call a motive."

"Call it what you like. You saw me the evening of the show, I'd gotten it out of my system. I was fine."

"I saw a lot of people that evening," Hugo said. "Everyone seemed fine, and yet someone killed Alia."

"How do you know it was one of the people who was at the exhibit? I mean, someone could have snuck in and done it."

"Extremely unlikely," Hugo said. "This was her first trip to Paris; she didn't know anyone in the city. Everyone she knew was at that event. Anyone and everyone who loved, admired, and hated her was in that small space, which means the person who killed her almost certainly had a ticket to get in."

"You can't be a hundred percent sure of that."

Hugo's phone buzzed in his jacket pocket, and he took it out, hoping to see Tom's name. Instead, it was Lieutenant Camille Lerens.

"Excuse me a moment," Hugo said to Reno. "I need to take this call." He stood and made for the exit, connecting with Lerens as he stepped outside. "Camille, what is it?"

"You have a sixth sense, Hugo?" she asked.

"I do sometimes, yes. You're not on this case, and you're not calling to invite me to dinner, so I'm assuming you have news. Probably bad news."

"I do. But first of all, you have to know that I didn't see this coming. If I had, I'd have told you beforehand."

"Told me what?"

"And that's the other thing. It's going to sound bad, but there are steps we can take, things we can do."

"Camille," Hugo said impatiently. "What the hell is going on? What've you done?"

"I haven't done anything. It's Lieutenant Intern Marchand. He's arrested Claudia."

"What?" Hugo felt a cold sickness in the pit of his stomach. "Arrested her? When and for what, exactly?"

"He arrested her not even an hour ago, for the murder of Alia Alsaffar."

CHAPTER SEVENTEEN

Hugo was halfway inside the taxi when he remembered Reno.

I'll pay you back later, he thought, slamming the Renault's door behind him. To the driver, he said, "*Préfecture de police, s'il vous plaît,*" but resisted the urge to offer a tip for faster service.

As the taxi started down the boulevard Saint-Germain, Hugo dialed Marchand's number.

"Monsieur Marston," Marchand said. "News travels fast."

"So do I. I'm on my way to talk to you."

"Make an appointment like everyone else, please, I'm very busy."

"You're busy arresting innocent people," Hugo snapped. "What the hell are you playing at?"

When he spoke, Marchand's voice trembled with anger. "How dare you speak to me this way. You think I am playing games? A woman is dead, and you think I have to bow and scrape to get your permission to do my job? That I have to drop everything to make time for you?"

Hugo regretted his own tone. Making Marchand mad would cause him to dig his heels in deeper, which in turn would mean Claudia would spend more time in custody. Precisely the opposite of Hugo's intentions. He took a deep breath and tried to start over.

"Look, I'm sorry, Lieutenant Intern, I didn't mean to be disrespectful. I know you have a job to do, but the idea that—"

"I don't have time for this," Marchand interrupted. "I will give you five minutes when you get here, and four of those minutes will be me talking and you listening. Understand?"

"I'll take it," Hugo said. "I'll be there shortly."

The Renault turned onto the wide and tree-lined boulevard Saint-Michel, home to designer stores, boutique shops, and expensive restaurants. But Hugo was immune to its charms for once, and so the bright-red canopies of its cafés, the orange glow of its bakeries, and crystal-blue sparkle of the Christmas lights in the storefronts were but impressionistic flashes of color on a too-slow journey to the prefecture. When the cab pulled to stop on Rue de la Cité, Hugo didn't wait to check the fare, just dropped twenty euros into the driver's hand.

"*Merci, monsieur, mais—*"

Hugo didn't hear the rest of the sentence, just hurried into the prefecture. Lieutenant Intern Marchand was waiting for him in the lobby, and they shook hands as formality required.

"Now you listen to me," Marchand began. "I know you think I am wrong. You are close with Claudia Roux, and have been for a while. To you she is not a suspect, could not possibly have done such a thing."

"That's all correct," Hugo said.

"But, I myself do not know her. That means instead of ruling her out because we are friends, I have to look at the evidence. I see just the evidence, not the person."

"What evidence do you think you have?" Hugo fought to keep his tone civil, but underneath he was fuming. In his book, a couple of weak coincidences did not amount to enough evidence on which to base an arrest.

"Everything that we discussed earlier," Marchand said. "Her proximity to the scene, her lack of an alibi, and you as a motive."

"No one saw Alia get killed," Hugo said. "Which means we don't know exactly when it happened, so *no one* has an alibi. Myself included."

"Not true, as it happens," Marchand said, a little smugly, Hugo thought. "We've not had you write or give a statement yet, but from talking to the guests we can put you in someone's line of sight from the moment you entered until the time you ran out to the ambulance."

"Well, I'm happy to hear that. But even so, we were all right there at the scene, and I can give you motives for half a dozen other people, ones that are infinitely stronger than the ridiculous notion that Claudia would be jealous enough to kill a complete stranger."

"You have motives for other people?"

"Oh, they're not great ones," Hugo said. "Not even particularly good ones. But they beat the hell out of yours for Claudia."

"Then entertain me, Monsieur Marston." He opened his arms expansively. "Tell me about these motives."

"Fine, I will." Hugo declined to remind Marchand of his five-minute deadline. "Let's start with Josh Reno. Spurned and rejected after years of loyalty to Alia. Also likely to face financial problems since he'll be on his own now and won't be able to piggy-back off Alia's shows."

"Not bad," Marchand said. "Who else?"

"How about JD Rollo next?"

"Please, tell me."

"Wealthy, older, distinguished. And by several accounts he holds a candle for Alia. Maybe a mix of mid-life crisis and unrequited love led to him losing his temper."

"Maybe."

"Then again, maybe you're right about jealousy being the motive. That might account for two other people who were there that night, Rachel Rollo and Rob Drummond. Two other people who don't have nailed-down alibis."

"Rachel Rollo being jealous of some relationship her husband had, or wanted to have, with Alia."

"Right."

"How was Rob Drummond jealous?"

"Successful, attractive stepsister. He's kind of a drifter who has no apparent direction in life, and who killed his own father with his bare hands. And I presume he inherits her estate, being the only living relative. Money, rage, and jealousy all present."

"Not to mention he was on coat-check duty at the event," Marchand said. "I can imagine that might be a little . . . humiliating."

"I agree," Hugo said. "Although to be fair to him, he said he offered."

"So he says," Marchand pointed out. "You know what all this tells me?"

"No idea."

"It tells me that you've been meddling with a police investigation.

Which, if this were any other case involving a different cast of characters, would be both irritating and inappropriate. But in *this* case, what you have been doing is almost criminal."

"Criminal? How the hell—?"

Marchand stepped closer, his eyes boring into Hugo. "I have arrested someone, and you are that someone's *copain*, or whatever label you wish to hang on yourself. Close friend, at the very least." He held up a finger to silence Hugo, who was about to speak. "I'm not finished. Not only are you her lover, but you would be the person called to testify at her trial, because you are the closest thing she has for an alibi."

"You can't possibly think—"

"And that," Marchand interrupted. "Makes you a material witness, does it not?"

Hugo stayed silent, not trusting what might come out of his mouth. In one small way, a tiny and abstract way, he knew Marchand was making valid points. But this was Claudia, in jail and being accused of murder. It was preposterous.

Marchand was still talking. "The idea that a material witness would be conducting his own investigation is, perhaps, not unheard of. But would you seriously expect the police to share the developments of an official investigation with such a person?"

"So you have more evidence than you've told me."

"Oh, yes," Marchand said. "I most certainly do."

"Evidence against a woman who wasn't there at all, wasn't even inside the building."

"So she says, anyway."

"You've interviewed her."

"At length, she was most cooperative."

"And?"

"Well, Monsieur Marston." Marchand pursed his lips as he thought about how to answer. "I can tell you one thing, and that is that she repeated her claim that she was never inside the museum. In fact, she says she never met or even saw Alia Alsaffar in person."

"And you have cause to doubt that?" Hugo asked.

"As a matter of fact, I do," Marchand said, a smug little smile appearing on his face. "In fact, I have considerable cause to doubt it."

Hugo's jaw tensed. He wanted to punch Marchand in the mouth, but more than that he wanted to know what cards the Frenchman was holding.

"And what considerable cause is that, exactly?"

"Three little letters," Marchand replied.

"Letters?" Hugo asked, confused for a moment at the cryptic reply. But then it struck him. "Wait, are you saying you have . . .?"

"Yes." Marchand nodded his head slowly. "We found Claudia Roux's DNA at the crime scene. Specifically, swabbed from the victim's right forefinger. I haven't seen the report yet, but I can only imagine it was taken from under Mademoiselle Alsaffar's fingernail, and got there when the victim tried to defend herself. As you know, that is quite common."

A coldness settled around Hugo's heart, and he found himself unable to reply.

"Now, if you will excuse me, I have work to do," Marchand said, and without waiting for a reply, he turned on his heel and stalked back into the bowels of the prefecture, leaving Hugo standing in the lobby, his mind at a loss for an explanation, and his body numb with shock.

Ambassador J. Bradford Taylor answered the knock on his office door at four o'clock that afternoon, his mind more on the bottle of Bordeaux he was planning to drain than the official papers in front of him.

"Come in." It was his secretary, Emma, and as soon as Taylor saw how pale she was, he gestured to one of the chairs across from him. "Sit. What's wrong?"

Emma sat and leaned forward. "Mr. Ambassador, I'm sorry to bother you, but I received a call for you but the man wouldn't give his name."

"We have a policy covering that. It involves hanging up."

"I did, sir, but he called right back and was very insistent. He said it was about Tom Green."

"Tom?" Taylor rubbed his chin for a moment. "What else did he say?"

"I wasn't going to put him through, since he wouldn't give his name, so I made him tell me why he was calling." Emma's eyes went to the desktop, and she clutched her hands together. "I'm afraid it's bad news."

"Spit it out, Emma, I'm a grown man. No need to sugarcoat whatever it is for me."

"Tom's dead, sir. This man said Tom was dead."

Taylor sank backward in his chair, his mouth falling open. "What?"

Emma had tears in her eyes. "He said Tom was dead."

"How? Where?"

"He didn't want to give me details, sir. But I took a number for you to call him back. He says he'll tell you what he knows, but he doesn't want to speak to anyone else."

"Jesus, how can this be . . .? He didn't say how it happened?" Taylor knew the answer, knew after his conversation with Hugo that if Tom had been shot, stabbed, drowned, or dropped from a building, Rick Cofer was behind it. The details might be important to an investigation, but Taylor knew who had done this.

"He was shot in the chest. Three times."

They sat in silence for a full minute, then Taylor asked, "Does Hugo know?"

"I don't know. I tried reaching him but had to leave a message. I told him to call you."

"Yes, thank you." Taylor took a long breath, then asked, "Did you know Tom well?"

Emma smiled. "I think everyone who ever met Tom knew him well. He was who he was." She wiped away a tear and looked at Taylor. "He was one of a kind."

"That's the truth," Taylor said. He frowned. "You know this might be some kind of sick joke. I need to talk to the caller and see what he has to say. Find out who the hell he is."

"I emailed you his number," Emma said. "It should be on your screen. Oh, and he said to use a secure line."

"Of course he did," Taylor said wearily. "Well, leave me to it; I'll let you know what I can when I'm off the phone."

"Yes, sir." She got up and walked to the door, then turned. "You knew him pretty well, didn't you?"

"Oh, yes," Taylor said. "Tom and I go way back. A long way back."

The ambassador waited until Emma had closed his heavy office door, then he looked over at his computer. He tapped out the phone number, mentally noting the code for Amsterdam, and waited as it rang. *Is this Cofer himself?* Taylor wondered. *Who else could it be?*

"Yes?" It was a man's voice.

"This is Ambassador Taylor in Paris. I was told you needed to speak to me about Tom Green."

"Yes, sir. Thank you for calling. This is a secure line?"

"The only kind I ever use."

"Good. Sir, my name is Brendon Fowler, and I have something I need to tell you."

The call lasted ten minutes, and Fowler did all of the talking. He answered Taylor's questions before they were asked, and he assured the ambassador he was telling him everything he knew.

"As soon as I heard, I knew that bastard Cofer was behind it," Taylor said grimly.

"Yes, sir."

"Well, I appreciate you telling me and arranging everything."

"Yes, sir. Tom and I go back a long way; I'll do anything I can to help. Call me back if you need anything."

They disconnected, and Taylor got up from his desk. He let himself out of his office and went to where Emma sat, waiting for him. She looked up, and he just nodded.

Emma straightened her back, but when she spoke, her voice cracked. "What can I do?"

"I'm afraid we have a funeral to plan," he said. "And if you could try again to get a hold of Hugo and have him come in as soon as possible."

"Do you want to just call him yourself?"

"No. This conversation needs to be here, in person and behind closed doors. Certainly not on the phone, and Hugo will make me tell him if I call to ask him to come in. That guy can read me like a book."

CHAPTER EIGHTEEN

Tom came to with his back to a large, concrete planter and his legs stretched out in front of him. His head throbbed, and he felt warm blood running down his cheek. He fought to make sense of what had just happened, a voice inside yelling at him that it can't have been Cofer because he'd been farther along in the alleyway. He'd heard him up ahead, whistling!

But when he blinked the vision back into his eyes, he saw Cofer leaning forward as he sat on a bench at Tom's feet.

"Long time no see."

"Fuck off, Cofer." Tom tried to shift his position, but a stabbing pain pinned him in place. At least he wasn't tied up. "What the fuck did you hit me with?"

"You're getting old and slow, Tom Green. It doesn't take much."

"Then why jump me from behind, you fucking coward."

"Says the man who's been hiding in a hat and oversized coat, sneaking around behind me all day."

The waves of pain were receding, just a little, and Tom groaned and sat more upright. "The orange outfit. Intentional, then."

"Well done." Cofer leaned forward and spat in Tom's face. "Genius fucking CIA agent."

"Great, now I'm getting Ebola from an ape."

"Oh, I wouldn't worry about that. You won't be living long enough to contract any diseases."

Something in Cofer's voice made Tom study the man's face. From a distance, he'd been right that Cofer had lost weight. But closer up, Tom guessed that it wasn't diet or prison exercise that had done it. And it all made sense now, the use of the brother's passport, the lack of care, the brazen shirt, and even the open-air attack in the middle of Amsterdam. There was a damn good reason Cofer was taking such risks.

"What've you got?" Tom asked. "AIDS? Cancer?"

"I wish it was AIDS, they can cure that shit these days." Cofer shook his head. "But that cancer, man, all they can do is fill you with chemicals, make you feel worse, and then tell you maybe you'll live an extra six months."

"That all the time you have left?"

"Maybe a year." He shrugged. "I don't need that long, though."

"How's that?" Tom asked, although he already knew the answer.

"How long does it take to kill a man?" Cofer sneered.

"You should fucking know already. Oh, wait. You kill innocent women, not men."

"I've killed more than that bitch at the bank, you asshole. And even if I hadn't, by the end of today, shit, by the end of the hour, I'd have one notch on my belt."

"Yeah, that's how you see other people, isn't it?" Tom sneered. "Notches. Not human beings, but expendable, for your own ends."

"You know, at the time, I had no idea."

"About what?" Tom touched the top of his head and was pleased that the blood flow seemed to have slowed.

"That I'd killed your sister. I had no idea that's who it was, and I was going nuts inside, trying to understand why you murdered my brother like that."

"Murder? Cockroaches don't get murdered—they get stepped on or dropped into the waste disposal."

"My lawyer told me. I tell you what, most inmates in prison hate their lawyers, did you know that? They figure they're on the take from the government or that they shook them down for high fees and then got them a shitty deal." Cofer shook his head slowly but never took his eyes off Tom. "No, sir, not me. My lawyer screwed you guys good. Used your dead sister and your cowboy past on those US attorneys, made them terrified of going to trial."

"And yet there you were in prison, and your criminal brother pushing up daisies."

Cofer nodded. "Yep, right next to your sister."

"I bet she reached over and cut his tiny balls off. Or was he like you, and didn't have any?"

"What're you going to do, Green, question my bravery so I throw down my gun and challenge you to a fistfight? Even a has-been like you could take a man dying of cancer—I'll give you that much."

"You don't have a gun." Tom moved his hands, just a little, just enough to confirm what he'd feared three minutes ago.

"I have yours." Cofer pulled Tom's .32 Beretta from a jacket pocket and let it dangle between his knees. "Good God, taking it from you couldn't have been any easier. You know how many times I'd imagined this moment? Pictured how this might go down?"

"You're really going to shoot me? Here?"

"You know, probably fifty percent of the time I got realistic and imagined you winning. I didn't hit you hard enough, fast enough, you saw me too soon, whatever the reason. And yet here we are, and it was *so* easy."

"Sorry to disappoint." Tom eyed the gun, wondered if he could move fast enough to kick it out of Cofer's hand. He doubted it. Not yet, anyway.

"Do you like the courtyard? I rented it. Well, the small apartment in the front, the courtyard comes with it. I bet it's nice in the summer. Shame you won't live to see it."

"That makes two of us."

"Oh, I'll make it to Christmas, I think."

"I was referring to one of my colleagues dispatching you, not your case of jail-contracted syphilis."

"Oh, were you?" Cofer shook his head with amusement. "Not if today is any guide. I really can't believe how easy it was to trap and disarm a former FBI agent. The orange shirt, the stroll through Amsterdam, and this place. Where, just so you know, I'd originally planned for your body to lie unfound for the remainder of my rental period, which is Sunday morning. You'd have been in quite a state by then, especially since there's a warm spell coming."

"You talk too fucking much."

"Right, sorry, I need to get to the good bit. See, you probably think this is all about killing you and Hugo Marston, but it's more than that. You see, I've had to live with the knowledge of my brother's death, and of course I witnessed it. I couldn't figure out how to trap you both in the same place and kill you, so the better course of action is to kill you, make Marston suffer, then kill him."

"If you like, you can kill him first, that'd work just as well for me."

"Funny man. Brave in the face of death, I like it."

"You really plan to kill Hugo as well?" Tom asked. "I'm the one who took out your brother, so unless you're actually the monster I think you are, why don't you leave him out of it?"

"Not a chance," Cofer snapped. "He's the one who covered for you. He's as guilty as you are." Cofer grinned, and Tom thought he'd never seen a man so evil. "The best part is, I'm gonna take him out when he's at his lowest. Dressed in black, long-faced, and teary-eyed. Then *pop*, and you and he can get together in whatever FBI hell exists in the afterlife."

"You're a piece of work, you know that?"

"Thank you," Cofer said. "It was meant as a compliment, right? After all, I've been planning this for a several years, thanks to lots of spare time and a good library in the prison."

"So much for rehabilitation," Tom said.

Cofer sat back. "It's true what they say about the federal pen, you know. I've done state time and federal time, and I much prefer the latter. Better food, more exercise available. Frankly, a better class of inmate. The politicians and money launderers make for better conversation than your common criminal."

"Like bank robbers, you mean."

"See, I don't know why you keep trying to antagonize me."

"Might as well have some fun before I die," Tom said. "I'm not known for my delicate manners."

"Don't you want to know if I had help? I thought you law-enforcement types were all questions. You know, *Nothing but the facts, ma'am.*"

"Doesn't seem like it'd change much."

"Well, I just want you to know that the Dutch police can be corrupt, too. I mean, as well as you Feds and the rest of the court system that helped you cover up my brother's murder."

"I told you, he was exterminated, not murdered."

"Funny. It's also funny that a certain member of the Dutch customs was open to financial persuasion. He's the one who ignored the fact that I used a dead man's passport. You probably didn't know about that, though, did you?"

"Actually, I did. For what it's worth." Tom adjusted his position, but a new jolt of fire pierced his skull and he winced.

"He couldn't get me a gun, wouldn't go that far. Funny where people draw the line when it comes to their morality, isn't it?"

"Please give the turd my thanks."

"All seems so random, so pointless, because here I am with a gun after all."

"And you're going to use it no matter what I say," Tom said. "You seriously expect me to play nice only for you to shoot me in cold blood at the end of our little chat? Fuck you."

"If your friend were here, I bet he'd be trying a little harder to stay alive. Mostly out of cowardice, but he'd be smarter about it."

"You leave him out of this. I shot your maggot of a brother. He wasn't even there."

"Sure he was. You and he chased us there, together. Yeah, you pulled the trigger, but who covered it all up?"

"There was nothing to cover up. Your shithead brother was trying to escape, and I shot him."

"You shot him in cold blood inside the house. Your buddy Marston walked away, turned his back and let you stage the scene to suit your story. And you knew he would; that's why you dared to shoot my brother. You knew he'd cover for you." Cofer sneered at Tom. "No, you may have pulled the trigger, but he's as responsible as you. And he'll pay just the way you're going to pay."

And that was the reason Cofer was in Holland, Tom realized. That's why he'd come to Amsterdam on a passport that could be tracked. He knew the difference between Tom and Hugo. He knew that Hugo had a job to do and that Tom was the reckless, shoot-from-the-hip kind of person. Cofer knew that once he'd been sighted in Amsterdam, Tom would head out there to confront him, whereas Hugo would stay in Paris and show up to his responsible, important, day job until there was definitive proof Cofer was in Europe. Despite himself, Tom couldn't help but respect the plan. An evil, twisted plan, yes, but one that showed him he'd underestimated Rick Cofer.

"Just so you know," Tom said. "Hugo Marston is not only braver than me, but he's about ten times smarter. Which makes him about fifty times smarter than you."

"And yet, as I said before, here we are. You bleeding on the ground, and me sitting comfortably with your gun in my hand."

"He'll get you. And he won't play the nice guy you think he is."

"Nice guy? I think he's an asshole. And, just like the asshole lying in the dirt in front of me, he's going to die in an alleyway in Paris. Two murderous cops dying on foreign soil, like the rats they are."

"It won't fire," Tom said, eyeing the gun. "Fingerprint trigger lock. I'm afraid you're going to have to beat me to death with it."

Cofer paused, uncertainty in his eyes. He looked down at the gun, then quickly back to Tom. "It's a normal trigger, a normal gun."

"Who was that whistling, by the way?" Tom asked. "You pay someone to do that?"

"Lots of starving musicians in Amsterdam, you know. Well, everywhere, I guess." He heaved the gun in his hand. "Normal trigger and a full clip, from the weight of it."

"It won't fire. So you better hit me over the head again, or take off running. I'd suggest the latter, since my legs will probably be wobbly for a while."

"You're bluffing, Green, and you're not very good at it."

"Not so." Tom held his eye. "And my legs are starting to feel a lot better, so it's time for you to go."

"I'm not much for running these days," Cofer said. "So, why don't we just try it, see if it works?"

From ten feet away, Rick Cofer raised the pistol, took aim, and shot Tom Green in the chest. Three loud cracks echoed around the courtyard, the sound lingering for several seconds after Tom's body crumpled sideways to the dusty cobbles, where he lay, absolutely still, his eyes open but unblinking.

Cofer stood and went to him, wondering if he should put an extra bullet in Green's temple just to make sure. But the man who'd killed his twin brother wasn't moving or breathing, so there was no need; it would only serve to attract more attention. Plus, he knew that Green was right. Hugo Marston was the smart one of the pair, and as soon as he heard about his friend's death, he'd use all of his power and resources to get to Rick before he could finish this mission. Which meant Rick might need every single one of those bullets, if it came to a shoot-out.

Cofer smiled. *A shoot-out with a Texan. What a perfect way to go.*

CHAPTER NINETEEN

At the same time Ambassador Taylor was dialing Brendon Fowler's number, Hugo took a seat in the jail visitation room in the bowels of the prefecture. He watched the other visitors take seats at the other small but sturdy tables, everyone's eyes on the iron door at the back of the room. When the visitors were all locked in, a bell rang and the heavy door clanked open.

Hugo's heart almost broke when Claudia walked through the doorway, pale-faced and dressed in the blue denim uniform of the jail. Her hair was pulled back into a ponytail, and even though she was trying to be brave, the dark smudges under her eyes told him she'd not rested or relaxed for even a moment since being arrested. He wanted to get up from the chipped and scarred Formica table and hug her, but the guards had made it very clear to the handful of visitors that there was to be no touching. *You touch, you leave* was the gist of things.

"Hugo." She smiled and sat opposite him. "You have no idea how good it is to see you."

"You too," he said. "How're you holding up?"

"I'm fine. It's a little cold back there, so next time if you could bring a nice bowl of hot chocolate. Maybe a few so I can share them around."

"Be glad to," Hugo said with a reassuring smile.

"Honestly, I'm surprised they let you in here at all."

"You really think they could stop me?" He gave her a small smile. "Not a chance."

"You are sweet, Hugo. But I wish you didn't have to see me this way. It's humiliating."

153

"You've done nothing wrong. And you know I don't care about what you're wearing; the fact you're here doesn't change a thing about you. I just want to help however I can."

"Thank you. And you know I mean it when I say I'm the luckiest person in here to have the great Hugo Marston working on my case."

"Well, if we're being honest," he said, "most of the people in here are probably guilty, so they wouldn't want me on their case."

Claudia laughed gently. "Oh, no, you're so wrong. I've come to learn that everyone in here is innocent. They told me so."

Hugo nodded, then became serious. "I know one person who is, that's for sure."

Claudia held his eye. "You do know that, right? That this is absurd and I would never have hurt that woman. I didn't even know her."

"Of course, there's no question." He clenched his fists to dispel the urge to grab and hold her hands. "Have you seen a lawyer yet?"

"Not seen, but talked on the phone. Twice, and the best one in Paris. She'll be in touch with you at some point."

"OK, good." He took a breath. "Claudia, there's something you need to know, something I don't think the police have told your lawyer yet."

"What is it?"

"They told me they have your DNA."

"Well, yes, I gave a sample just like everyone else did."

"No, not that way," Hugo said. "They found your DNA on Alia. On her hand, probably under her nail."

Claudia's mouth opened, but for a moment she just stared at Hugo. Finally, she said, "But that's not possible. I never went into the museum, the exhibition."

"Is there any way you could've bumped into her outside?"

"No, of course not. I did my training run up there, felt faint, and passed out. I didn't even run past the museum, let alone go in."

"You didn't stop for a moment, maybe walk for a bit, talk to anyone?"

"Hugo, no. Stop. You know I didn't. There must be some mistake with the DNA, that's all."

"He seemed pretty certain. Confident."

"Was it Marchand who told you?" she asked.

"Yes."

"I'm not his biggest fan," Claudia said.

"Nor am I, but I'm told he's good at his job."

"Then he'll figure out it's a mistake."

"If he doesn't," Hugo assured her, "then I sure as hell will."

"Just find whoever did this. If you find out, they'll see it wasn't me." She paused, then asked the question he'd hoped she wouldn't. "Do you have any good suspects for it?"

"Not right now," he said. *Sadly, no one else left their DNA behind*, he thought but didn't say. "I'm still working on it, but now that Marchand has his sights set on you, he's told me to back right off. He says that since I'll be your alibi witness at trial, I'm a material witness and can't be investigating."

"Which is true, isn't it?"

"Technically, yes." He looked her in the eye. "But you know I'm not going to stop, right? You know I'm going to figure out who did this, don't you?"

"I do," she said quietly. Then she looked up and smiled again. "But please hurry up. The accommodations are awful, and the food is even worse."

"Plus, you have a marathon to train for," Hugo said, returning the smile. "You want me to stay and keep you company for a bit longer?"

"I'm fine, Hugo, really. I'd rather you get back to finding whoever did this, and you can't do that from here."

"You said you're allowed to make phone calls, right?" he asked.

"Only to my lawyer. But I can get her to contact you if I need something. And if you have any questions for me, whatever they are, go through her. I'll call her right now and give her your contact information."

"What's her name?"

"Nicola Dumont."

"I hope she's good," Hugo said.

"She is. For what I'm paying, she has to be. More to the point, *you're* good."

"And cheap."

"Oh, I wouldn't say that." She winked and started to slide her hand across the table, stopping after a few inches and glancing past Hugo toward the guards. "Damned jail rules. Go back to work, Hugo, get me the hell out of here."

"I will. I most definitely will."

She nodded and stood, and he watched as she got up and went to the back of the visiting room and was let through the sliding iron door. She didn't look back, but he noticed her straighten as she walked through the doorway, walk away from him and back to her cell.

Hugo hurried out of the jail and checked his phone to see several texts and missed phone calls, all from Emma. He dialed her number.

"Hugo, there you are. What're you doing?"

"Visiting someone. Where's the fire?"

"Can you come to the embassy?"

"Now? It's quitting time." Although Hugo had no plans to stop just yet, he wanted to talk to Rob Drummond again. And maybe Lieutenant Intern Marchand.

"I know. But the ambassador wants to see you. Says it's urgent."

"What's urgent?"

"Hugo, please. Just come back to the embassy."

Something in her voice, a slight break or tremor, gave him pause. "Emma, is everything all right?"

"No, it's not," she said. "So I'll see you here soon."

And then she hung up on him.

It was a straight shot to the embassy, not quite two miles along Rue de Rivoli, a route that Hugo would walk on any other day. But the wobble in Emma's voice, the way she hung up so quickly, told Hugo something was very wrong indeed, so he jumped into a cab outside the prefecture.

He was about to give the driver his destination when the ambassador texted two words: *Chez Maman*.

Hugo smiled. They hadn't been to Chez Maman in a while, but it was closer than the embassy and would serve him a drink. Hugo got out of the cab, apologizing to the driver and slamming the door shut so he didn't hear the man's frank expressions of surprise.

He walked quickly, crossing Pont Saint-Michel with his head down against the wind, and in five minutes he was leaning against the anonymous door of Chez Maman, a one-room bar that you wouldn't know was there unless you did. Its customers were locals only, although Hugo had been in there drinking with Tom once when a foursome of tourists wandered in. Eastern Europeans, Hugo had guessed right away from their cheap jeans and bright, white sneakers. They come to a jarring halt once inside, wide eyes taking in the worn stone floor; the low, smoke-stained ceiling; and the sturdy wooden furniture that had supported the drinks, and backsides, of serious drinkers for more than a century. Maman, always stationed behind the bar with her rolling can of oxygen within reach, had ignored them the way she ignored every first-timer in there, the way she'd ignored Hugo until Tom had charmed the orange-haired battle-ax into loving them both. When the tourists entered, the other ten people in the bar—some playing dominoes, some cards, and some just drinking—glared so hard that a force field seemed to appear. The drinkers at Chez Maman put up with tourists like this in every other part of their city, but not in their bar. The force field grew with every passing second, and pretty quickly the foursome exchanged panic looks and backed out of the door, closing it quietly but firmly behind them.

Hugo got a few appraising looks when he stepped into the bar, but the briefest of waves from Maman put everyone at ease. Hugo took a seat at the bar.

"Been a while," Maman said in her raspy voice. "Whisky?"

Hugo looked at his watch, even though the answer was always going to be yes. He nodded and watched as Maman poured generously from a bottle with no label. She put a separate glass of ice next to the whisky.

"*Merci, Maman,*" Hugo said.

"Where's your handsome friend?" she asked.

"No one's ever called him that before. But he's in Holland." Hugo glanced at the door, wondering if it was news of Tom that the ambassador was about to give him. A deep worry nestled in the pit of his stomach, and Hugo only burned away the edge of it with a mouthful of whisky.

"Looking for pleasures of the flesh?" Maman rasped.

"Looking for . . . an old acquaintance."

"That could be the same thing."

"Not in this case, I can assure you of that."

"Well, he's too young and energetic for me anyway," she said with a lascivious wink.

Hugo smiled. "No one's ever called him that, either. Not for a few years, anyway."

They both looked at the door as it opened, and Ambassador Taylor walked in. Maman blushed at the sight of him, and turned to Hugo.

"You didn't tell me *he* was meeting you here."

"Oh, well," Hugo joked, "Tom has some competition?"

"Not in the slightest," Maman whispered. "The ambassador has him beat, hands down."

Hugo chuckled, and once Taylor and Maman had exchanged pleasantries, and she'd poured him an extra-large whisky, they found an empty table at the back of the room. Before Taylor could say anything, Hugo spoke.

"It's about Tom, isn't it?" he said.

"Yes, it is." Taylor took a gulp of whisky, grimaced, and started in on the story, telling him what Brendon Fowler had said, as close to word-for-word as he could make it. When the ambassador had finished, Hugo realized both of their glasses were empty, though he'd not noticed either of them drinking. His mind was both numb and buzzing, not wanting to process what he'd been told, not wanting to accept it, so he stood and went to the bar. Maman took one look at his face and poured two large ones. When Hugo put his money on the bar, she pushed it away.

"On the house," she said. "You look like you need them."

"*Merci*," Hugo said. "We do, and I'll explain it to you when I can."

"You know where to find me."

Hugo nodded and went back to the table. He put the drinks down and sat. "Well, thank you for telling me in person," he said finally. Then he picked up his glass and raised it to eye level. The ambassador did the same.

"To Tom," they said together.

CHAPTER TWENTY

Hugo held the door for his neighbor Ashley Errico, this time unburdened by dog or groceries, and she flashed him a grateful smile. Then she gave him the once-over.

"Never seen you in a black suit before," she said. "You going to a funeral or something?"

"Actually, yes," Hugo replied.

Her face fell. "Oh, I'm so sorry, I was just . . . I wasn't thinking."

"Please, it's OK," he said with a kind smile. "You couldn't have known."

"Except I guessed, so I could have. I'm sorry."

"It's fine, really. Not someone I knew that well."

"Oh, OK." She started to turn away but stopped. "So where's your friend Tom these days?"

"He's . . . traveling," Hugo said.

"Been quiet around here without him." She winked. "Haven't needed to open the door to any hookers for ages."

"Enjoy the respite," Hugo said. He gave her a wave and headed out onto Rue Jacob, looking up at the gray sky as big, fat raindrops started to fall. *Thanks, Tom. You would have your funeral on a rainy day in December, wouldn't you?*

They'd decided against a church ceremony for a devout atheist. Or, as the ambassador had put it, "We'd be making the place a target for lightning strikes, for sure."

Instead, they decided to hold a memorial at noon on Thursday, in a quiet corner of the Luxembourg Gardens. In past discussions with Tom, he'd always been adamant about being cremated instead of buried, but Hugo and the ambassador had agreed that the following day a graveside burial would be held for just a handful of close friends, in the famous cemetery of Père Lachaise. Tom might not have approved of the fact of a burial, but he'd have liked the impressive grounds and his famous neighbors.

The memorial service was open to everyone, though, and Hugo was shocked at the number of people who were there. More than a hundred, maybe a hundred and fifty, most of whom Hugo didn't recognize. Hugo caught sight of Camille Lerens and gave her a warm hug.

"Impressive turnout," she said.

"Bartenders and prostitutes, if I had to guess," Hugo said.

"In that case, pretty thin turnout," Lerens said with a smile. She squeezed Hugo's arm. "You doing OK?"

"Yep. Let's get things going, shall we?"

They moved to the front of the group, shaking hands and hugging those they recognized, grateful for the presence of those they didn't. At the front, two rows of chairs had been set up, not nearly enough for the attendees, and facing them a temporary podium. Next to it stood Ambassador Taylor and a woman Hugo didn't know. Ambassador Taylor spotted Hugo and gestured for them forward. He extended a hand to Lerens.

"Lieutenant Lerens, nice to see you again. Apart from the circumstances, of course."

"Of course. Good to see you, Monsieur Ambassador." They shook hands and Taylor introduced them to the serious-faced woman in a dark suit and long black wool coat who stood next to him.

"This is Assistant Director Danielle Tierney, from the CIA. Please meet my RSO Hugo Marston and Lieutenant Camille Lerens of the Brigade Criminelle."

They shook hands, and Tierney spoke directly to Hugo. "I know you and Tom were friends, good friends. Please accept my condolences, and those of the agency."

"Thank you," Hugo said. "It was good of you to come."

"I knew Tom well, too," she said, and allowed herself a small smile. "Wouldn't miss this for the world."

"You want to sit up front, Hugo?" Taylor asked.

"Sure. Am I speaking first?"

"Yes," Taylor said. "I'll introduce you, then let you speak. Then I'll say a few words. Then Lieutenant Lerens on behalf of the Paris Police, and finally Director Tierney."

Hugo nodded and looked at the sky. "Rain's holding off, for now. Let's get started. And, if you don't mind, once I'm done I'll just mingle with people, maybe hang nearer the back."

"Understood. Have a seat, we'll get on with it."

Hugo sat between Lerens and Tierney, and the crowd fell silent as Ambassador Taylor took up position behind the podium. Hugo glanced over his shoulder and caught Emma's eye. She sat bolt upright on the row behind him, looking pale but determined. If Hugo was like a son to her, then Tom was the cheeky best friend she'd doted on. The best friend, she knew, who'd always look out for her Hugo. Hugo felt a pang of regret, of guilt, at seeing the pain on her face. He turned his attention to Taylor who was starting to speak.

"Ladies and gentlemen, thank you all for being here. It's cold out, and Tom would hate it if we piled on too much sentimentality, so we'll keep things short. We'll start with Tom's best friend, who I'm sure you all know, or have at least heard of. Hugo Marston."

Hugo stood and went to the podium, his eyes scanning the crowd. He took a breath and spoke from the heart. "If you don't mind, I will speak as if Tom is still alive, and use the present tense." The crowd murmured its approval. "Tom Green is a jerk. He's a mooch, too. He has the moral compass of a moray eel, and I have no idea how his liver didn't kill him long ago. He's also my best friend. The man I can count on no matter what. I've never thought about life without Tom, because he was a giant in mine, as I'm sure he was in yours. It never seemed possible that Tom could ever disappear." Hugo smiled. "Even when, just sometimes, we wanted him too." Several people laughed gently. "Here's the thing. This memorial and tomorrow's private burial will not be the end of things. The man who shot him is still out there, but I promise he won't be for long." Another murmur from the mourners, and Hugo paused. "On that, I give you my word. Thank you again for being here, for showing your love and respect for Tom."

There was a gentle, respectful ripple of applause as Hugo nodded to the ambassador and walked to his right, around the two rows of chairs. He shook a few more hands as he made his way to the back of the crowd, and he heard Ambassador Taylor's strong voice sweep over the mourners, saying nice things about his former CIA colleague.

Hugo looked behind and to each side, into the park, where several people had stopped what they were doing to watch the proceedings. One was a man feeding pigeons, his hand still clutching a broken baguette, and two women had stopped on the path, their strollers in front of them, plastic covers over their wrapped-up babies.

Hugo turned his attention to Taylor's eulogy but noticed an old man slowly making his way toward him from the middle of the crowd. He had a wool cap pulled low over his ears and a scraggly white beard that hadn't seen a comb in a month or two. The man stationed himself beside Hugo and watched in silence for a moment. Then the old man spoke.

"Any sign of him?" he asked.

"Not yet."

"How many eyes do we have?"

"About two dozen, I'm not sure exactly," Hugo said.

"The pigeon feeder and the two ladies with strollers?"

"Yep. They're that easy to make?"

"That used to be my job, remember, but I doubt that asshole will notice."

"You don't think so?" Hugo asked. "Why not?"

"In part because he's just an asshole who doesn't know shit about surveillance. But mostly because he thinks Tom Green is dead and so he'll be fooled by your lovely memorial."

"Let's hope so." Hugo said. He smiled at the scraggly beard. "I hope you appreciate the turnout."

"Fuck you," the man muttered back. "You just couldn't resist, could you?" He shook his head slowly. "A mooch, a drunk, *and* a jerk ... really? At my own funeral?"

"Well, you're always telling me to be more honest and less politically correct." He put a hand on Tom's shoulder. "And, hey, you never know, when you really do get yourself killed, maybe I'll try a little harder to be nice."

Hugo and Tom stood side by side in silence as Taylor finished his remarks and ceded the podium to Camille Lerens. She was in on it, too, the whole scheme, so Hugo's eyes picked out the strong shoulders of Emma, who wasn't. *As soon as I can, I'll tell you everything. I promise.*

Hugo flexed his cold fingers inside his gloves and adjusted the scarf that was failing to keep the chill breeze from his neck. Something tickled the end of his nose, and when Hugo glanced up at the gray sky, he saw that it had started to snow.

CHAPTER TWENTY-ONE

After the memorial, Hugo tried not to glance around as he started his walk home. The women with the stroller had been replaced by a pair of businessmen, and the birdman . . . Hugo couldn't tell. Maybe the priest? Cops did love to dress up when they got the chance, and Hugo was grateful that Camille Lerens had quietly commandeered a select group of officers to watch over him, more than a dozen police officers surrounding him as he walked. They either were on foot or looked down from strategic points higher up. And those guys watched through the telescopic lenses on their sniper rifles.

Despite the cold, Hugo was beginning to sweat. He wore heavy clothing to disguise the bullet-proof vest he was wearing, the same make as the one that had stopped three .32 rounds fired at his best friend. Tom would be sporting a giant bruise for a week or two, but no ribs were broken, which meant that that if Cofer jumped out of the shadows, and Hugo's security couldn't stop him in time, Cofer would still be wielding Tom's relatively small-bore weapon, and once again aim for center mass. That was the dilemma: bring security in too close, and Cofer would know the gig was up, and either try something incredibly reckless or disappear into the ether. Hugo had requested his bodyguards err on the side of invisibility. A trap was good only if the mouse had eyes only for the cheese.

Hugo's phone rang in his pocket, and he checked the display. It was Lieutenant Intern Marchand. Hugo knew better than to answer, though. He had to keep alert, not assume that the people looking out for him would do their jobs. Sure, Cofer had promised to kill Hugo at Tom's funeral, and the memorial at least was over without incident. But Hugo knew better than to take Cofer at his word, even if the man thought he'd been talking to a corpse. Plans change, opportunities come and go . . . Until Cofer was in handcuffs or dead, Hugo wasn't safe.

He breathed a sigh of relief as he reached his apartment building, and after he'd stepped into the lobby he leaned against the door for a moment.

"Monsieur Marston, are you all right?" Dimitrios, the building's concierge, stepped out from behind his desk.

"Yes, thank you. Rough morning." Hugo straightened. "Did someone come by and explain what's happening?"

"Yes and no. A man, Monsieur Pierce, came from the embassy. He said to keep an eye out for someone, a Richard Colter."

"Cofer," Hugo corrected.

"Yes. He told me to call the police and then him if I see the man."

"That's right."

"But he did *not* tell me," Dimitrios started, a little huffily, "why this man is a problem. I am responsible for the people living in this—"

"I know, I know," Hugo interrupted. "And I also know I can trust you." That calmed the concierge and prompted a *harrumph* of agreement, so Hugo continued. "He was a bank robber in the United States. Monsieur Green and I put him in prison, and now he's out, and he may be here in Paris looking for revenge."

Dimitrios's eyes widened at the story. "I had no idea. Is he truly dangerous?"

"Potentially. So do what Monsieur Pierce asked, and call the police the minute you see him."

"I most certainly will," Dimitrios said. "I will call the police, the embassy, and you if you are home."

"Thank you," Hugo said.

"By the way, where is Monsieur Green? I've not seen him in a while." Dimitrios, like everyone in Tom's life, held a powerful affection for the man, and, given the size of Tom's personality, his absences never went unnoticed.

"He'll be back soon," Hugo assured him. "He's on one of his trips." Hugo winked to bring Dimitrios into an imaginary conspiracy, then he turned and walked up the stairs to his apartment. Once inside, he stripped off his layers, including the bullet-proof vest, and sank onto the couch. He thought about the next day's burial service, going over the details in his mind, and then remembered the call he'd missed from Marchand. Marchand had left a message for Hugo to return his call, but said nothing else. Hugo hit *Call Back* and waited for Marchand to pick up.

"*Allô, oui?*" Marchand's voice was gruff.

"Hugo Marston here."

"Ah, yes." His voice softened, and Hugo thought to himself, *Here come the condolences.* "I just wanted to say that I'm sorry for the loss of your friend. I know you were very close, and I have heard many great things about him."

"Thank you, Lieutenant Intern, that's kind of you."

"I know he was killed in Amsterdam, but if there's anything I can do for you, either personally or on behalf of the Paris Police, please do not hesitate to let me know."

Hugo was moved by the words and the obvious sincerity in Marchand's voice. He would have liked to tell him the truth, and knew there might be some fallout if he didn't, but Camille Lerens had sworn her officers to silence in case of another breach, in case some of Cofer's dirty money had found its way into the prefecture.

"I'll take the heat for this," Lerens had said. "After all, if we manage to take Cofer down, or even out, I'll get the plaudits for catching an international criminal mastermind."

Hugo had laughed. "You're giving him too much credit. He'd sure love to hear you call him that."

Now Hugo asked Marchand, "Is there anything you can tell me about the investigation?"

"I would like to, really. But since you are so closely aligned to a witness, I'm afraid my hands are tied."

"Nothing at all?"

"Well, I suppose I can tell you that we managed to obtain a copy of Mademoiselle Alsaffar's will. It was with the lawyers of Monsieur and Madame Rollo in America."

"Anything useful in it?"

"I don't think so," Marchand said, and Hugo could hear the smile in his voice. "That's why I'm telling you about it."

"Then tell me more. Who gets what?"

"There is no single beneficiary. Her brother gets her cash reserves, which her bank records indicate amounts to about five thousand dollars, and any real estate she owned, and we haven't finished figuring out if that's something or also nothing."

"She got a flat in London from her stepfather; she told me that herself."

"That's not shown up yet, but if you say so, we'll come across it. Anyway, Josh Reno gets some sculptures that might one day be valuable but aren't now, and the same goes for the Rollo couple. Some other specific items are left to museums."

"No motive for murder, then?"

"It doesn't look like it. And, before you ask, there was no life-insurance policy." He paused, then said, "I need to ask you something, and I would like the truth."

"Ask me," Hugo said.

"Did you advise the Americans not to cooperate? I know you are supposed to assist them, so I am wondering about this."

"No, not at all. Quite the opposite. Why do you ask?"

"Not only did Rob Drummond refuse to give his fingerprints, but the Rollo couple did, too. In fact, they seemed outraged I would ask."

The question got Hugo's attention. "Did you find prints at the scene?"

"I cannot tell you that yet. Please answer my question."

"I didn't say anything to any of them about prints," Hugo assured him. "If I had, I would have asked that they give them as a way of being eliminated from the investigation."

"Which is precisely how I phrased it, and yet no cooperation."

"Not my doing, I promise you."

"Very well, I believe you. I know you Americans are very big on asserting your rights when it comes to it, even when it works to the detriment of a larger picture."

"Well, I'm not going to argue with that," Hugo said, smiling to himself. "But that's a discussion for another day." He thought for a moment. "Can you tell me whether you are retesting the DNA that you say matches Claudia Roux?"

"It *does* match Mademoiselle Roux. And yes, I can, but only because that is normal procedure. We do not charge based on DNA unless it's been tested twice, and both are positive."

"When will that result be back?"

"Today or tomorrow. We submit specimens to two labs at the same time, and I asked them both to hurry, given the circumstances."

"You mean, given that you're holding an innocent woman?" Hugo kept his tone light, but the meaning was clear.

"Tell me. In my shoes, would you have done anything differently?" When Hugo didn't reply immediately, Marchand went on. "DNA doesn't lie. People lie, but DNA doesn't."

"And you think Claudia Roux is lying."

"What else am I supposed to conclude? I gave her every opportunity to tell me she'd bumped into Mademoiselle Alsaffar outside the building, in the street, anywhere at all. I gave her every chance to explain it, yet she insisted she'd never met her, had never been in contact with her. So, if you can, explain to me which is more believable, her or the DNA?"

"I can't. Not yet. But I *can* tell you she is innocent, so while I don't necessarily blame you for pointing the finger at her right now, I am telling you point blank: do not stop looking for other suspects."

"I gather you have been doing just that," Marchand said drily. "Even after I told you not to."

"A minute ago, you asked me to put myself in your shoes. So now put yourself in mine. Imagine you have a friend charged with a serious crime in another jurisdiction. You know with every fiber of your being that there's no way that friend is guilty. What would you do?"

Marchand was quiet for a moment. "I hear what you are saying," he said finally. "I don't blame you for wanting to exonerate your friend, Hugo. Just do it without interfering with my witnesses or investigation."

"Doing my best," Hugo said. "You have my word."

"Thank you. Again, I'm sorry for your loss; I hope tomorrow's service brings you some peace."

Me too, Hugo thought. *Me too.*

Hugo paced his apartment, wanting the afternoon to pass quickly but slowing time by looking at the kitchen clock every minute or two. He almost jumped when his phone rang, but he hesitated to answer when he didn't recognize the number. *Even a telemarketer would help pass the time*, he thought, and he picked it up.

"Hello?"

"Mr. Marston, Josh Reno here."

"Call me Hugo. And I'm glad you called, I meant to apologize for running out on you like that. I'll pay you back for the check, too, of course."

"Oh, sure, that's OK. But I'll take the money, thanks."

"Of course. So what can I do for you?"

"I hesitated to call but . . . you know, figured I should."

"About what?"

"Well, I went out this morning, took a walk and went by the museum . . . I don't know why, I just wanted to. Then I took the metro down to the river, wanted to walk along it. You know, clear my head and see a bit more of Paris at the same time."

"Sure," Hugo said. "Did something happen?"

"Not while I was out. It was when I got back to the hotel."

Hugo gritted his teeth. "What happened, Josh?"

"Well, I'm pretty sure someone broke into my room."

"What makes you think that? Is something missing?"

"That's why I hesitated to call. As far as I can tell, nothing is."

"Why do you think someone broke in, then?" Hugo pressed.

"Because it's obvious. My stuff has been moved, and a few bags gone through."

"Did you report it to the police?"

"No, should I?"

"Yes, you should." Hugo thought for a moment. "But not yet. Where are you now?"

"I'm in the hotel lobby. I figured it was better not to touch anything, to talk to you first."

"Good thinking. Is the room secured?"

"Well, it's locked if that's what you mean. But if they got in before, I guess they can again. What should I do?"

"Sit tight," said Hugo. "I'll be there in thirty minutes."

It took him thirty-five, but ten of those were spent arguing with Lieutenant Lerens about leaving his apartment.

"I put together a team to get you there safely," she said. "Now you want to take the metro to Montmartre?"

"No, silly," Hugo said. "I'll take a taxi."

"Oh, much safer."

"Look, I've told you when he'll make his move."

"You gave me your opinion, you mean."

"I'm right, Camille. Trust me on this."

"Why wouldn't he shoot you the way he did Tom? Surely he'd get more satisfaction watching you die up close."

"No. If it wasn't today at the memorial, it'll be tomorrow. He's not going to hit me in some back alley or in a taxi cab. This guy wants to go out in a blaze of glory in front of as many people as possible. Where's his satisfaction in shooting me when no one's watching?"

"But that's what he did to Tom."

"Right, because he didn't have a choice. He had to lay low until he could get to me. Tom was his primary, sure, because he killed Cofer's brother, but he's being practical in his psychopathy. In other words, he couldn't go all out with Tom, because then we'd catch or kill him. With me, he *plans* to die. He's not going back to prison, Camille, so this is his grand finale."

"You're assuming he's being logical."

"He is, sort of," Hugo insisted. "He's a maniac and on his way out of this world, but he's intent on doing it on his terms."

"That's your profile?" Lerens asked.

"Pretty much. Like I said, blaze of glory, maximum impact."

"Well, I can't stop you, Hugo. But if you get yourself shot while you're up there, I'm going to have some explaining to do. And a budget shortfall, for that security team."

"Send Ambassador Taylor the bill. Better yet, send it to me and I'll bequeath it to you in my will."

"Funny. But I'm serious," Lerens said. "Keep an eye out, Hugo. We need you in one piece tomorrow."

"Just tomorrow?"

"And ever after," she said. "Stay safe."

Hugo stood in the doorway of Josh Reno's room. Reno stood behind him, peering over his shoulder as if he'd never seen his own room before.

The bed was made, and the room was tidier than Hugo would've expected for an artist on the road. A few framed paintings were stacked against the wall beside the bed.

"Your work?" Hugo asked.

"Yep. I'd hoped to display them, but . . . you know."

"I do." Hugo stepped inside and wondered whether he was imagining the resentment in Reno's tone. "You're a hundred percent sure nothing was taken?"

"I mean, I looked pretty carefully. Nothing important, for sure. None of my art, or Alia's. No money or credits cards."

Hugo pointed to a white travel trunk. "That's yours?"

"Alia's stuff is in there. Right after it happened, the hotel wanted her room because there was a big party of people coming, so they put some of her stuff in her trunk and gave it to me. I guess they changed their mind and gave the room to Drummond, but I kept the trunk."

"Why didn't you give it to him, since it's hers and was in her room?"

Reno shrugged. "Because he's an asshole, I don't know."

"Could something have been taken from it, and you not notice?"

"No. I locked it with a padlock as soon as I'd filled it and moved it in here. My keys were with me when the person broke in, and the locks are intact, as you can see. And why would someone want any of that stuff of hers?"

"No idea," Hugo said. "But if there's one thing I know, just because I can't come up with a reason for someone to steal, that doesn't mean the thief doesn't have one of his own."

"I guess."

"Maybe he was looking for something he *thought* you had, but it wasn't here."

"Such as?"

"Art is the obvious answer."

Reno frowned in thought. "Nothing comes to mind. She just brought stuff for the exhibition."

"Show me how you know someone was in here."

"OK, so." Reno moved to the table beside the trunks and pointed to a canvas shoulder bag. "This was closed up and hanging off the back of the chair, that's how I left it. But I get back and it's here on the table, so I'm betting someone went through it. Also, the lamp on the desk was unplugged, and my passport was visible when I opened the desk drawer."

"What do you mean?"

"I'd put it in there, I always do, put I put things on top of it so it's not obvious."

"Why not use the room's safe?"

Reno snorted. "Last time I did that, it got stuck closed. Even the hotel people couldn't open it, so no thanks. I figure if I keep my room locked and the passport in the drawer, that's as good as a safe."

"Apparently not," Hugo said. "What else was touched that you know of?"

"You're thinking fingerprints?"

"Not at this stage, necessarily."

"Then what?" Reno asked.

"He or she looked in your bag and the desk drawers. Now we know that whatever they were after is small enough to fit into both." Hugo shrugged. "It's not much, but it's something."

"Some clothes were moved, too."

"What exactly? And from where to where?"

"I put a sweatshirt, jeans, and sneakers on the chair. Sweatshirt on the top." Reno pointed to a floral armchair in the corner of the room. "They were on the floor when I got back."

"Just thrown there?"

"No, it was odd. They were in reverse order, but still neatly folded."

Hugo nodded, processing the information. "Do me a favor. Have one more look through everything before you call the police."

"You think it's worth me calling them? I mean, if nothing was taken . . ." He looked around. "I don't really want people, the police, going through all my stuff. I feel like I've done nothing but answer questions for the past few days. Endless questions, and I don't want any more if I can avoid it."

"You can do as you wish," Hugo said. "But if anyone says anything, I'm telling you to call."

"Sure, right. I'll think about it."

Which means you won't, Hugo thought. "Do you mind opening the trunk?"

"No, I guess not." Reno pulled his keys out of his back pocket. He went to the trunk and put one of the keys into the padlock. "It's not working."

"Whoever broke in swapped out the lock," Hugo said. *Unless you're playing some game I'm not aware of . . .*

"What should we do?" Reno said, looking over his shoulder.

"Nothing for now. But if you think of anything else, you have my number." He turned to go but hesitated. "If you do call the police, do me one favor."

Reno smiled. "Don't tell them I told you first?"

"Don't mention me at all, if you can help it."

"Right, no problem. Hey, don't you know the lady they arrested?"

"She's not been formally . . . But yeah. I know her."

"You think she did it?"

"I know she didn't," Hugo said firmly. "As surely as I know my own name."

CHAPTER TWENTY-TWO

Hugo left Reno to look over his room one more time, and rode down alone in the elevator. His thoughts were on Claudia, wondering how she was doing, and what more he could do to help her. And even though it was stupid, he felt guilty because if he'd not had that dinner with Alia, one of the pegs supporting Marchand's theory of guilt wouldn't be there. No dinner, no jealousy. Mostly, though, he felt frustration, much of it because he had no leverage with the police, since she was a French citizen. The best thing he could do, Hugo knew, the *only* thing he could do, was find the real killer.

The elevator doors opened, and he stepped out into the lobby of the hotel just as the sliding glass doors opened and Rob Drummond stumbled through. At first, Hugo thought the man was drunk, but the blood coming from his nose and the swelling around his eye told of injuries, not alcohol. Hugo hurried forward, as did the two receptionists.

"Rob, are you all right?" Hugo asked.

"Yeah," Drummond said, but leaned his considerable body weight on Hugo. "My legs feel kinda wobbly, though."

"What happened, *monsieur*?" one of the hotel staff asked. Hugo glanced at her name tag, which said *Clarice*. "Do you need a doctor, or ambulance?"

"Some guys in a bar. They wanted my wallet."

"The police, then," Clarice said.

"No, no. Not necessary. I handled it, they didn't get anything."

"If you are sure, *monsieur*," Clarice said, sounding dubious. "Which bar was it? Most around here are safe."

"I don't remember. It has a picture of sunflowers on the front. Shitty little place, not a sunflower in sight."

"Ah, you should have asked us for recommendations." Clarice shook her head. "That place would not have been one of them."

"Not good for American tourists?" Hugo asked with a smile.

"Not unless they want to buy drugs, gamble with dice, or pick up certain diseases."

"Or get mugged," Drummond added, with a groan of pain.

"I'll help you to your room," Hugo said. "You sure you don't want to report it?"

"Thanks, but no. What're the police gonna do about it? I'll hopefully be back in London by the end of the week, so even if they catch them, they can't prosecute. I'm not coming back, that's for damn sure."

"You don't like Paris?"

"I know it puts me in a club of one, but no. My sister is murdered and I'm beaten up in a bar. What's to like?"

"Fair enough." Hugo put an arm around Drummond, and they started toward the elevators. "But look at it this way, if you do decide to come back, next time has got to be better."

"I guess," Drummond grunted. He leaned against the wall, then shuffled into the elevator when the doors opened.

"How many of them were there?" Hugo asked.

"Three."

"And they mugged you inside the bar?"

"As I was leaving. One of them asked for money, when I said no, he got pushy and two of his friends showed up out of nowhere. They waited until I was outside to really let me have it."

"You fought them off?"

"Fought them off, ran away. A combination, you might say." He winced as he shifted his weight. "One of them had brass knuckles, pounded me in the leg after I'd pushed him over. Gonna be some kind of bruise there tomorrow."

The elevator dinged as they reached his floor.

"Here we go," Hugo said. "Just lean on me."

"Oh, I will, don't worry." He groaned again as they started forward, but managed to say, "Thanks for this, by the way."

"All part of my consular duties."

They shuffled slowly down the hallway, and Drummond fumbled in his pocket for his key card. His phone and a set of keys fell out onto the floor, and Hugo picked them up as Drummond finally got the door open.

"Thanks again, man, I appreciate it." Drummond said, stumbling into the room and promptly collapsing onto the bed. "That's better."

"I'm going to grab you some ice. You should put it on your eye and leg to reduce the swelling." Hugo picked up the ice bucket from the desk. "You have a spare key? If not, I can prop the door open so you don't have to get up."

"I do." Drummond pointed to a pair of expensive brogues on the floor under the desk. "In the left one."

"You keep your spare key card in your shoe?"

"Along with my passport, yes. Money and house keys in the other one," he said. "That way I know where they all are, and no one else wants to touch them."

"Right," Hugo said, wrinkling his nose. "I think maybe I'll just prop the door open."

Hugo took the bucket to the ice machine, which sat opposite the elevators. It rattled and whined for a moment, then spat out ice as if it were angry and didn't care how much made it into the bucket and how much went on the floor. When he got back to the room, Drummond was propped up on the bed.

"Not the prettiest nurse I've ever had," he said.

"You get what you pay for." Hugo popped into the bathroom and grabbed a hand towel.

"Seriously, though, thanks again."

"You're welcome." He threw the towel to Drummond and put the ice on the nightstand beside him. "Wrap some ice in the towel, it should help."

"I will."

Hugo paused at the foot of the bed. "So if you don't mind me asking, maybe not for the first time, how well did you know your sister?"

Drummond shrugged. "Not very."

"I'm just struggling to find anyone who didn't love her, even mildly dislike her, let alone want to kill her."

"No shit." Drummond snorted, but when he laughed it was good-natured. "Story of my life, people telling me how wonderful she is. Apart from Reno, he may have changed his tune after she basically cut him off, shutting him out of the Dali exhibition. But otherwise, it's true."

"I can believe it," Hugo said. "Although it's my understanding his exclusion from the museum wasn't her fault at all. Be that as it may, I'll leave you to rest. If you think of anything that might help, you have my number."

"I do."

Hugo took the stairs, too impatient to wait for the elevator. He paused by the reception area and asked Clarice a question. "What's the name of that bar?"

"*Les Champs de Tournesol.*"

"I should have guessed," Hugo said with a smile. "Thanks."

"I wouldn't recommend you go there, though."

"Maybe a quick look. I don't like my countrymen being abused by thieves."

"Just make sure they don't get their hands on you, too."

"Thanks, but I'll be fine."

He looked at his phone when it buzzed, and was surprised to see Claudia's name on the screen. He thanked Clarice and moved away from the reception area.

"Claudia? Are you OK?"

A female voice spoke, but it wasn't Claudia's. "Is this Hugo Marston?"

"Yes, who is this?"

"My name is Nicola Dumont. I am Claudia's lawyer. She wanted me to call you, since she's not allowed to."

"Not allowed . . . what do you mean?"

"She is out of jail. But there are certain conditions she must abide by, and one of them is not talking to any of the witnesses in the case. That includes you."

"I'm hardly a witness."

"That's not your decision," Dumont said, her voice brusque. "You were there that night, and you are on the list of people she cannot talk to. That is what matters."

"Fine. But how is she?"

"Happy to be at home."

"I bet. Has she been charged with anything?"

"Yes, with the murder of Alia Alsaffar."

Hugo felt a hot flash of anger. "That's just so ridiculous, ludicrous."

"I tend to agree," Dumont said mildly.

"Well, since I can't speak to her myself, please give her my love and tell her I'm doing everything I can to help her."

"I will. She tells me you are good at what you do."

"I'd like to think so. For her sake, I'd better be."

"Again, I agree."

"Well, thank you for calling," Hugo said, "and please let me know if there's any way I can help you."

"Wait, there's one more thing," Dumont said. "Claudia wanted you to know this."

"Know what?"

"The police retested the DNA found on the victim."

"I know, they told me they always do that in . . . serious cases."

"Yes, and the results just came back," Dumont said. "I'm afraid that the findings were the same as the first test."

"You mean . . . ?" Hugo's voice trailed off as the news sank in. He felt a band close around his chest, and his voice was thick with emotion. "Surely not. I mean, there must be some mistake. Can you have it retested as her lawyer?"

"I can, and I will. But that will be a formality. We have to face the reality that it was most definitely Claudia's DNA on the victim's finger. I'm afraid there can no longer be any doubt about it."

CHAPTER TWENTY-THREE

The snow was falling when Hugo stepped out of his apartment building on Rue Jacob, small flakes that shifted and danced in the light wind that blew down the street. A black Cadillac, his ride to the cemetery, sat idling by the curb, but he lingered for a moment, turning his face to the sky to feel the tickle of snowflakes on his skin, feel the chilly pinpricks of water sting his forehead and cheeks as they melted.

He heard the whir of a window being lowered, and then his second-in-command, Ryan Pierce. "Everything all right, sir?"

"Yep," Hugo said, not moving. "Just a weird morning is all."

"Weird, sir?"

"Burying a friend who's not dead instead of getting to work to clear the name of another friend, one who's been wrongly accused of murder."

"You can be thankful for one of those things." Pierce was glancing around, subtly but noticeably. "Climb in, sir, if you don't mind."

"There aren't any snipers, Ryan," Hugo said, amused. "And if I tell you one more time to call me Hugo instead of *sir*, I'm going to fire you."

"Yes, sir," Pierce said unapologetically. "Roger that."

Hugo rolled his eyes and climbed into the front seat of the car. "Do you know Tom well?"

"I didn't until last night," Pierce said.

"Meaning?"

"I was on babysitting duty. And that one can be a big baby."

"He can." Hugo buckled himself in, and Pierce pulled away from the curb. "What did he get up to?"

"Well, first he complained about the lack of booze at the safe house, so I had one of the other guys go get a six-pack of beer."

"Just a six-pack?"

"Yes, sir." Pierce flashed a grin. "Of French beer."

"French beer?" Hugo whistled. "You sure like to live dangerously."

"He was pretty unhappy. Oh, and then he tried to get an escort."

"Yep, that sounds like him."

"I had to take his phone away."

"He probably had a spare," Hugo said.

"That was the spare. His phone was the first thing to go before they moved him to the house, and since he didn't seem to mind too much, I figured he had another one."

"Smart guy," Hugo said.

"Those aren't the words *he* used." Pierce turned onto the boulevard Saint-Germain, where the traffic was light and the pedestrians on the sidewalk were wrapped up in wool coats and colorful scarves.

"He didn't try to sneak out?"

"Nope."

"How'd you manage that?" Hugo asked. "I mean, no booze and no women, that's not Tom's idea of an evening."

"I took his pants away."

Hugo snorted with laughter. "Are you serious?"

"Yeah. Once he realized we were serious, he settled down."

"Next you'll be telling me you got him to read a book."

"I'm not that good," Pierce said with smile. "But we played cards until midnight and then he went to bed."

"You know he probably cheated, right?"

"Oh, yes, he absolutely cheated. But we let him, since that was a safer outlet than him getting wasted or bringing an escort to the house."

Hugo laughed. "I knew I hired you for a reason."

They drove in silence for a while, angling north across Pont de Sully as the snowflakes grew larger and filled the air around them, making the colorful lights over the *boulangeries* twinkle, and dusting the displays of Christmas trees that were for sale on the sidewalk here and there along the route. Somehow, though, Hugo couldn't escape the chill that sat inside him, the cold and very real knowledge that Rick Cofer was out there waiting for him, and with one purpose in mind: putting a bullet in Hugo's heart. Hugo was confident in the plan, but no plan was fool-proof, and there was little room for error.

They were headed to Père Lachaise cemetery, which had been picked because it was easier to surveil than anywhere else. The entrances were easy to watch, and the high walls surrounding it eliminated the risk of Cofer slipping in unnoticed. Or out. This time of year, the few tourists wanting to wander the cemetery's cobbled streets would be easier to turn away, and the fewer disappointed visitors, the better.

Not that Cofer would realize. The cemetery would have fifty offi-cers in plainclothes, wandering singly, in pairs, and in small groups, all looking out for Cofer. And by the time Hugo was inside, Camille Lerens had promised they would have their man in their sights.

"He won't get close to you," she'd assured him.

"I'm wearing a vest just in case," Hugo said, then smiled. "Although I trust you completely with my life."

A vest and Ryan Pierce, Hugo thought. And when they pulled up on Avenue Gambetta, he saw that Lerens had assigned him another policeman as a bodyguard.

The *flic* opened Hugo's door. "Good morning, sir." His uniform looked new, newly pressed for sure, and he saluted as Hugo stepped out of the car.

"Paul Jameson, how are you? Good to see you again," Hugo said.

"And you, sir." The *r* rolled softly off the Scotsman's tongue, and they shook hands. Jameson was Lerens's most trusted subordinate, a wiry and bald man about to hit fifty, but who looked ten years younger. He'd grown up in Toryglen, a rough-and-tumble section of Glasgow south of the River Clyde and east of Hampden Park. Famous, as Jameson liked to say, for the band Simple Minds and not much else. Jameson had served in the British Navy for several years, but said little about it other than his job involved "nukes." Hugo never asked for details, understanding that often people had done things, in jobs or in their lives, they couldn't talk about. That went for Hugo himself, Tom, of course, and even Ambassador Taylor. What Hugo did know about the Scotsman was that he'd talked his way into the police force many years ago and impressed since the day he'd hit the streets.

"Snow seems appropriate somehow," Hugo said. "Thanks for arranging it."

"Aye, you're welcome."

"You hanging out with me today?"

"Never more than two steps away. And jumping on top of you, if I have to."

Pierce rounded the front of the car. "That's my job," he said. "But if there are bullets flying, we may both have to do it."

"Paul, meet Ryan Pierce, my number two."

The two men shook hands, and Hugo felt a sense of security for the first time since finding out that Tom had been shot. He looked at the stone steps leading up to the cemetery gates, and said, "Gentlemen, shall we?"

The cemetery was cold. Not just because the snow was settling, which it had started to, but because the narrow alleys and walkways funneled the wind so that when it hit, it hit hard. Hugo hunched down into his coat, and his eyes watered as he scanned the crypts around him. They'd commandeered a vacant gravesite a couple of rows off Avenue de la Chappelle, and Hugo stood shoulder to shoulder between Jameson and Pierce. About forty people, all police, surrounded the gravesite, even "Father Galvan," who wasn't there yet, would be packing a pistol under his frock. Ambassador Taylor had wanted to be there for authenticity, but Hugo had resisted, saying he couldn't protect him, and that an ambassador missing the funeral of someone not even affiliated with the embassy would not raise any red flags with Cofer.

Hugo nudged Jameson. "You gonna let me have an earpiece? I'd like to know what's going on."

"No spare, sorry. But I'll let you know if they spot him."

"I like hearing the radio chatter," Hugo pressed. "Knowing who's where, what they're seeing. Even if it's not him."

"Lerens said you'd ask," Jameson said. "Which is why she didn't give me a spare. It's too obvious. If he's watching, he might spot it, and why the hell would you be wearing an earpiece at your friend's funeral?"

"If he's watching me, that means he's already inside and your boys and girls have failed."

"Relax," Jameson said. "We've got our best people out here, no one's gonna fail you. This needs to be convincing."

"He's right," Pierce chipped in. "Not worth the risk."

Hugo dug his hands deeper into his pocket and pressed his forearm against the Glock on his hip.

"I heard that you caught the crypt thief in here," Jameson said.

"Not quite, although he shot at me in here," Hugo corrected. "He also shot at me in a different cemetery, in Montmartre. We caught up with him at his apartment."

"Aye, yes," Jameson said. "I remember now. Sick puppy, that one." He thumped his gloved hands together to warm up.

"That he was," Hugo agreed. "I thought you Scots were used to this weather."

"There's a reason I left the motherland."

"Was it just the weather?" Pierce asked. They were making casual conversation, Hugo knew, to distract him, a measure of comfort and familiarity at a dangerous time.

"It was mostly a woman," Jameson replied. "But that didn't last. The weather here was an added bonus, also less harsh and more predictable."

The three of them chuckled, but they went silent as Jameson tensed and put a finger to his ear.

"They've spotted him. Southeast corner."

"At an entrance?" Hugo said.

"No, which is weird. How the hell did he get in without being seen?"

Hugo waited until Jameson had stopped listening to his radio, then said, "They closed up the tunnels, right?"

"Tunnels?" Jameson asked, his expression blank.

Hugo and Pierce exchanged glances, and Hugo said: "Yes. The crypt thief you were asking about. He moved around the city using the tunnel system. He knew them better than anyone—it's how he popped up in here to rob those graves."

"Yeah, I know about them, of course."

"After that case, the authorities were going to work with the police to block the ones leading in here, and a bunch of others."

"I didn't know about that part of it," Jameson said. "Lemme ask Lieutenant Lerens."

Jameson stepped away and spoke quietly into the mic on his uniform. Hugo couldn't hear the words, but the worried looks he was getting from the Scot told him plenty.

"Some of them," Jameson said when he stepped back beside Hugo.

"Can you be any more specific?"

"No. Bottom line is, some tunnels were walled up, some weren't, and some of the ones that were, well, they did a shitty job, so who knows how effective they are." Jameson shuffled his feet. "Also, they lost sight of the suspect. They weren't sure it was him," he added hurriedly, "but whoever that was, he's no longer on our radar."

Hugo looked around at the rows of telephone-booth-sized crypts, hundreds of them filling the leafy cemetery. Snow had settled on the tops of most of them, but too many had their doors broken down, and too many gaped darkly at him, potential entry and exit points for a man intent on killing him.

"Where's the damn priest?" Hugo muttered. "We need to force things a little, get the program started and hope Cofer's not quite ready."

Jameson put a hand to his ear again. "Fuck. The priest isn't coming."

"Meaning?" Hugo said.

"They found him in the funerary chapel. He's dead."

"How?" Hugo pressed.

"Hang on." Jameson listened again, then said, "They don't know. Could be a heart attack—there are no signs of violence."

"Which leaves open strangulation or suffocation," Hugo said.

"Does seem like quite the coincidence," Pierce agreed.

All three of them shifted, looking around but trying not to be obvious about it. There was a chance, a slight chance, that their plan was still in place, could still work, but the tension was palpable. The air around them had become still, as if the falling snow had blocked any breeze and shut out the rest of the world. Their breath steamed in the chill, and Hugo felt exposed, unprotected.

"Any chance of a radio now?" he asked.

"I'll see if someone can bring you a spare," Jameson said, and made the request into his mic.

"Thanks," Hugo said.

"Shit, they found a body behind a crypt." Jameson relayed the information quietly, still listening. "Homeless man, stabbed once in the throat."

"Maybe that's how he got in," Hugo said. "He suspects this is a trap, that we're looking for people here by themselves, so he either paid or forced someone to walk in with him."

"But we're blocking the entrances, not allowing *anyone* in," Jameson insisted. "Singles, couples, groups, no one has been allowed in this morning."

"So he is using the tunnels?" Pierce asked.

"Sowing confusion," Hugo suggested. "Maybe the homeless guy and the dead priest are coincidences; maybe they're meant to send a message; or maybe he's trying to create confusion."

"He's succeeding," Jameson muttered. "How hard can it be for fifty cops to find one person out here by himself?"

"It's more than a hundred acres," Hugo reminded him. "Trees, crypts, mausoleums. And tunnels. He won't go unspotted for long, but in the meantime there are plenty of places to hide. He just needs to make his way here slowly, get close enough."

"How close is that?" Jameson asked.

His question was answered a second later when a shot rang out, a sharp *crack*, that froze everyone in place as the sound echoed off and between the stone crypts all around them. Except one man wasn't still. Hugo saw him start to topple beside him, and he reached out instinctively as one of the men sent to guard him, one of his friends, collapsed to the ground.

CHAPTER TWENTY-FOUR

A second shot rang out, and Hugo threw himself on the fallen man.

"Ryan, can you hear me? Ryan!"

Pierce didn't respond, and Hugo looked at his subordinate, his colleague, and saw a neat hole in the man's cheek. Hugo called his name again, and Pierce's eyes rolled toward him, but they were full of confusion. A moment later, Pierce jerked in Hugo's arms, and the confusion left his eyes, replaced by an empty stare that Hugo had seen plenty of times before. Panic rose in Hugo's chest, and he was about to start chest compressions when someone tugged hard on his shoulder.

Kneeling behind him, Paul Jameson was shouting and pointing away to their left, but when Hugo raised his head, he couldn't see anyone. The body of his second-in-command lay inert beneath him, and despite the danger Hugo wanted to stay where he was, shield and protect his friend.

But Jameson was shouting still. "Hugo, get up, go!"

"I can't, we need to—"

"Someone will give him CPR, but you need to come with me!" He gestured frantically for a uniformed *flic* to run over and begin lifesaving measures, and Hugo allowed himself to be rolled off Pierce for that to happen.

Another shot zipped past them—Hugo felt it cut the air—and a moment later, Jameson was dragging him to his feet. Hugo scrambled backward, shielding himself between the stone crypts and behind a tall, stone mausoleum. As he scanned the graveyard, desperately looking for

Cofer, a third shot rang out and Paul Jameson dropped to the earth. Hugo started forward, but strong hands grabbed his coat and pulled him back. Hugo turned and stopped short at the ridiculous disguise Tom was wearing, the wool hat and large brown mustache that drooped past his chin. But two men had been shot and were lying in the open, and Hugo knew he had to get to them.

"Stop!" Tom said, seeming to read his mind. "He's not after them. He's after you, and he has a limited number of bullets."

Both men looked to their left as the sound of voices and running feet cascaded toward them, the plainclothes officers summoned by the shots or by a cry for help from one of the *flics* around the grave.

Hugo realized Tom was right, that Cofer was after him and him only. "He'll have moved," Hugo said. "Follow me."

"Let's do this." Tom threw his hat to the ground and tore off the fake mustache. "That's more like it."

Hugo turned and ran, angling between the ten-foot-high crypts and away from Avenue de la Chappelle, where the police would soon converge on the shooting scene, and where they would be able to help Jameson and Pierce. He guessed that Cofer would head the same way to put some distance between himself and the police, find somewhere he could hide again until he regained his target. Hugo's mind flashed back to the stocky little man who'd shot at him before in this place, a man who didn't even know his name and who disappeared into the ground before Hugo could catch him, the man they still called the crypt thief.

Tom was panting behind him, and Hugo heard him shout, "To the left."

Hugo glanced across and saw a figure fifty yards away, dodging between the crypts and heading toward them at an angle. He stopped and put a hand on Tom's heaving shoulder.

"Let him chase me," Hugo said. "You come up behind him."

"Why not just holler for the troops?" Tom panted.

"I don't want him going to ground."

"OK, but, fuck, I'm pretty much gassed already, so don't make him run too much farther."

"I won't." Hugo slapped him on the shoulder. "Let's get the bastard."

Tom sank to one knee and peered over a stone tomb. "I'll spot him, let him go after you. Just make sure he doesn't shoot you before I get there."

"I'll try." Hugo gave his friend a grim smile, turned, and ran into the forest of crypts, going slowly enough to be seen by his pursuer, but fast enough not to be shot by him. *He'll have to be close to shoot that .32*, Hugo thought, but somehow that was little comfort each time he emerged from behind a stone sepulcher and stepped into an open space. He kept his head low out of instinct, and caught flashes of movement to his left and back a little, Cofer closing in. Hugo scanned the tombs ahead to find one that would suit his plan, and he spotted it just as he crossed the empty Avenue Neigre and disappeared again into the cemetery's interior.

It was a waist-high, stone crypt that sat beneath a willow tree, whose spindly branches hung down, trailing across the top of the gravesite. It was set in a little space, too, apart from the resting places around it. Hugo rounded it and sank to one knee, drawing his gun and watching intently for Cofer. He spotted the tall figure twenty yards away as Cofer leapt from behind one tall crypt to hide behind another.

"I'm over here," Hugo called. "You don't have much time; reinforcements are on their way."

"That so?" Cofer's voice floated across to Hugo. "Isn't that what Custer said?"

"I mean it. Give it up, Cofer, or get on with it. This is a long way to travel just to end up in a French prison."

"Dutch prison, you mean. And I hear they're very comfortable." A flash of movement and Cofer dodged behind a closer crypt. There were just two rows between them now.

"How many shots do you have left?" Hugo called out.

"Enough. Your fat little friend only needed three to die. I'm guessing two will suffice for you."

"You're gonna need to get closer then. You're a shitty shot."

"Shitty? I just killed two more of your friends, didn't I?"

I don't know, Hugo thought, *but if you did . . .* "You were aiming for me."

"True. You gonna play by the rules this time, Marston? Just curious, if I give you the chance, are you gonna kill me in cold blood like you did my brother?"

"I didn't do that, Cofer." *Where are you, Tom?* Hugo wondered.

"You're as guilty as your fat friend was. And you know it." Another flash of movement, and Hugo dropped a little lower as Cofer moved up one row. "Hey, let's do this like they used to back home," Cofer said.

"How's that?"

"Quick draw. Face-to-face."

"This isn't a game, Cofer."

"You're too scared? Or don't you trust *me* to play fair?"

"Damn right I don't." Hugo spotted Tom finally, moving low and quietly across Avenue Neigre, directly behind where Cofer was standing. *Keep him talking, and make some noise*, Hugo told himself. "After all, you put three bullets into an unarmed man. Why the hell would I trust you not to do that to me?"

"How about I give you my word?" Cofer laughed. "That worth anything to you?"

"About as much as your life," Hugo responded. "Which is to say, no."

"Yeah, well, how about—What the . . . ?"

Hugo heard a scuffling sound and two soft thumps and, just as he stood up, Tom appeared with Cofer at the end of his gun, hands raised and eyes wide with surprise.

"You should've seen his face!" Tom said. "Fucking classic." He shoved Cofer forward, and they watched as the ex-con stumbled and fell to his knees. He stayed like that for a moment, then seemed to regain his composure, and he looked up at Tom, eyes still wide.

"How did you not die?"

"I was wearing a vest, you moron."

"A vest?" Cofer shook his head slowly. "Well, shit."

"I'm not known for my forward thinking," Tom said. "Hugo made me promise to wear it, even though I wasn't planning on you seeing me first."

"I could've shot you in the head. I *should* have."

"Hindsight is a bitch, huh?"

"I told you I was coming here." Cofer shook his head slowly, and Hugo could almost see his mind working. "So all this. And yesterday's event. It's all been a ruse to get me?"

"A successful one," Hugo said. "Wouldn't you say?"

"I suppose so." Cofer rocked slowly to his heels, then looked back and forth between Tom and Hugo. "So what now, the execution?"

"It'd be my pleasure," Tom said, and aimed his gun at Cofer.

"No!" Hugo held up a hand. "We're not doing it that way, Tom."

"Not this time, you mean," Cofer snarled.

"Don't push your luck." Hugo snapped. He looked at Tom. "Dude, no. He goes back to prison. We can send him postcards every now and again to remind him how much fun we're having in the free."

"Hugo, this is bullshit." Tom kept his gun pointed at Cofer's head. "He shot Ryan and your Scottish pal. Fuck, he shot me!"

"Yeah, he did. And for that he'll die in prison."

"A cushy Dutch one," Tom snapped. "Not happening." He reached into his jacket pocket and pulled out the gun Cofer had taken from him in Amsterdam, the one he'd just taken back.

"What are you doing, Tom?" Hugo asked.

"I think I'm about to commit suicide," Cofer replied.

"Not exactly." Tom threw the gun to the ground, and it skittered to within three feet of Cofer. Tom put his own gun back into a pocket. "That quick draw you wanted."

"Hardly." Cofer gestured to Hugo, who was still covering him with his Glock. "He drew already."

"Then I suggest you draw real fast," Tom said mildly. "And aim for him first."

Hugo took a small step forward. "Tom, pick up that gun. He's going to prison."

The air quivered with tension, the breath of three men puffing out like smoke as they watched each other, three statues waiting for someone else to move first. The sounds of voices and police sirens drifted over to them but seemed so very far away.

"Prison?" Cofer said quietly. "Fuck that." He lunged forward, his body flattening out and rolling as he grabbed the gun from the earth and twisted toward Hugo, still lying down but his arm getting halfway up before a shot rang out. Cofer's head snapped back, then slammed down into the cold, hard ground. His arm seemed not to know the rest of him was dead, and for a few seconds he pointed the gun at the sky. Then the weapon dropped from his hand and hit the earth with a thud.

"Nice shot," Tom said. He stepped forward and stood over Cofer, looking down. "Yep. Dead as a doornail."

"What the hell were you playing at?" Hugo moved to the .32 and picked it up. "What if my gun had jammed?"

"Oh, please. I thought of that. It's unloaded."

"I shot an unarmed man?"

"A man you reasonably thought *was* armed," Tom corrected.

They both turned as four police officers ran between the crypts, guns in hand. Camille Lerens was at the front of the pack.

"You guys OK?" she said, looking back and forth between them.

"Yeah, we're fine." Hugo glared at Tom, who plucked the .32 from his hand.

"We sure are, just dandy," Tom said. He handed the gun to Lerens. "Here, take this, it's evidence."

"Who shot him?" Lerens asked. She didn't wait for an answer, just barked orders at the men with her, who pulled back and cleared the crime scene.

"I did," Hugo said. "He had that in his hand, was bringing it up to shoot me."

"Head shot," Lerens said matter-of-factly. "Impressive. And it looks like a clear case of self-defense, but we'll have the crime-scene people come out here, and you'll both have to give a statement, of course."

"Of course," Hugo said.

Hugo knew his written statement would be thorough, but it might have a gap or two as to how and when Cofer pulled the gun. Apparently his friend hadn't evolved much from the previous encounter with the Cofers, but Hugo had. And he was angry with Tom for that. The rules were there for a reason—not just to protect dirtbags like Rick Cofer and his brother, but to protect cops, too. Play by the rules and you get to keep your badge, and your freedom. Of course, Tom didn't have a badge to lose. His ire at his friend was tempered, though, by the knowledge that they'd both breathe easier with Cofer permanently out of the picture. And Dutch prisons, he'd heard, *were* pretty plush when compared to American ones.

Lerens holstered her weapon, then dropped the magazine out of the .32 and inspected it. "Empty. That's odd, why would he go for an empty gun?" She pulled back the slide. "Ah, there it is. One left in the chamber."

Hugo, Tom, and Lerens left two men standing guard over Cofer's body and hurried back toward Avenue Neigre, where a few officers lingered, huddled in small groups, talking and smoking cigarettes. Somewhere ahead of him, in the direction of Avenue de la Chappelle, Hugo heard an ambulance siren start up, and a stab of fear ran through him.

"How're Ryan and Paul?" Hugo asked. "Give me good news, please."

A voice behind him spoke up. "Ach, it'd take more than a flimsy .32 bullet to take me out." Jameson stepped forward and shook Hugo's hand. "Glad you're OK, too, I heard you got him all by yourself."

"Oh, I had some help," Hugo said, and nodded toward Tom. "But I thought you got shot, Paul."

"I did." Jameson thumped his own chest, and winced. "Got hit in the sternum. That's why we wear those vests, though, eh?"

"Exactly. And thank heavens. You had me worried for a moment there." Hugo was still deeply concerned, though. "What about Ryan?"

"He took a round in the face," Jameson said, suddenly somber. "It didn't look good, but that siren was him on his way to hospital."

"Good. Is anyone—" Hugo began, but Jameson interrupted him.

"Aye, one of my boys is with him, don't worry."

Hugo turned to Lerens. "Can you have someone drive me to wherever they're taking him?"

"Of course," Lerens said. "Paul, are you all right to do that?"

Hugo and Lerens looked over at Jameson, who stood stock-still, one hand on his earpiece and the blood visibly draining from his face. He shook his head slowly, and his jaw clenched as he acknowledged the radio message. He reached out to put a hand on Hugo's shoulder.

"I'm so sorry," the Scotsman said. "That was my man in the ambulance. Pierce didn't make it."

Hugo closed his eyes, and a wave of exhaustion washed over him. He felt his legs give way, and Lerens guided him to the flat top of a moss-covered tomb behind him.

He looked up at Jameson and asked the question that everyone asks. "You're sure?"

"Yes, sir. I'm afraid so. He didn't make it out of the cemetery gates. My man tells me the bullet went straight into his brain."

Hugo lowered his head and sat there, his elbows on his knees, staring at the ground. He felt as much as saw Tom sit down beside him.

"I'm glad I put that bullet in that bastard Cofer's head," Hugo said quietly. He thought, but didn't say: *Thank you for making me do it.*

"Yeah," Tom said. *You're welcome.*

After a moment, Hugo looked up at Jameson. "I'll still take that ride, Paul, if you don't mind."

"Of course. But why?"

"Someone will have to identify him formally," Hugo said. "And I'm sure as hell not going to make his wife do it."

CHAPTER TWENTY-FIVE

Hugo didn't recognize the number, but he answered it anyway. He'd been sitting on his couch just staring at the walls since returning from the hospital, and it was from there that he'd called Louisiana, where Ryan's wife, Katie, was visiting family with their three kids. He hadn't known she was away, and it was the hardest call he'd ever made. Hugo sat there quietly, with tears streaming down his face, as this strong woman sobbed into the phone, and eventually her father had taken it from her. Hugo told him what had happened.

"I'll take care of her, of the kids," the old man said finally.

"Thank you. I can arrange for him to go home in the next couple of days; I'm assuming he'll want to be buried there."

"He will. Mr. Marston, can you tell me something?"

"Of course."

"The man who shot him, you said he was an American. Will he go to prison here or there in France?"

"Neither," Hugo said. "I killed him."

"Ah. Thank you. Thank you for doing that."

For the next two hours, Hugo grew increasingly restless in his apartment, and when his phone rang, he all but leapt at it. Hearing Claudia's voice for the first time in days sent a new rush of emotion washing over him, a mixture of relief, joy, anger, and frustration.

"I'm so sorry about Ryan," she said. "I know you thought the world of him."

"Thank you, I did."

"You shot Cofer. Are you OK with that?"

199

"Very much so. It's about the only thing I'm OK with right about now."

"Hugo, please. If you're worried about me, don't be."

He laughed softly. "It doesn't work that way."

"I know, but I'm telling you I'll be fine."

"You shouldn't even be talking to me," Hugo said. "You could get in a lot of trouble for that."

"We're not talking about the murder case, which is what they care about." It was her turn to laugh gently. "Plus, they won't know. I'm using a burner phone."

"You are?"

"Yes. Untraceable."

"And why did you decide to do that?"

"So I can talk to you." She paused, then said, "Hugo, I don't mean to put too much of this on you, but are you having any luck looking into my case?"

"Some progress, but not as much as I'd like."

"I don't understand how my DNA got on her—I really don't."

"Me neither," Hugo said. "You haven't remembered any interaction, a chance meeting, anything between the two of you?"

"No, I haven't." There was irritation in her voice. "I'm sorry, but we've been over that. And my lawyer keeps asking me, too. Should I make something up?"

"No, don't do that. I know it's hard, but the truth will out, I promise."

"It doesn't feel like it from here."

"Hang in there," Hugo said. "I have a few ideas, things to check out."

"Such as?"

"I'll let you know, if and when they work out. Now go put that phone under your pillow."

"You think they'll search my house again?"

"Wait, they searched your house?"

"Yes, while I was in jail. You didn't know?"

"No." It made sense, of course they would search the home of a murder suspect. But Captain Marchand hadn't told him, not out of courtesy nor as an aid to the investigation.

Which gave Hugo an idea. When they hung up, he typed a name into a search engine on his phone. That gave him an address and phone number, which he dialed immediately. He was put on hold for a few minutes, but then he finally got through to the person he needed.

"Hello?" the woman said. "Is this Hugo Marston?"

"It is," he replied. "And I have a proposition for you."

By six o'clock, Hugo knew he had to get out of his apartment, needed to kick some life into himself and maybe get his brain back into gear to help Claudia. Tom had disappeared, as he was wont to do, despite having promised to buy Hugo a drink or two to celebrate his return to Paris, and to life.

Hugo showered and dressed in a white collared shirt, dark-blue slacks, and an even darker gray jacket, and he was just about to grab his keys from the kitchen counter when his phone rang.

"Tom, I thought I'd lost you again."

"Stuff to take care of. You ready for that drink?"

"More than ready. But I get to pick the place—you promised."

"I was thinking Chez Maman, it's been a while."

"I was just there with Ambassador Taylor," Hugo said. "No, I was thinking somewhere a little more upmarket."

"Where?" Tom's voice was laden with suspicion.

Hugo told him, trying not to laugh.

"Hugo, seriously? You trying to bankrupt me?"

"You said I could choose."

"Come to think of it, I'm pretty sure I'm banned from there."

"One way to find out. I'll be there around seven. Don't make me wait."

Hugo hung up and then called one of the cab companies he used, and by seven was walking into Les Ambassadeurs bar at the Hôtel de Crillon. Over the years, he'd sipped cocktails at many of Paris's finest bars and restaurants, usually alongside the ambassador or Claudia, but the recent remodel at the Crillon had resulted in a place that felt more like a palace than a bar. The carpet was thick underfoot, and the muted beige and cream tones allowed the marble and gold décor to glow. A line of crystal chandeliers ran down the middle of the room, sparkling like diamonds. *Maybe sparkling* with *diamonds*, Hugo thought.

Hugo started toward the bar itself, suddenly wondering if his credit card would stretch to more than one drink. *Tom better hurry*, he thought.

"Mr. Marston, what a nice surprise." The voice came from behind him, and he recognized it instantly. He turned to greet her.

"Mrs. Rollo, how are you?"

"Fine, thank you." She took Hugo's hand and looked him up and down. "You look very handsome."

"Thank you, so do you." He smiled. "I mean, beautiful."

She wore her hair up in a French twist that somehow emphasized the fineness of her features, especially her eyes. Her dress was a deep burgundy color and slightly off the shoulder, hugging her body down to her knees. A four-strand pearl necklace wrapped itself close around her throat, the pearls the size of marbles.

"I assume from your attire you are meeting a date?" she asked coyly.

"No, actually. Just a friend. He's rather uncouth, so I like to make him uncomfortable from time to time. How about you?"

"Well, if any other man had asked, I'd say I'm waiting for my husband, but that would be a lie." She put a hand on his arm. "He's working in the suite, so maybe I can buy you a drink and flirt with you until your friend comes."

"That's very kind, but I couldn't—"

"Oh, you're so old-fashioned. I bet you've never let a woman buy you a drink in your life, have you?"

He thought of Claudia immediately, the first person to challenge what he called chivalry and she labeled sexism.

"One or two," he said meekly.

"Bullshit," she said with a laugh, and steered him to the bar. The bartender waited attentively. "Champagne for me, please. Hugo?"

"I'll have the same, thank you."

"A bottle of Cristal, then."

The bartender gave a small bow. "*Oui*, Madame Rollo, if you care to find a table I will bring it to you immediately."

"And some olives and nuts, if you please, Jorge."

The bartender gave a small bow and turned to collect the champagne, glasses, and plates for their nibbles. Hugo led the way to a small table close by and pulled out a chair for Rollo.

"This OK?" he asked.

"You like to sit with your back to the wall," she said.

"Most law enforcement do."

"And how is that going, the investigation?" she asked. "I heard that they arrested someone, but no one's telling us anything."

"They arrested the wrong person," Hugo said. "So, in my opinion, the investigation is going very poorly indeed."

"Oh, really? How do you know it's the wrong person?"

They fell quiet as the bartender arrived. He put an ice bucket in a stand beside the table, and popped the bottle in front of them. The champagne hissed as he filled their glasses. He sank the bottle into the ice bucket with a satisfying crunch, and said, "I will be right back, excuse me."

Hugo raised his glass. "*Santé.*"

"Bottoms up," Rollo said with a wink.

They sipped, and when they put their glasses down, Hugo said, "So how long will you be staying in Paris?"

"JD keeps changing his mind. And the police haven't said we can go." Jorge appeared again and put two bowls on the table, one full of black and green olives, the other holding nuts of various kinds. "*Merci*, Jorge," she said with a smile, and Hugo was sure the young man blushed.

"Very welcome, *madame*."

When the bartender had returned to his station, Hugo took another sip and said, "Can I ask you some rather-direct questions?"

"What about?"

"Alia Alsaffar."

She pursed her lips. "I suppose so. I was hoping that my police interrogation was over, though. Or are you hoping to get me drunk and have me spill the beans?"

"Are there any beans to be spilled?"

"Oh, there are always some, don't you think? Is there a person alive who doesn't have at least one skeleton in his or her closet?"

Hugo shifted in his seat, glad that his particular skeleton had been consigned to the grave. Or at least the mortuary. "True," he said. "That was true of Alia?"

"Yes and no." Rachel Rollo picked out a few nuts with her delicate fingers, popped them into her mouth, and chewed slowly. She took a sip of champagne, as Hugo waited patiently, then she said, "But those are not my secrets to tell, are they?"

"I don't know. But if there's something that can help me find out who killed her . . ." Hugo watched her carefully. Her body language had changed completely. She now sat hunched forward, with her legs crossed and her arms across her chest. She held her champagne glass in front of her like a shield. "Or maybe it'd help me rule someone out," he said.

"You have a list of suspects somewhere?"

Hugo tapped the side of his head. "Up here."

"And who have you ruled out so far?"

"Just one person."

"And who is that?" she asked.

"The person they arrested."

"You never did explain why you're so sure that person's innocent." Rollo looked at him. "I'm pretty sure someone said they had DNA."

"Ah, yes, DNA." Hugo smiled. "Those damned cop shows make it seem like DNA is the silver bullet for crime detection. You have DNA and that's your man; you don't and he walks." He shook his head. "That's just not how it works."

"It's not?" She sounded genuinely surprised. "Tell me."

Hugo took a sip and let the bubbles fizz on his tongue. "Well,

DNA usually just means someone was at a particular place. Or touched a particular thing. It can't tell you when, and it certainly can't tell the larger story, either what happened or who did what to whom."

"Right, it puts the murderer at the scene. That seems pretty huge to me."

"It can. Or it can mean nothing."

"How so?"

"Let me tell you about a case I had. It was a cold case where the suspect had strangled his ex-girlfriend to death, twenty years previously. Long story short, we managed to undo his alibi and establish that he'd lied to police when first interviewed. We also had a witness who said he'd confessed to her, while drunk, that he'd done it."

"Sounds pretty convincing."

"All circumstantial, but yes, it was as decent a case as we could make it."

"There's a 'but' coming," Rollo said.

"Right. And it's to show you how people are getting this DNA thing wrong—not understanding it or even wanting to."

"I'm all ears."

"The case went to a jury trial, and I worked closely with the prosecutor. Dimple Malhotra, was her name. Great lady, cute as a button and sharp as a tack. Had a habit of wearing leather pants on Fridays, but without question, one of the best prosecutors I've ever worked with. They picked a jury on the Monday of trial, and she was asking the panel of eighty people the usual questions, you know, to see who'd be appropriate and who wouldn't.

"Dimple talked about DNA, because she knew jurors expected to hear about it in cold cases. Many of them have been proven that way, so it's not surprising someone would bring it up. But she explains that the prosecution can prove its case with other evidence, and that DNA isn't required. This one lady puts up her hand and says, 'Well, it's a cold case, so I'd expect DNA evidence.'

"Dimple takes a breath and explains why DNA isn't always useful. The example she gives is a brother murdering his sister. Even if it happens in her bedroom, and some of his DNA is on her neck, her clothes, that doesn't tell you much, because you'd *expect* it to be there. He lives in the house, his DNA is going to be in every room."

"I guess so," Rollo said.

"I know so. Thing is, this woman kept saying she'd expect the state's prosecutors to present DNA evidence in every cold case. The judge even explained that the state got to choose what kind of evidence it put on, that prosecutors weren't required to present DNA evidence, but she stuck to her guns and so, of course, she never made it to the final jury of twelve. The trial lasted two weeks and, sure enough, no DNA evidence was put on by Dimple or her colleagues. She explained, several times, that the defendant had lived with the victim, so his DNA would be all over the place, including any clothes that were preserved. Hence, there was no *point* testing for it. It wouldn't have added anything."

"I can see where this is headed."

"I imagine so." Hugo drank some of his champagne and ate two black olives. "Anyway, the jury deliberated for one day, then another day. On the third, the judge declared a mistrial and both sides, along with the judge, talked to the jurors about why they couldn't reach a decision."

"Let me guess," Rollo said. "The lack of DNA."

"Ten jurors wanted to find him guilty, but two wouldn't convict without DNA evidence."

"Why didn't they speak up before, like the woman?"

"I don't know," Hugo said. "The defense team made it a big deal once the trial started, of course; maybe that persuaded them that the state hadn't been thorough enough. Point being, it's not a thing of magic that determines whether or not someone is guilty."

"It's like a fingerprint," Rollo suggested. "Just shows someone was there at some time."

"Precisely. Except it's a little more . . ." It hit him like a blast of cold air, and he just sat staring at her as his mind worked. "Fingerprint," he repeated slowly. "Oh my God."

"Hugo, are you OK? You've turned white."

His eyes gained focus again, and he put his glass down on the table. "I'm fine," he said. "But I have to go."

"You do? Things were just getting interesting."

"I really do, yes. And don't worry, they'll be even more interesting when my friend Tom shows up, believe me."

"Well, thank you for . . ." Her voice trailed off and she seemed upset that he was leaving so suddenly.

"No, thank you. You just helped me solve a mystery, and saved a woman who is charged with the most serious crime there is." He took her hand, kissed it once, then stood and walked quickly out of the bar, his cell phone in hand and already trying to connect with Lieutenant Intern Adrien Marchand.

CHAPTER TWENTY-SIX

At the prefecture the next morning, Hugo was led to a small and windowless room. It was on the first floor, but it felt more like the basement. Or dungeon. The walls were light green from the floor to about waist height, then painted a cream color that had turned to yellow as it aged. The place smelled musty and contained one wooden chair and a rectangular table that took up 70 percent of the floor space. The only modern item in the room was a security camera that trained its beady eye on him from the far corner.

Hugo thanked the uniformed officer who'd let him in, and looked at the two boxes and three file folders that lay on the table.

"Please do not touch those yet," the officer said. "There are instructions you need to be given first. Someone will be here soon."

"Soon" in police time, as Hugo well knew, meant within two hours, so he pulled out a copy of Robin Yocum's *A Perfect Shot* and made himself as comfortable as he could on the hard but sturdy chair. Twenty minutes later, Lieutenant Intern Marchand threw open the door and strode in. He glared at Hugo.

"Monsieur Marston. I thought I made myself perfectly clear that you were not to involve yourself directly in this investigation."

Hugo pulled a letter from his jacket pocket and handed it to Marchand. "This is from Claudia Roux's lawyer, Nicola Dumont. As you can see, it confirms that I am a member of the defense team. Their investigator, you might say."

"This is preposterous." Marchand scanned the letter, then waved it angrily at Hugo and threw it onto the table. "Clever, I'll give you that, but preposterous."

"If we're talking preposterous, we should discuss you arresting Claudia in the first place," Hugo said mildly.

"We have. Several times. And not once have you been able to offer a rational explanation for the DNA of Claudia Roux being found on the victim's hands."

"Give me thirty minutes with these files, and assuming you've been as thorough in your work as I expect, I will have an explanation for you."

"Seriously?" Marchand looked at him in disbelief. "You think you can explain that away?"

"Yes."

"With my own investigation files?"

"I do. Thirty minutes."

"I see." Marchand stared at him for a moment, chewing his lip. "Fine. I will be back in thirty minutes. But please know the rules for you being in here. Nothing gets photographed or copied in any other way. You may make notes about what you see, although you don't even seem to have a pad or pen."

"Don't need either," Hugo said. "I know what I'm looking for, and if I find it I'll show it to you."

"And if you don't find it?"

Hugo smiled. "Then your investigation hasn't been as thorough as I would have expected."

It took twenty-five minutes for Hugo to find the pages, and to satisfy himself that he was right. He left those papers on the desk and put everything else neatly back into the boxes and folders, winked at the camera, and picked up his book. When Marchand let himself in, somewhat less enthusiastically than before, Hugo had his feet on the table and was just starting chapter eleven.

"You found what you were looking for?" Marchand asked. His tone was neutral, but Hugo could see curiosity burning in his eyes.

"I did." Hugo swung his feet off the table to the floor. He stood, picked up the papers, and gestured for Marchand to perch on the table beside him.

"This should be good," the Frenchman said.

"I think it is. So, the question is, how did Claudia's DNA get on the body of Alia Alsaffar, most notably her hands?"

"That is the question, yes."

"And here's where specifics matter. Specifics I didn't ask for and you didn't give. Frankly, it didn't occur to me to ask until . . ." He waved a hand. "No matter, it occurred to me eventually."

"What are you—?"

"The thing that's important," Hugo interrupted, "was that I needed to see the forensic and medical reports to get as much detail as I could. And, as I expected, you have all those in your case file."

"Of course."

"You were thorough enough to get not just the victim's medical records but also Claudia's." Hugo reached into the breast pocket of his jacket and pulled out some folded-up papers. "I brought my own copies in case you hadn't, so congratulations for making that unnecessary."

"Where are you going with this?"

"In America, we call these run sheets." Hugo held up the papers from his pocket. "The standard report from the ambulance crew that tended to Claudia when she fainted. From you, I was able to review the run sheet from the crew that attended the murder scene. They got there before the police, as you know, but found Alia dead."

"Yes, of course. I know that."

"Well, what you either don't know or didn't spot yet, is that the same ambulance that helped Claudia also went to the museum."

"I hadn't made that connection. Yet." Marchand's eyes narrowed. "So what?"

"We'll get there in a moment. After looking at the run sheets and making that little discovery, I then looked at the forensics reports. Specifically the crime-scene tech who swabbed the victim for DNA. She was very thorough because she swabbed each finger separately, and also the palms of her victim's hands separately. Each swab went into its own tube and was sealed, and then sent for processing."

"Perfectly standard," Marchand said. "Nothing improper about that at all."

"I'm not suggesting there was. Quite the opposite—I'm thrilled to pieces she did it that way."

"Why?"

"Because," Hugo said, enjoying the confusion on Marchand's face, "she marked every tube with a number and letter, enabling me to match each one up with the findings of your DNA lab."

"Again, standard."

"You have great standards, no doubt. My point is that Claudia's DNA was found not on either of Alia's palms but on one of her fingers. And *only* one. Which, if you think about it, is odd if it got there while Alia was defending herself from an attack by Claudia. But, that aside, what's more interesting is that it was from her index finger."

Marchand furrowed his brow in thought, and Hugo gave him a moment. Finally, the Frenchman's head jerked upright and he snapped his fingers.

"*Mon dieu*, I know what you're saying!" His eyes were wide and he stared at Hugo.

"Good." Hugo nodded. "Because I think what happened is that the same ambulance crew that treated Claudia rushed to the museum to attend to Alia Alsaffar, and when they got there . . ."

"Yes, I see it now." Marchand nodded. "They had no time to clean their equipment, probably didn't think they needed to since Mademoiselle Roux declined any real treatment."

"Right," Hugo said. "Except they did use a couple of things, probably without even thinking about it. The blood-pressure machine, a stethoscope . . ." Hugo left the sentence open, letting Marchand finish his thought.

"And the oxygen monitor, whatever you call it, that they put on Mademoiselle Roux's finger!"

"Pulse oximeter," Hugo said. "And, yes, the very same one that minutes later they put on Alia's finger."

"*Merde*, show me." Marchand turned to the papers on the table. He leaned over them as he looked at the ambulance's two run sheets.

"Fortunately, they are very thorough," Hugo said.

"Yes, yes. It says right here in the notes, both times the pulse oximeter was placed on the index finger of the patient."

"Even paramedics have habits, I guess," Hugo said. "This guy puts
the oximeter on his patients' index fingers and, thankfully, makes a
record of it."

"Yes, and . . ." Marchand straightened and picked up the forensics
report, turning to the back page. "You're right, it was Alsaffar's index
finger that the DNA was found on." Marchand put the report down
and stood, staring down at the papers, slowly shaking his head. "That
fool! How can he not clean his equipment?" He looked up at Hugo,
anger in his eyes. "Thanks to his laziness, I charged a woman with
murder!"

"Don't be too hard on him," Hugo said. "His job is to get to his
patients as quickly as possible, and he did so that night. Plus, if not
wiping the inside of the pulse oximeter was so obviously a danger, then
you, or I, should have figured this out earlier."

"Perhaps, yes." Marchand sighed. "You are right about that, too.
It was my error and not his. And now, apart from a possible motive,
which," he looked away sheepishly, "I admit was never very persuasive,
this was our main evidence. Our only real evidence."

"So you'll withdraw the charges?"

"I will have to inform my superiors, but then, yes, immediately.
Right away."

"One more thing," Hugo said.

Marchand cocked his head, then a smile spread over his face. "Ah,
but of course. Please, say it."

"Thank you." Hugo cleared his throat dramatically. "I told you so."

Marchand nodded his head. "Yes, you most certainly did." He gave
Hugo a wry smile. "You know, you're quite the boyfriend."

"Hang on, I never said I was—"

Marchand laughed. "I was a fool to miss this evidence. But I am not
a fool when it comes to affairs of the heart. She is lucky to have you."

CHAPTER TWENTY-SEVEN

The cold nipped at Hugo's face as he stepped out of the prefecture and headed toward his Saint-Germain-des-Prés apartment on the other side of the river. As he walked away, he felt like a huge weight had been lifted from his shoulders, and even the cold couldn't suppress the delight he felt. Mostly at knowing Claudia was free from suspicion, and criminal charges; but, to a lesser degree, from the satisfaction of putting together the clues, solving what for him had been at one time an utterly inexplicable mystery. It was true, in Hugo's experience, that even the most difficult puzzles often had simple explanations, but he refused to chide himself for not spotting it sooner.

As for Claudia, he'd called her before leaving the prefecture, and she'd echoed Lieutenant Intern Marchand's sentiments about his worth as a boyfriend, and promised him unnamed but glorious rewards the next time they were alone together. Until then, they agreed to meet right away for an early lunch at a new place that had opened up in the Sixth Arrondissement, not far from Hugo's apartment. "I'll get us the best table in the house," she'd said, laughing. "I'll leave now. Can you call Nicola and let her know?"

Even the tough façade of Nicola Dumont cracked a little when Hugo told her the news.

"That's fantastic," she'd said. "Very impressive work, Monsieur Marston."

"Thanks, Claudia is happy. And I'm sure you'd have figured it out once you saw the documents."

A pause, then the first, and very gentle, laugh he'd heard from her. "I certainly hope so."

Hugo started across Pont Neuf, but stepped to one side at the sound of a bell behind him. He watched in amusement as a slender young man dressed in black, but topped off with a brown fur hat with a tail, swept past on a bicycle as spindly and upright as he was.

Hugo slowed his walk to enjoy the sights and sounds a little more than he had recently, and partway down Rue Dauphine, he slowed even more to watch a burly man about fifty yards ahead of him. The man wore green coveralls and stood on top of his van. He was in animated discussion with a smiling and rotund woman who was wearing a powder-blue robe and leaning over her second-story balcony. As Hugo got closer, the woman laughed at something the man said, twirled her hair in her fingers, and then threw something down, which the man caught with both hands.

A key? Hugo wondered. He resisted the urge to linger, to see if the man disappeared into the building, and instead he minded his own business and turned down Rue du Pont de Lodi.

The café Claudia had chosen was almost empty when he got there. One hardy couple was sitting at a sidewalk table outside, hands clasped around bowls of *chocolat chaud*. Overhead heaters were built into the green-and-gold canopy above their heads and, as at so many cafés, the shift toward customer service was enhanced further by the red blankets folded over the backs of the outdoor chairs.

A waiter stepped out toward him, hands cupped around a cigarette, and he nodded at Hugo as he moved away from the entrance for his smoke break. Inside, Hugo asked for a table by the large picture window that looked out over the narrow street. He'd barely sat down when he spotted Claudia outside, heading for the door. He stood as she came in, and she threw herself into his arms.

"My hero!" she said.

"Why thank you, my lady."

"I always knew you were a genius."

"That might be a little generous." He pulled a chair out for her, and she sat. "But I'll take it." He sat, too. "How're you feeling?"

"Amazing." She reached across the table and took his hands. "Seriously, Hugo. Thank you. I don't think anyone else could have figured that out. You saved me from prison."

"Possibly. But I think Nicola would've got there and, even if not, with no other evidence against you . . . pretty weak murder case."

She sat back as the waiter arrived. "Champagne?" she asked Hugo.

"I'll take coffee for now. I still have a murder case to solve."

"Two coffees, please," Claudia said to the server, and they waited for him to leave. "So is Marchand letting you back into the fold?"

"Yes, basically. I think he was upset with himself for arresting an innocent person, and he is now a little more willing to accept help."

"Your help, specifically."

"I suppose so."

"Good. Whoever killed that poor girl is still out there."

"And I got the sense Marchand doesn't really know where to look next." Hugo picked up the leather-bound menu. "We should order, then talk. All this freeing innocent damsels has made me hungry."

"Get two of everything," Claudia said with a smile. "It's all on me."

When the waiter returned, Hugo ordered the veal *blanquette* over basmati rice, and Claudia chose the cod *brandade* with salad. They stuck with water and coffee to drink.

"I guess Claudia the journalist has a story to write now," Hugo said. "Quite the perspective, if you think about it."

"I'll wait until you catch the killer," she said with a wink. "Like I usually do."

"Fair enough."

"Let me ask you something, though." She sipped her coffee and peered at him over the rim. "Marchand made a big deal out of you having dinner with Alia. It was my motive, right?"

"Right."

"Be honest with me. Did you have any feelings for her?" She wagged a finger at him. "And it's perfectly all right if you did. You're still my hero."

"Good." Hugo laughed, then said, "I suppose I was attracted to her. She was beautiful, smart, talented. Maybe a little young for me, though."

"This is France, my dear, we don't care about those silly things."

"Age is just a number, eh?"

"Unless one of you is a child, then yes." She sat back. "Have you been seeing other people lately?"

"No."

"Why not?"

"I don't know." Hugo stirred his coffee absentmindedly. "No time. No real interest."

"Don't you want to . . . I don't know, settle down with someone? Get married?"

"Again." It was his turn to laugh. "I can't really say that I do."

"I guess I want to know if you're happy," she said. "I want to make sure you are."

"I'm happy. Are you?"

"Yes. Especially today." She turned and looked out of the window as a young woman walked past. "She's pretty. I do love Paris—it's the only city in the world where you'll see pretty girls wearing berets." She waved a hand. "Maybe Lyon, I don't know, but you get what I mean."

"And only in the winter," Hugo said.

"Right. If a woman is wearing one in the summer, she's probably a tourist." She laughed, then fell silent as their food arrived. When they were alone again, she said, "So, back to business."

"Business?" Hugo asked.

"Yes. The business of murder." She took a sip of water and asked: "If I didn't kill Alia Alsaffar, who do you think did?"

That question was still weighing on Hugo's mind when he stepped into his apartment building's foyer. The concierge, Dimitrios, looked up.

"Monsieur Marston, *bon après midi*," he said. *Good afternoon.* "I have something for you."

"You do?"

"A package. Envelope, I mean." He bent down and pulled out a yellow, six-by-eight-inch envelope. "Here you go."

"Thank you." As a matter of habit, Hugo pulled out a handkerchief and used it to take the envelope.

"Oh, I didn't think . . ."

"It's fine," Hugo reassured him. "I'm probably being overly careful; it's in my nature. Do you know who delivered it?"

"No. One of the tenants brought it in from the doorstep, where it was left. I'm surprised it didn't get wet out there."

Which means it wasn't out there long, Hugo thought. "When did you get it?"

"Maybe an hour ago."

Hugo thanked him and climbed the stairs to his apartment. Inside, Tom sat on the couch with his nose in a book.

"I've heard that near-death experiences can do strange things to men," Hugo said. "But you reading? This I find hard to believe."

"It's true." Tom grinned. "Not sure I've read a book since college, and then it was because I had to. Dickens, Faulkner, God knows what else. The more turgid it was, the more we had to read it. Oh, that Macbeth dude from Scotland."

"Really, that hack? Poor you."

"But this." He held up Steve Goble's novel, *The Bloody Black Flag*. "A murder mystery on a pirate ship? That's genius."

"I know, and it doesn't even have pictures in it."

"Funny. Very funny." Tom sat up. "But you know what wasn't funny?"

"Do tell."

"That chick last night."

"If we're talking about you and some chick, you're going to have to narrow it down a little."

"The one you left me with at the Crillon bar. I'm for sure banned from there now, by the way."

"Oh, Tom. What happened?"

"Well, she was so beautiful and friendly, I made a wrong assumption. Or two."

"No. You didn't . . ."

"I kinda did. Anyway, I can testify to the fact that she has beautiful hands that are much more powerful than they look." He turned his face sideways. "You can probably still see the outline of one of them."

"No, but then if there's a face that's used to being slapped, it's yours."

"First time in ages," Tom said huffily. "Just so you know." He nodded toward the envelope in Hugo's hand. "So, what's that, and why the forensic countermeasure?"

"It's an envelope, and just in case."

"What's in it?"

"Let's find out, shall we?" Hugo took it to the kitchen and placed it on the counter. He took a knife from the butcher's block and sliced the top of the envelope open.

"Shout if you see a puff of anthrax," Tom said, hanging back.

Hugo threw him a dirty look and used the tip of the knife to widen the opening of the envelope.

"No anthrax," he said. "Looks like just photos."

"Of what?"

"Bring me some gloves from my desk drawer and I'll tell you. Top left."

"Yeah, I know," Tom said. "The only one you don't lock." He walked into Hugo's room and appeared a moment later with a pair of surgical gloves. "Here you go."

"Thanks." Hugo snapped them on and, with his fingertips, pulled out two four-by-six glossy photos. They were color but not great quality, as if shot from a distance and enlarged. But what they showed was unmistakable.

Tom sidled over and peered at them. "That's the dead girl, right?"

"Alia Alsaffar, yes."

"Beautiful. Who's the dude?"

"That's her . . . benefactor, I suppose you might call him. His name is JD Rollo."

"They had a thing going on?"

"Nope," Hugo said. "At least that's what I thought. What they told me."

"These photos . . . I dunno, man, they seem to indicate otherwise."

"Possibly," Hugo agreed.

The pictures were both taken outside, in a street Hugo couldn't name. Narrow and cobbled, so maybe one in Montmartre, near the museum. Alsaffar and Rollo stood face-to-face, closer than friends usually stood. They seemed to be looking into each other's eyes, and from the photo Hugo couldn't tell if one of them was talking. It was a frustrating moment in time, a split second caught on camera. Maybe in the next moment they kissed; maybe one of them wanted to and the other pulled away. The only doubt in Hugo's mind was whether friends stood that close to each other just to talk.

The second picture was taken from behind, and they appeared to be walking along the same street. JD Rollo had his arm around Alsaffar's shoulders, and their hips must have been touching.

"Dropped off anonymously?" Tom asked.

"Afraid so."

"A little ambiguous, to be honest. Don't tell you all that much."

"Quite the opposite." Hugo gave Tom an enigmatic smile. "As long as Mr. Rollo himself didn't drop them off, they tell me plenty."

"What the hell are you talking about?" Tom frowned. "You *just* agreed with me that they're ambiguous as to whether or not they were doing the dirty."

"Correct."

"God, you're frustrating."

Hugo took out his phone and photographed each a picture, then reached into a cabinet and pulled out a box of gallon-sized resealable plastic bags. With still-gloved hands, he pulled out the first two bags and set them aside, then he opened the third and slid the envelope inside. He made sure the bag was air-tight, then peeled off the gloves. He called Lieutenant Intern Marchand and filled him in, asking that the envelope and contents be forensically examined.

"Of course, I'll send someone to collect it from you now, and have it tested straightaway."

"Do me a favor," Hugo said. "There's one part of the envelope I'd like your tech to be sure not to miss."

"*Absolument,*" Marchand said, when Hugo told him. "I'll make sure of it. So, what do you think?"

"About what?"

"About whether they were in a relationship."

"I'd say you have to ask him about it."

"I already did." A note of frustration sounded in Marchand's voice. "He said not."

"He told me the same thing."

"I'll bring him in to the prefecture. He'll tell the truth while in one of our little rooms."

"No, he won't," Hugo said. "He'll clam up and ask for a lawyer."

"Why do you say that?"

"He's rich, powerful. You won't be able to bully or intimidate him." Hugo paused, then said. "Let me talk to him. I can play the embassy-approved role. People like JD Rollo enjoy thinking they have friends in high places, and they like to avoid trouble if they can. I just think he's more likely to talk to a friendly American diplomat than a pushy French policeman."

"No offense taken," Marchand said, humor in his voice.

"And none meant, as you know."

"Inviting yourself back into the heart of the investigation team, I see." The humor remained in Marchand's tone.

"If that's all right with the lead investigator," Hugo said.

Marchand appeared to think for a moment before speaking. "In this instance, maybe you're right. When will you talk to him?"

Hugo looked at his watch. It was just after three. "Well, in America we have a saying: no time like the present."

CHAPTER TWENTY-EIGHT

Rollo opened the door to his suite, and Hugo stepped past him.

"I thought our business was concluded," Rollo said. "And by that I mean with you *and* the police."

"Very nearly," Hugo assured him. He followed Rollo and sat in a plush cream armchair as Rollo sank onto the sofa. "Your wife isn't here?"

"Does it matter?"

"Not at all. I always talk to people however they are most comfortable. Some prefer their spouses to be present, some prefer not."

"I gather you were buying her a drink last night." His tone remained neutral.

"I was, but had to run."

Rollo smiled. "Your friend made quite the impression when he showed up."

"Tom? Yes, he wouldn't give me many details, but I gather he mistook your wife's politeness for . . . a different kind of interest. My apologies, on his behalf."

"You've nothing to apologize for. She can take care of herself—I'm not worried about that." He cleared his throat. "Now, what exactly can I help you with?"

Hugo took out his phone and pulled up the images of Rollo and Alsaffar that he'd photographed before bagging and handing the pictures to Paul Jameson. He'd been surprised to see the Scotsman, who explained his presence: "Since the Claudia Roux bad arrest, Lerens is keeping a closer eye on things. Through me."

"Everyone makes mistakes," Hugo told him.

"Aye, but not everyone makes high-profile ones. He's a good cop and he'll go far, but right now he's on a short leash."

"Is that why he's letting me get more involved?" Hugo asked.

"Partly. And because you're good at what you do. Like I said, he's a good cop and he knows who can help him solve a case."

Hugo had almost blushed at the praise.

Now he passed his phone to Rollo. "There's that one, and if you swipe left there's another."

Rollo held the phone up and studied the first picture, then the second. He handed the phone back to Hugo. "What of them?" he asked.

"Oh, hang on, I need to record this conversation, if you don't mind."

"I suppose not," Rollo said, but suspicion lurked in his eyes.

Hugo started the record function on his phone, and announced the date and time, along with his presence and that of JD Rollo. "So, these photos," Hugo said. "Do you know when they might have been taken?"

Rollo held Hugo's eye for a moment. "That seems like an odd question."

"It does?"

"Aren't you going to ask if I was having an affair with Alia?"

"No, because you weren't. I just want to know when the pictures were taken."

Rollo smiled, amused by Hugo's certainty. "You're pretty confident of that. Why?"

"Does it matter?"

"Let me guess. Because my wife is so beautiful, I couldn't possibly be sleeping with Alia."

"Not at all. Beautiful women, and men, too, find their spouses in bed with other people all the time."

"The age gap, then."

"These days?" Hugo laughed gently. "I hardly think the decade or so between you qualifies as a prohibitive age gap."

"Whatever your reasoning, assuming you have one—"

"I do."

"—you're right. We were close, like brother and sister. Or father and daughter, depending on your view of that age gap."

"So can you tell me when the photos were taken? From the clothing, location, and lighting, both at around the same time."

"If I remember right," Rollo began, his brow furrowed in thought. "Yes, I think the only time she and I went out by ourselves was the day before she . . . you know."

Hugo nodded. "About what time?"

"It would've been around lunch. Afterward, I think."

"And where did you walk, do you remember?"

"Not really," Rollo said. "We were near her hotel, and we just kind of wandered hither and thither. She was upset about Josh, the way she'd handled things. And the way he'd reacted, of course."

"I don't blame her."

"Me neither. But we were both surprised by how angry he was. Anyway, I wasn't paying attention to where we were going, I was more focused on trying to make her feel better the day before her big exhibition."

"Quite naturally, of course."

"That reminds me, for some reason. I heard that the woman they'd arrested is now free. You don't think it could've been Josh, do you? Given how angry he was. Or did they release her but expect to charge her still?"

"Oh no, she's in the clear. As in, wrongly arrested and completely innocent."

"How awful for her."

"She'll be fine. But, yes, not much fun while it was going on."

"So are you officially part of the investigation?" Rollo asked. "I'm just wondering whether the Paris police will be hammering on my door asking about those photos, and coming up with a different conclusion about our relationship."

"No, that's why I'm recording this interview. I'll hand it to the police so they can add it to their case file. Unless I forgot to ask you something they want to know about, I don't think they'll bother you. Not about the photos, anyway."

"Good. Any idea whether we can leave the city yet?"

"Not just yet, I don't think." Hugo looked around. "This suite must be burning a hole in your pocket, though. I can facilitate a change to a more reasonably priced room, if you like."

"No, no need for that."

Must be nice, Hugo thought. He stood. "Well, thank you for your time, I do appreciate it."

"Hang on." Rollo stood too, a worried look on his face. "Do those photos make me a suspect now? I mean, I can see how someone would look at them and assume they mean something they don't. I promise you, there was nothing going on between Alia and me."

"Like I said, I know that," Hugo reassured him. "And I'll make sure the detective in charge understands that, too."

"Thank you, really. I'd hate for them to go down the wrong rabbit hole, especially if it leads to me. Those photos . . . I just worry they'll put me in the frame." He grimaced. "If you'll excuse the pun."

"Not at all. In fact, I think it's fair to say that these photos cut *two* people off my suspect list."

Hugo decided to walk to the Dalí museum. It was probably three miles away, and mostly uphill, but there was a picture forming in Hugo's head, and he knew that a long walk was the best way to help the puzzle pieces fall into place. And the best way for him to figure out what to do next.

The sky was already darkening when he walked out of the hotel, the chill of dusk settling over an already-cold Paris. She responded, though, by turning on her lights—the streetlamps that lit the way for drivers, the spotlights that kept her monuments alive and glowing, and the storefronts that jollied their entrances with strings of colored or ice-white Christmas strands.

Hugo headed up Rue Royale, where Bentleys and sleek Jaguars swept slowly past him on the cobbled road, chauffeurs easing off the gas to let their wealthy passengers eye the store fronts of L'Oréal and luxury jeweler Heurgon, and perhaps contemplate dinner at Maxim's. Hugo slowed as he passed a boutique shop selling crystal vases and ornaments, and it gave him an idea. He stopped to text Rob Drummond and Josh Reno, separately but with the same message: *Can you meet me in an hour at the Dalí museum?*

He continued on his walk, buttoning up his coat and pulling his hat down as the wind buffeted him. He put his leather gloves on, too, and, five minutes later, Drummond replied: *Sure. Why?*

Hugo ignored the question, waiting for Reno to respond, which he did just as Hugo turned into Rue Blanche: *At 5pm? We getting a drink there??*

Hugo smiled, and thought, *Kind of.*

The wind died down a little as the sky greyed into evening, and Hugo smiled at the couples and family units who were out looking for a place to eat, lingering at the menu stands in front of the bistros and restaurants that had just started to grill. Hugo breathed it in, too, the tempting aromas of steak, garlic, and simmering wine.

Close to the museum, he stopped at a small grocery store and bought an old-fashioned glass bottle of Coca-Cola, tucking it into his coat pocket and being careful not to let it slip from his gloved hands.

Josh Reno was already leaning against the stone wall opposite the museum when Hugo turned the corner onto Place du Calvaire.

"It's closed," he told Hugo. "Is it still a crime scene, or something?"

"No idea," Hugo said. "It could just be that there's no replacement for Alia's exhibition. Maybe it's out of respect for her, I don't know."

"Well, it's cold out here, should we go find someplace warm to sit?"

"I wasn't planning on staying long, just wanted to show you guys something." He looked up as the burly figure of Rob Drummond approached.

"Fellas." Drummond rubbed his hands together and eyed Reno warily. "We not going in?"

"It's closed. But we can talk out here; I won't keep you long." Hugo took his phone out and pulled up the photos of Alia Alsaffar and JD Rollo together. "Josh, do you recognize these pictures?"

Reno glanced at them, then at Hugo. "What do you mean by 'recognize'?"

"Well, any idea where they were taken?"

"How should I know?" He said it a little too sharply, and his eyes wouldn't meet Hugo's.

"Let me see," Drummond said. He peered at the screen, and swiped to the second one when Hugo told him to. "Somewhere in Montmartre, I'd guess. Narrow streets, cobbles. But this is your city, not mine."

"Yeah, Montmartre is what I thought."

"You didn't show these to Rachel, I hope," Drummond said.

"Why not?"

"Well, it looks totally harmless, but out of context . . ." He shrugged. "Seems like she can be kinda fierce, but then what do I know? Maybe it's fine."

Hugo nodded. "You agree, Josh?"

"With what?" His tone was more subdued now.

"That they look like they were taken in Montmartre?"

"Sure, I guess. But, like he says, you know Paris better than we do." His eyes narrowed with suspicion. "You really brought us out here just to see those?"

"Partly," Hugo said. "Something else I wanted you to see, too." He put the phone into his inside jacket pocket, then patted the outside of his coat. "Somewhere in here." He pulled out the Coke bottle and handed it to Drummond. "If you don't mind, I think it must be . . ." He dug deep into the vacated pocket, then frowned. "I guess not, dammit. Well, shoot, gentlemen, I'm sorry. I seem to have drug you out into the cold for nothing."

"What was it you wanted us to see?" Drummond asked, handing Hugo the bottle back and blowing warmth into his ungloved hands.

"Some documents. Stuff we found in Alia's belongings at the museum." He stuffed the Coke bottle back into a pocket and gave them both a bright smile. "Well, another time. Again, sorry to have brought you out here for just those photos. Oh, and just for the record, neither of you took these, right?"

"Not me," said Drummond.

"Why would I?" Reno said.

"No idea," Hugo said, still wearing his friendliest smile. "That's why I needed to ask."

CHAPTER TWENTY-NINE

The next morning, Hugo dressed in a dark suit, a white shirt, and a blue tie that was so dark it looked black from any distance. A car from the embassy idled on Rue Jacob, waiting for him as he stepped onto the sidewalk. A heaviness settled around his heart and, after bidding good morning to the woman who was his driver, he sat in silence as the car took him toward the embassy.

He gazed out of the window, his mind off the case for the first time in days. Instead his thoughts centered on the people he saw on the sidewalks and behind the steering wheels of their cars. Ordinary people, doing ordinary business. Teachers, lawyers, accountants. Safe jobs. Stressful, maybe, but ultimately safe.

His job at the embassy was supposed to be safe, too. Or safer than working for the FBI. But in the last couple of years he'd lost two colleagues, two friends who were dear to him and had no reason to die.

Too many bodies, he thought. *Too much pain.*

Both men had had families, and Hugo wondered for a moment about a world where a good husband and father got shot instead of a single man like him. Tom even.

Outside the embassy, they sat quietly with the engine running as they waited for the rest of the convoy to pass out of the gates and begin the journey to the airport. Ryan Pierce's final trip home, where his wife and kids would be waiting to greet the most important man in their lives, lying dead in his coffin. Hugo's throat closed, and he felt warm tears run down his cheeks. There was no shame in mourning a man like Ryan, a man who'd made the lives of everyone he met better, personally

231

and professionally. A loyal friend, willing to give everything, including his life, to make others safe.

As they waited, Hugo felt the eyes of his driver, a young embassy staffer Hugo had met maybe once, watch him in the rear-view mirror. A moment later, the young woman offered him a box of tissues, which Hugo accepted.

"I heard great things about Mr. Pierce, sir," she said.

"I'm glad to hear that. I'm sorry, remind me of your name."

"Cecilee Walker, sir. From Austin, Texas, like you."

"That so?"

"And my dad was a cop."

"Me too."

"I know, sir. FBI. You're kind of a legend."

Hugo smiled and dabbed at his eyes. "You ever see a legend cry before, Ms. Walker?"

"Yes, sir," she said. "I saw my dad cry many times. And like he told me, for a lawman it often takes more guts to cry than not."

"Smart man, your dad."

"That he is." She put the car in gear. "Here we go, sir."

From out of nowhere, a dozen police cars appeared around them, half taking the lead and the other half tacking themselves onto the rear of the emerging convoy of six black embassy cars. They couldn't bury Ryan, have a funeral for him, but they were sure as hell going to drive him to Charles de Gaulle Airport in style.

As they got close, Walker peered back at Hugo. "Can you tell me more about him, sir?"

"Who, Ryan?"

"Yes, sir."

Hugo smiled. "Only if you stop calling me *sir*."

"Yes ... Mr. Marston." Her eyes crinkled and he knew she was smiling, too.

"Take the next step. Call me Hugo. How old are you, Cecilee?"

"Twenty-five, s— Hugo."

"I don't even know how old Ryan was." Hugo looked out of the window at the traffic as he talked. "Forty-something, I guess. He was one of those guys who look and act young, no matter how old or mature they might be." He was quiet for a moment. "You know, it was his day off."

"When he was shot?"

"Yes. He knew I'd been shot at in that cemetery before, and he insisted on coming. Acted like he was there for the adventure, but he'd been in combat before. He knew that gunfights are ugly, dangerous things, not movie-style action. He was there because he wanted to protect me."

"You're not blaming yourself, are you?"

"No, nothing like that. In the old days, maybe, but there's only ever one person responsible for a murder, and that's the murderer."

"Why was that guy after you anyway?" She changed lanes expertly, the snaking line of cars whipping as one into the lane to exit the highway. "If you don't mind me asking."

"A long story. One for another time, maybe."

"Sure," she said hurriedly. "I didn't mean to pry—sorry if it came across that way."

"Not at all. Please, don't worry, it's actually a pretty interesting story."

"Just not one for today, I'm with you." She gave him a reassuring smile, and they rode the last ten minutes in silence. Eventually the convoy pulled through a mesh gate at the east side of the airport and made its way slowly toward the C-130 Hercules aircraft that would take Ryan Pierce, and a squad of US soldiers, back to America.

The cars lined up in some preplanned sequence that Hugo hadn't been told about, but when he climbed out of the back seat he saw his boss, Ambassador J. Bradford Taylor, at the rear of the black Cadillac that contained Pierce's body. Hugo joined him, and with the silent assistance of six soldiers in dress uniform, they slid the coffin out and onto the conveyor belt that would take it into the belly of the plane. Either side of the conveyor, a line of soldiers stood to attention, joined by the black-suited members of the embassy who had come to say farewell.

Hugo and Taylor stood side by side close to the tail of the plane, both oblivious to the cold, but their eyes streaming anyway as the flag-draped coffin moved slowly past them. Every man in uniform saluted as the head of the coffin reached him, and Hugo and Ambassador Taylor did the same.

"Goodbye, my friend," Hugo said, his words barely even a whisper as the coffin moved past him, and into the plane.

"Ride with me," Taylor said, as the C-130 turned slowly away from them and toward the runway. "I want to know what's going on with you."

"Meaning?"

"Meaning you just lost a good friend, almost lost another, and had the only woman in the world who'll put up with you arrested for murder."

Hugo nodded. "Well, when you put it like that . . ."

"I do." Taylor started walking toward the giant Cadillac that had brought him. "Just because you're a tough-guy, profiling, FBI agent, doesn't mean you can't crack. And that's something you definitely don't need to happen. Nor do I."

When they reached the car, Hugo gave Cecilee Walker a wave to show he was riding with the ambassador. She gave him two thumbs-up to acknowledge the message, and Hugo climbed into the back of the car beside Taylor.

"Take us home via the Champs, please, Mike," the ambassador said to their driver. Then he turned to Hugo. "Well, that fucking sucked."

"Yeah. Losing good people seems to get harder and harder, not the other way around."

Taylor nodded. "And he sure was good people."

"That he was." Hugo looked over at his boss. "Did you know he was a great baseball player? Starred for LSU back in his college days. Could've turned pro, but I think an injury ended his career."

"I knew he loved the game, didn't know he'd played at that level."

"That was Ryan for you, too modest for his own good."

"Yeah, I got that impression." Taylor looked at Hugo, then asked, "There's no shame in talking to someone if you need to do that. To relieve the stress, vent, whatever you need."

"Really, I'm fine. Not at my best this morning but, larger picture, I'm good. I promise."

"Not about to crack up on me?"

"No. I'll give you advanced warning if that changes."

They exchanged tight smiles, then Taylor asked, "So who killed our artist, figured it out yet?"

"Getting there."

"Who looks good for it?"

"Well, let's see. We have a limited pool of suspects, so I suppose we can start with Rachel Rollo. Beautiful, wealthy, and maybe ten or twelve years older than the talented artist she and her husband have been patronizing."

"Anything between her husband and Ms. Alsaffar?"

"No. Admiration, friendship, but no real evidence of a sexual entanglement."

"So possibly she's jealous, but probably not."

"Right," said Hugo. "But things are complicated by the fact that, supposedly, Alia was about to leave them behind."

"As in?"

"As in not take their money anymore."

"That sounds like cause for celebration, not motive for murder."

"You'd think so," Hugo agreed. "But I've done some reading on the art scene. For a lot of those benefactors, their identity is strongly aligned with the people they are supporting. One older gentleman committed suicide when his protégé found success and left him behind. Although one article about Alia and the Rollos did suggest maybe there was a love affair, so who knows?"

"That'd be a reason for the husband to kill her, too, then."

"In theory, it would."

"What about the murder itself?" Ambassador Taylor asked. "Crime of passion or premeditated?"

"Can it be both?"

"Stop being coy, Hugo. No one reads a crime scene better than you, and you've made up your mind which one it is."

"I have," Hugo admitted. "But we've not finished going through the list of suspects."

"Fine." Taylor sighed heavily. "What about the brother?"

"Rob Drummond. Afraid of germs, didn't know her very well, and with no eye for art."

"Jealous of her talent, maybe?"

"Oh, I'm sure. But everyone was. And in theory he stood to gain from her being alive, because if she gets rich, maybe she helps him out. A rising tide lifts all the family boats."

"Does he have a temper, maybe?"

"That would only matter if the crime was one of sudden passion . . ."

" . . . which you're not prepared to tell me yet," Taylor finished. "Damn you, Marston."

"Which leaves us with Josh Reno, who certainly seems like our best candidate."

"How so?"

Hugo stared out of the window as the car turned onto Avenue des Champs-Élysées. "Well, he devotes years of his life to helping Alia make it big. He shows his artwork at her shows, gives up any semblance of a life to travel with her. If anyone's hitched a wagon to her train it was him."

"And now she's making it big, he's out."

"Right. And there can be no doubt that he was mad about it—he yelled at her in a busy restaurant."

"But mad enough to kill her?" Taylor asked. "And yelling at your intended victim in public is not the act of a premeditated killer, either."

"So that's your analysis of the crime scene?" Hugo asked with a wry smile. "It showed premeditated murder?"

"I was a spy, not a profiler, so I'd just be guessing. I want your opinion."

Hugo stroked his chin exaggeratedly. "Wait, so you're telling me that you, a spy, were at the museum where an American woman was murdered . . ." Hugo grinned, enjoying the moment, this crack of light in their dark moment of bereavement. "How very peculiar that you're not listed as one of the suspects."

"Oh, very funny—"

"I bet you pulled rank at the crime scene and acted all outraged that you, the United States Ambassador to France, were so improperly detained. Trying to deflect attention from yourself, no doubt."

"Yes, Hugo, that's exactly—"

"And here you are, trying to pry information from me, to find out which poor sap will be taking the fall for your homicidal inclinations . . . Very clever, Mr. Ambassador."

"Are you quite finished?"

Hugo chuckled. "I think so."

"Good. Now you can tell me whether it was a crime of passion or premeditated, and who you think did it."

"I would, sir, I really would."

"But?"

"I'm not big on sharing ideas or theories until I'm sure about them." Hugo's phone rang. "Excuse me."

"Monsieur Marston. Hugo. Marchand here."

"Lieutenant Intern, what's going on?"

"Where are you right now, are you free?"

"I'm in a car with the ambassador, heading to the embassy."

"Would you be so kind as to ask His Excellency if he would mind a brief detour?"

"Where, and why?"

Marchand explained briefly, and when Hugo hung up, he made the request.

"Sure, I guess," Taylor said. "What's going on?"

"He didn't give me all the details, but said a fisherman pulled a bag of personal belongings out of the river."

"Personal . . . so what?"

"He thinks maybe there'll be a body floating somewhere nearby. He wants me to take a look at the scene."

"All right then, let's do it," Ambassador Taylor said. "Rather fun to be involved in the action again." He leaned forward to speak to the driver. "Lights and sirens, Mike, activate the lights and sirens. We should make the most of it!"

CHAPTER THIRTY

The bag had been pulled out of the River Seine opposite Parc de Bercy, which lay on Paris's right bank, in the Twelfth Arrondissement, southeast of the city center. It took them twenty minutes to get there, with Hugo's curiosity rising by the second. Eventually, they pulled off Quai d'Austerlitz and drove down beside the water. Four police cars sat silent in front of them on the narrow bricked quayside.

Marchand opened the Cadillac's rear door, and when they'd stepped out, Hugo reintroduced him to the ambassador. The two men shook hands, and Taylor said, "I would say it's my pleasure, but under the circumstances . . . I know you have work to do, so I'll let you get to it. I'll just hang back and watch."

"Thank you, Monsieur Ambassador." Marchand led Hugo to a picnic table that was covered with plastic sheeting. A large, see-through and sealable bag sat closed on top of it. Two crime-scene techs hovered nearby, and, toward the water, a dozen policemen and women in uniform wandered along the riverbank.

"You've opened it already?" Hugo asked.

"Opened it, catalogued, photographed, and inspected the contents. Dusted for prints and swabbed for DNA, then put back as it was found, as best we could." Marchand handed Hugo gloves and a surgical mask. "Put these on, and look for yourself."

"Are you going to tell me whom it belongs to?"

"Someone who was at the museum the night Alia Alsaffar was murdered."

"Clearly, otherwise I wouldn't be here," Hugo said. "Keeping me in suspense on purpose?"

"Yes, I suppose I am." Marchand smiled. "These items belong to the brother of Mademoiselle Alsaffar. Rob Drummond."

"Well." Hugo stared at the bag. "I wasn't expecting that."

"We've not located a body, but as you can see we're looking up and down the riverbank, and will be dragging this part of the river."

"Makes sense." Hugo put on the gloves. "Interesting."

"What is?"

Hugo didn't answer him, instead circling the table, his eyes on the bag. "A fisherman found it, you said?"

"Yes."

"He didn't open it?"

"*Non*, he saw the passport, and what he thought was blood, and called the police."

"Good." Hugo pulled up the surgical mask, reached for the bag, and opened it. He tipped it on one side and slowly pulled out the contents, spreading them on the plastic sheeting. He then picked up each item and inspected it. "Half a passport," he said, opening it. "With blood smeared on several pages." He moved onto the next objects. "Bright yellow scarf, looks new. Red, wool sweater, also new-looking. A novel." He flicked through the pages, but it contained nothing except an inscription from the author to "J.S." and the innocuous bidding that authors always seemed to write: *Best wishes!* He put it down and picked up the next object. "Ah, what's this, a gold necklace?" He held it up and it glinted in the sunshine. "I don't remember seeing him wearing this, but it's very thin, so maybe I just didn't notice." He turned to Marchand. "You already collected photos from people at the museum, right?"

"From the night of the murder, yes we did. Several hundred in all."

"Can you have someone look through them and check the ones that have Drummond in them? I want to know if he was wearing this necklace."

"A step ahead of you." Marchand smile at him. "The same thought occurred to me. I already have people looking to see if they can spot any of the clothing or the necklace."

"The sweater is too casual, and I don't recall him wearing such a gaudy scarf that night. Our best bet is definitely the necklace."

"Hey, you never know." Marchand glanced at his phone. "Ah, they've finished. No sweater, no scarf, and no necklace in any of the photos."

"He wore an open-necked shirt that night. No tie. So if he'd worn it, your people should have seen it."

"Maybe he just didn't wear it."

"People don't usually take *off* their jewelry for fancy events. Quite the opposite."

"True," Marchand conceded. "Oh, I forgot to tell you, that lot was all double-bagged, one clear bag inside another. I sent the outer one to the lab already, figured you didn't need to see the same bag twice."

"Double-bagged?"

"*Oui.* Both sealed tight. That tell you anything?"

"It does. A hell of a lot, actually."

"Do you mind sharing?"

"All in good time," Hugo said. "When exactly was this found?"

"About two hours ago. It took a while for the responding officers to connect the dots."

"They did so through the passport?"

"Correct."

"Good police work." Hugo winked at Marchand. "Time for you to do some. What do you make of it all?"

Marchand took a deep breath. "Well, if we can rule out accident, which I think we can, and if we're sure this is all Drummond's property, which it likely is given the passport, then I think we have to conclude there has been more foul play, and whoever dumped the bag in the river also put Drummond in there."

Hugo waved toward the policemen stretched in a line along the riverbank. "Which is why you've got those men out here, and a dive team on the way."

"*Exactement.*"

"If you're right, then who exactly do you think put poor Rob Drummond into the river?"

"Well, I suppose our list of suspects just narrowed. It must have been one of three people: Rachel Rollo; her husband, JD; or Josh Reno."

"I'd agree, they do seem like the best suspects. But which one?" Hugo pressed.

"Was Mademoiselle Alsaffar having an affair with JD Rollo? If so, then his wife did it. Drummond finds out, he needs money so he tries to blackmail her. She lures him out here . . ."

"And if her husband wasn't having an affair with Alia?"

"Then perhaps that's why Monsieur Rollo killed her. He was spurned, rejected. He decides that if he can't have her, no one will. Again, Drummond finds out somehow, and gets himself killed."

"Does each of your scenarios include Drummond discovering the identity of the killer and being murdered for that?"

Marchand bristled. "You asked for possibilities, and I am giving them."

"You met and interviewed Rob Drummond. Does he strike you as the detective type?"

"People find things out by accident, by chance. Like I said, maybe he tried blackmailing the killer."

"I could see him more as blackmailer than detective, I'll give you that much."

"Which means it would be one of the Rollos."

"Why do you say that?"

"Josh Reno wouldn't make for a great blackmail target, would he?" Marchand said. "That guy has less money than I do."

"Good point. So which Rollo is it?"

"I don't know," Marchand said. His eyes narrowed. "Why do I feel like you're playing games with me?"

Hugo ignored the question, and asked: "How do you explain the bag of Drummond's stuff floating in the river? What's the point of that?"

"Simple. The river is fast, full, and takes everything to the sea. If the killer is trying to get rid of Drummond, of everything to do with him, then the sea is a better dumping ground than a relatively narrow river."

"For half a passport and two pieces of wool clothing, fire would work much better."

"Perhaps." Marchand conceded. "But where are the Rollos going to light a fire without attracting attention?"

"Ah, so you have them working together now?" Hugo asked with a smile.

"Another perhaps." Marchand shrugged. "Why could it not be two people?"

"Two people," Hugo repeated, his voice distracted. He picked up the passport and studied it. "Yes, that's one way to put it."

"What?" Marchand stared at Hugo. "You know who the killer is?"

"I believe I do."

"Who? Which one of them was it?"

"It's like you said." Hugo smiled at him. "It was two people. Sort of, anyway. And depending on when this clever little duo dumped the bags, we might want to hurry."

CHAPTER THIRTY-ONE

Two police cars sped from the embankment, tires squealing, and Hugo waved out of the window from the rear seat of the lead car to his boss. For his part, the ambassador stood wide-eyed and his arms apart. *Where the hell are you going?*

Over the next two minutes, Hugo tried texting to let him know, but the car was jerking too much, swinging from side to side as the diver changed lanes, the firm chassis of the little Renault shaking the phone in his hand. Hugo gave up and looked through the front window. Overhead, the sky had darkened and he hoped it wasn't about to rain, because Paris had one thing in common with the rest of the world as he knew it: as soon as rain hit the roads, people drove like idiots. And that meant accidents, jams, and maybe their quarry getting away.

"Gare du Nord, you're sure?" Marchand asked, after Hugo had given the driver directions.

"I am."

"How do you know we'll be in time?"

"I have no idea if we will be," Hugo said patiently. "All I can tell you is I'm pretty damn certain this is the exit plan."

"You don't think they'll try and shake us, take a convoluted route?" Marchand sat beside him and stared intently out of the front window as the rear end of an eighteen-wheeler loomed over them. "*Merde*, don't get us killed!" he yelled at the driver, who ignored him.

"No," Hugo said.

"Then do you mind explaining who we're looking for, and why they won't?"

"Be happy to," Hugo said. "If we're successful, though, mind if I sit in on the initial interrogation? I think you're going to want me to, anyway."

"You are welcome to. Assuming you're right, and assuming you stop torturing me and tell me what you think is going on."

"Thank you," Hugo said. "I have some questions for our quarry."

"I thought you had all the answers," the Frenchman said, almost under his breath but not quite.

"Some of them. Most of them. But not all."

"Well, I don't have many right now, so if you've kept me in the dark long enough, can I hear your theory . . . ?"

"Sure thing." Hugo gave him a sideways glance. "But I only share my thoughts when I'm positive, which means it's no longer a theory."

"Fine." Marchand raised his hands in surrender. "We can call it whatever you want."

Hugo looked out of the side window as he spoke. "It's funny, despite being such a gifted artist and sweet person, everyone had a motive to harm Alia. It could've been a lover's jealousy, a friend scorned and left behind, or revenge for destroying a money-making venture. And a marriage. Any one of those could've fit."

"Let me guess, it's none of those." The impatience in Marchand's voice was plain.

"Correct."

"Instead it was . . . ?"

"A combination of greed and desperation. Mostly greed."

"And the killers?"

Hugo looked out of the window for a moment, then turned to Marchand. "Our killer is Rob Drummond. And my guess is, he's on his way to England right now."

"Which is why we're going to Gare du Nord, for the Eurostar. In that case, I should also alert the border agents, and have our people look out for him at ferry ports and airports." Marchand had his phone in his hand.

"You can, but it'd be a waste of resources. He won't try to fly anywhere."

"Because he has no passport?"

"He does have one. A British one. So start with Gare du Nord, then other train stations, and finally the ferries. If his little plan gets held up, it's easier to turn and run from those places than from deep inside an airport."

Hugo sat quietly while Marchand called Lieutenant Lerens and started the process of stopping up the city's escape routes. When he hung up, he looked at Hugo. "Who is the second person? You said there were two."

"No, you did. I agreed. Sort of."

"Please, Hugo, this is no time for games. You should tell me everything."

"Fair enough. The first sign, and one that I missed completely at the time, was the book Rob Drummond was reading at the museum."

"A book? What does that have to do with anything?"

"It was called *The Paper Trip*," Hugo said. "At the time I thought it a good name for a novel, but it's not."

"Not a good name?"

"No, it's not a novel. It's an expression, one that I've come across a few times, but it's not well known. It basically means you disappear from your own life by creating a paper trail that belongs to someone else. You take a paper trip."

"To a new identity?"

"Precisely. You need one or two key documents, and from there it's just a matter of patience and attention to detail."

"Drummond faked his own death—is that what you're saying?"

"Yes. Think about what we found. Bright clothing and half a passport, all of it double bagged. The bright clothing and bright book cover were designed to make sure someone spotted the bags. And he used two bags, of course, to make sure his little distraction didn't sink to the bottom of the river or otherwise get damaged."

"Why half a passport?"

"I'd be willing to bet there's another bag out there floating its way down the Seine containing the other half."

"You mean as a backup?"

"Right. The gold chain that we can't find him wearing suggests he bought it recently and, I suspect, put it in the bag to ensure someone fished it out, the promise of reward or perhaps more valuables inside. And the bloody passport, well, who wouldn't call the police on seeing that?"

"It makes sense," Marchand conceded.

"Much more sense than the idea that some other killer double-bagged his victim's clothing . . . *some* of his clothing, sprinkled in a piece of jewelry and half a passport. For the life of me, I can't imagine why anyone else would do that—can you?"

"I admit, my theory of floating his belongings out to sea sounds a little . . . well, unrealistic now."

"Again, note how only bright clothing made it into the careful bagging, for visibility."

"Makes sense," Marchand said again. He frowned. "If you're right and it's him, even if we get fingerprints from the bags or the contents, since Drummond refused to give us his, we'll have nothing to compare them to. That's frustrating."

"Actually, not true."

"What do you mean?"

"I have an old-fashioned Coca-Cola bottle in a plastic bag in my fridge," Hugo said. "It has his prints on it, and I can authenticate they are his in a court of law if I need to."

Marchand's eyebrows rose. "How did that happen? And why?"

"Sleight of hand. And because I don't like not having everyone's prints in an investigation. He had a right not to give them, sure, but he also had a right not to hold the Coke bottle when I handed it to him."

"I see." Marchand laughed gently. "You said he has an English passport, thanks to his English father. He'll be using that to get across the Channel."

"He will." Hugo almost toppled onto Marchand as the driver took a last-second swing off the road they were on, arrowing them through an intersection with a blare of lights and noise.

"Put your seatbelt on," Marchand said, as he pushed Hugo upright and back into his own seat.

"Good idea." Hugo did so. "Thanks."

"Lerens will have flagged his name; the customs people will stop him."

And then it hit Hugo, the wash of certainty, the pistons in his brain firing and slotting all the moving parts into their rightful place. The tenant in London, the book in the bag, and the advice from *The Paper Trip*. "No, they won't," he said.

"What? Why not?"

"The passport he's using. It'll be in a different name, not Rob Drummond."

"Then who?"

Hugo's mind worked overtime. "Drummond broke into Josh Reno's room after Alia's death, but Reno said nothing was missing."

"Right, I know."

"So either Drummond didn't find what he was looking for, or he did and Reno just didn't know."

"Go on," Marchand said.

"At the time, I was thinking in terms of a piece of art, something obvious."

"But now?"

"Paperwork. Rob told me that he killed his father, Alia's father. He was abusive, but when he died he left her an apartment. Rob Drummond got some cash, and she got an apartment in London."

"Wasn't Drummond living in London before he came over here?"

"He was. And I'd wager he was living at her place."

"Did she tell anyone about that?" Marchand asked.

"She did. In a way, yes she did." Hugo took out his phone and called Lieutenant Lerens. "Camille, this is Hugo. When your people are canvassing the train stations and airports, they're not looking for Rob Drummond."

"Wait, what? Jesus, Hugo, I just printed out a hundred or more flyers with his photo on them. So who the hell are they looking for?"

"Use the flyers," Hugo said. "Just change the name. Your officers are looking for that face still. But the name on his passport will be John Smith."

CHAPTER THIRTY-TWO

They didn't want him going to ground, so Lerens made sure the dozen uniformed officers at Gare du Nord strolled casually from concourse to concourse and looked as uninterested as they could when they passed through the station's small cafés and restaurants. They talked quietly into their mics as they went, and by the time Hugo and Marchand arrived, they had cleared half of the public areas. Two men stayed on the platform where the train departing for London would soon be arriving, just to make sure Drummond didn't sneak aboard.

"Take the northwest entrance," Lerens told Hugo as they climbed out of the police car. "I have two guys there but most of my men are making their way in that direction, if he spots them he'll be flushed toward you."

"Got it." Hugo relayed the instructions to Marchand and they walked briskly to the heavy glass doors leading into the station. They stopped for a moment to let their eyes adjust to the light, and to roam over the crowds of people drifting every which way around them.

"No idea what he's wearing, I suppose," Marchand said.

"I'm guessing gray and black." Hugo gave him a tight smile. "After all, he disposed of all his colorful clothing, didn't he?"

"I suppose so," Marchand said. "You want to wait here or go look around?"

"The latter. The *flics* by the door will catch him if he tries to get out this way."

"Did Lerens say if she has people covering the entrance to the metro? If he heads down there, he's gone."

"She did. He can't get through there, or shouldn't be able to. Come on."

They started forward, separating slightly so they could cover more ground, but staying close enough to watch each other's back. Hugo stopped when an older woman in front of him tripped on her own rolling suitcase, sending it to the floor and her on top of it. He helped her up and picked up her bag, too.

"I'm so clumsy," she said in French, her face red with embarrassment.

"As long as you're not hurt," Hugo said.

"I don't think so." She patted herself down to check for hidden injuries. "My son always tells me I travel with too many things, that I need to pack more lightly."

"I think your son may have a good point," Hugo said, separating himself from her with a friendly smile and wave. He glanced over at Marchand, who'd stationed himself to make sure Drummond didn't slip by. The Frenchman nodded, and they both set off again.

Somewhere overhead, the station's PA system announced the imminent arrival of the Eurostar from London, and Hugo felt his stomach tighten. That train was a deadline. It was Drummond's escape route or, if he spotted the cops before he boarded, it would mark the moment he went into hiding.

"There!" Marchand pointed ahead and to his right.

Hugo stopped in his tracks and looked where Marchand was pointing. He saw several couples and a family of four, two priests in earnest discussion as they walked, and . . . Drummond. He was heading right toward Hugo, his head down and half his face hidden by a new fedora and what looked like a gray, drooping mustache plastered to his top lip. Hugo almost smiled at that, because Drummond was the epitome of a man trying not to be recognized, and therefore stuck out like a sore thumb. Hugo gestured for Marchand to stay put, and they waited for the American to get within grabbing distance. Drummond was big, and probably strong, but with every step forward Hugo grew more confident that Drummond would not be able to outrun either him or Marchand. Five seconds later, Drummond looked up to get his bearings, and his gaze passed right across Hugo's face.

And then returned to it.

Drummond's mouth opened, and his eyes grew large with surprise. He turned on his heel and began to march back the way he'd come, but he stopped after ten yards when a pair of uniformed *flics* arrowed in toward him. Hugo was close behind, and when Drummond turned to his left looking for another escape route, Hugo called out.

"Rob Drummond, stay still! Do not move!"

Drummond's body did remain still, but his head was on a swivel trying to spot a way out. Hugo sped up and in a moment was on him, a strong hand on Drummond's shoulder, spinning him and putting them face-to-face. Hugo reached up and pulled the mustache off Drummond's upper lip, and the big man cried out, either from the sting of that or the surprise of Marchand putting a hand on him, too. Drummond stiffened as if squaring himself for a fight.

"Rob, please don't do anything stupid," Hugo said. "This place is crawling with cops all looking for you, so even if you get away from us . . ."

"I'm not . . . My name isn't Rob Drummond," he said weakly, but from the look in his eye, Hugo knew that he was abandoning any pretense, forgoing the farcical defense of, *He must be my doppelganger.*

"What did he say?" Marchand asked. He pulled a set of handcuffs from a clip on his belt.

"Nothing," Hugo said. "He won't resist. You know it's over, right, Rob?"

Drummond's head dropped, and he stared at the ground as four more *flics* ran over to where they were, surrounding them and at the same time ushering the slowly gathering crowd away. Hugo spotted Paul Jameson making his way toward them, and smiled. He should've known Lerens would put her best man on this job.

"Hugo, all ok?" Jameson asked. He nodded a greeting at Marchand.

"It is now." Hugo gestured to Drummond's bag. "Can you have someone take possession of his belongings? Treat everything as evidence, not inventory."

"Aye, will do it myself, sir."

"Thank you." Hugo let Marchand know what he'd asked of the Scotsman, and Marchand nodded but gave Hugo a look that seemed to suggest the American shouldn't be giving orders.

"We'll take him straight for questioning," Marchand said, a hand on Drummond's cuffed wrists. "Assuming he'll want to cooperate."

"I'll have to notify the ambassador, since he's a US citizen," Hugo said. "He may want to send legal counsel to the prefecture."

"Fine by me," Marchand said. "And you should call the British Embassy, too, since he's a UK citizen. With any luck, they'll get into a turf war and give us a few moments alone with him."

Rob Drummond sat slouched in the chair, and he barely looked up as Hugo entered the interview room and sat across the steel table from him. A red mark spread across Drummond's lip from where the fake mustache had irritated it, or, more likely, from Hugo's ripping it off. Drummond's sat with his elbows resting on the table, and his wrists shackled to a metal rail atop the table.

Hugo turned to the jailer who'd let him in. "Can we take the cuffs off him? He didn't run when he had the chance, so he's not going to now."

The jailer looked uncertain for a moment, then said, "*Oui, monsieur.*"

His wrists free, Drummond rubbed them and mumbled a thank you to Hugo. Then he glanced up and asked, "Can I get some water or something?"

Hugo nodded. "I think Lieutenant Intern Marchand is bringing you a bottle."

"He's the French guy, the main detective?"

"He is."

"Why isn't he here already?"

"He's putting a couple pieces of the puzzle together, at my request."

Behind Hugo, the door opened and Marchand appeared with a

bottle of Évian in his hand. He stopped short when he saw that Drummond's hands were free but handed him the bottle before sitting beside Hugo.

"*Merci*," Drummond said. He unscrewed the cap and gulped a third of the water. He then put the cap back on and placed the bottle on the table. He stared at it, as if afraid to lift his eyes to his interrogators.

"You understand this interview is being recorded, right?" Hugo said.

"Yes."

"And you have been told what your rights are."

"I have."

"Mind if I ask you some questions, then?"

"Sure," Drummond said sulkily. "Ask what you like. Doesn't mean I'm going to answer."

"True. Thing is, this isn't the usual situation where you're a suspect and we're trying to find out if you did it. We know you killed Alia Alsaffar, so the only question left is what happens to you."

"You don't know anything, because I didn't kill her."

"Oh, come on now." Hugo sat back. "You can't possibly expect me to swallow that."

"I didn't," Drummond insisted.

"Right. You were just fleeing the country under an alternative passport, and wearing a fake mustache, for giggles."

"I owe some people some money is all."

"Oh, I don't doubt that, so let's talk about it. You're prepared to admit you have a gambling problem, right?"

"I guess."

"I mean, who else, what other American, would go to the sunflower bar, an obvious gambling den, unless they had a problem?"

Drummond looked up. "How did you know that's what it is?"

"I went there. Jesus, Rob, this isn't rocket science, and you're not a very sophisticated criminal."

"I'm not a criminal at all; I didn't do anything."

"You gambled at the sunflower bar, and lost all your money, right?"

Drummond didn't respond, so Hugo went on. "That's why you got beat up—you couldn't pay your debt to whoever you'd been betting with."

"No, they robbed me."

"Problem is, your gambling addiction runs a lot deeper than a few hundred euros in a Montmartre bar."

"Meaning?"

"Well, your stepfather was a jerk, and you killed him in self-defense. Right?"

"That's right, so what?"

"We got some information from the executor of his estate that indicated he left you more than four hundred thousand pounds in his will."

Drummond's eyes widened, but he didn't say anything. Hugo glanced at Marchand, who said quietly, "I am understanding things so far. Go on."

Hugo did. "So I got to wondering. Why were you in Paris? Why were you staying in a flea pit of a hotel miles from the tourist areas? More specifically, why would someone who has a phobia about germs stay in a place like that? Simple answer is you had no money. And why else would you go to a run-down, filthy bar known for gambling if the idea of just touching a fingerprint pad grossed you out? Not because you wanted to, but because you needed to. And then I wondered, well, how did you manage to live in London, in one of the most expensive cities in the world, with no money?"

"What did you come up with?" Drummond asked, his tone still petulant.

"I came up with your stepsister's flat."

Drummond's eyes closed, and after a moment or two his shoulder sagged, which told Hugo he'd hit the mark. A quick glance to Marchand showed that the French detective was still understanding, and was as captivated as their prisoner.

Hugo went on. "You've been living there as John Smith, right? I'd guess you were late on payments to your sister, who had no idea you and Smith are the same person. Him being a hermit and all, refusing to meet in person. Of course, in reality there was a good reason for that."

Drummond's breathing deepened, and a film of sweat covered his brow, but he stayed quiet.

"Rob, this stuff is really, *really* easy to prove. A lease agreement here, a neighbor seeing you there."

"It's not a crime," Drummond said suddenly. "Well, it's not murder. If I did that, it doesn't prove anything."

"Oh, come on now, Rob. That's not all we have." Hugo turned to Marchand and spoke in French. "Did you hear anything from my embassy?"

Marchand looked directly at Drummond as he replied. "*Oui.* It's as you thought. On both subjects." He smiled at Hugo. "And here's your apartment key back."

"Thank you for checking on those so fast."

"What's going on?" Drummond asked, confusion on his face.

"Turns out your John Smith passport showed up in America last year," Hugo said to Drummond. "Why?"

A pause. "Business."

"What business is that?"

"I forget what exactly. I do a lot of things."

"Like trying to run down your sister in a rental car that you switched the plates on?"

"What? No!"

"No? You sure? What I'm sure about is that when we go through your belongings at the hotel, we'll find a key. A key to the padlock on your sister's chest that's in Josh Reno's room, right?"

"I don't know what you mean."

"How'd you manage that?" Hugo pushed him. "Swipe a key from the cleaner's cart?"

"I wouldn't—"

"We also have your prints from the room where Alia was killed. Remember, Rob, that room wasn't open to people yet, so you're gonna have to come up with an explanation if you keep up this nonsense about being innocent."

"But . . . but . . . I didn't give the police my prints."

"That's right, you didn't." Hugo smiled. "You gave them to *me*, when you kindly held that Coke bottle for a moment outside the Dalí museum."

Drummond shook his head in disappointment, but Hugo couldn't tell whether it was at himself for falling for the trick, or at Hugo for being sneaky.

Hugo continued: "And speaking of prints, I'm sure you wiped down the photos and the envelope you left on my doorstep, but so many amateur criminals make the same mistake. When they open the envelope, they leave a thumbprint inside. Think we'll find one?"

Drummond visibly paled. "Photos?"

"Yeah, thanks for that. They helped me rule out JD and Rachel Rollo. A clumsy attempt to implicate both of them that had the opposite effect."

"Explain that to me," Marchand said.

"The picture suggested, very vaguely I have to say, a relationship between JD and Alia. That gives him a motive, for leaving him; and Rachel one: jealousy. That being the case, JD wouldn't leave them for me, and neither would she. Which left me with Reno and Rob. Very helpful, like I said."

"It must have been Reno," Drummond said, surly again.

Hugo sighed. "You're not helping yourself here, so let me explain how this works. When we find bad things out about you, have to collect all the evidence ourselves, we put it in a stack, and eventually that stack will collapse on you and bury you. Maybe forever. And in a French prison. Now, I don't think you speak French very well, and I certainly don't think you want to be the pasty American who gets a life sentence and has to learn from scratch from a xenophobic cellmate. Do you?"

"I don't know what you're talking about."

"If, on the other hand, you cooperate, and tell us what happened, things can be made much better for you. For example, we're not there yet, but I'm betting the car that drove at Alia in Washington, DC, was rented to, or can be connected to, someone called John Smith. Now, we can go to the trouble of getting all that paperwork, doing the legwork, sure. But if you tell us what happened, Rob, I promise it'll go easier on you."

Drummond looked back and forth between them. "Easier, how?"

"Maybe you can go home, to America. You're going to have to face the consequence of your actions, but right now, and only for a short time, you have some leverage. A modern US prison instead of an eighteenth-century French one." Hugo held up his hands. "Now, I'm not promising anything here and now; I can't. But I can assure you that we know the truth, and we'll dig up the details. Being honest now can't possibly bury you any deeper than you are." Hugo softened his tone, and reached over to Drummond, putting a hand on his forearm. "Rob. You're not a psychopath. You're not some natural-born killer. I have seen evil people, and you're not one of them."

"I'm not, I'm really not." Drummond's head dropped and his whole body started shaking.

"I know that," Hugo said. "I know that for a fact. But you have to tell me what happened, and why it happened. Rob, I don't want to see you locked up here, but I truly can't help you if you don't help yourself."

Drummond raised his head slowly and looked Hugo in the eye. "I don't even know why. Why I did it."

"You do, Rob," Hugo said, his voice almost a whisper. "Tell me what happened."

"You were right, I do have a problem." Drummond's voice turned plaintive. "But it's not my fault, addiction is a disease, it really is. Anyway, you were right about me spending all the money my father left me. And using Alia's apartment without her knowing. But she wouldn't have minded, I'm sure of that."

"Is that why you broke into Josh Reno's room?"

Drummond nodded, then he said, "Yes. I figured she had the paperwork with her, since she was going to go from here to London."

Marchand looked confused, so Hugo took a moment to explain in French. He added, "Reno told me nothing was missing, but he must not have known about the apartment, the papers for that. He looked for material items that might have been taken." He turned back to Drummond. "When did you legally change your name in England?"

"About two years ago. With dual citizenship, I realized I could be two people, use two different passports to get a second identity. To be Rob, and also be someone completely different."

"John Smith."

"Yes. Once I had my English passport, it was so easy to change my name by deed poll. That's what they call it, the name change."

"You chose that name because it's so common, right?"

"Right." As so often happened, in Hugo's experience, once that desire to talk, to confess, had been tapped, the words flowed like water. "I knew it'd be easier to hide with a common name like that, knew it'd be harder for people that I owed money to find me."

"Did you get that from the book you were reading at the coat-check counter?"

"*The Paper Trip*, yes, that was one of the things it taught me."

"Rob, tell us what happened. That night at the museum."

Drummond took a deep breath and sat back, his head bowed so that his chin almost touched his chest. "It wasn't premeditated, you have to believe me. I even offered to help with the coat checking. I admit, I did it mostly to get in her good graces because I wanted her help. Needed it."

"Her help with what?" Marchand interjected.

"Money." Drummond's head snapped up. "I mean, come on, for Christ's sake. She'd hit it big with that show. She was about to get a London exhibition, and you know what it's like, how it works. Once you're famous, your shit sells for thousands, millions even. And she had that apartment in London, that's worth a million, at least. More."

"And you wanted a share," Hugo said.

"I wanted *my* share. It was my father's after all, not hers. Why did she get the fancy apartment, when all I got was some cash?"

"Four hundred thousand is a lot of money," Hugo said.

"It's not a fucking million-dollar flat, though, is it?" Drummond said, his face reddening with anger. "Why should she have that, and not let me stay there while I'm down on my luck? Especially when she's about to hit the big-time with her stupid art."

"Is that how you put it to her?" Hugo inquired.

"No, of course not. And, look, don't get me wrong, I don't begrudge her the success she had. I mean, I don't get it, I'd never pay for her sculptures no matter how rich I was, but if other people want to, good for them." He sighed heavily. "Anyway, I took her to one side, she seemed happy, and I thought maybe she'd be in a generous mood. She wasn't. She got annoyed that I was bugging her at her opening. Then she asked me about the money, where it'd gone, and you should've seen how condescending she was. Jesus, I was opening up to her, telling her about my problems, and she just acted like I was an idiot, like it was my fault and nothing to do with her. And, yeah, I know you think it wasn't her business to look after me that way, but when a family member asks for help, you give it. You fucking give it. And all she did was stand there and act like I was a disgrace. A loser."

"Is that what she said?" Hugo asked gently.

"She didn't need to. It was written all over that perfect fucking face. And I just snapped. I lost it. I wanted to shake her pristine world, make her see things from my perspective. Just fucking *see* me, you know?"

"So you hit her," Hugo said.

"I took the globe from her hand, someone had left it in there and she was irritated because it wasn't supposed to be in there. It wasn't a part of her precious display." He shook his head. "It shouldn't even have been in there."

"And when she fell, you put your hands around her neck."

"Just for a minute. To make her . . ." His voice fell away. "The next thing I knew, she wasn't breathing."

"What did you do then?"

"I left her there. Honestly, I couldn't believe no one had come in, no one had heard anything. I was shocked. I even thought about calling for help, I really did, but I knew no one would believe it was an accident. And then I realized that if she was dead, the apartment would be mine. Her sculptures, too. It just came to me in that room, that there was nothing I could do to help her, to save her, and if I called for help, I'd get blamed and go to jail. But if I walked away, just turned and walked up the stairs and threw away the globe, my life would be saved. I mean, literally saved."

"Literally?" Hugo asked, not hiding the skepticism in his voice.

"You don't know the people I owed money to. You think you do, but you don't. So, yeah, saved."

"What else did you take from Reno's room?" Hugo asked.

"Nothing."

"Yes, you did. We'll find it, Rob, so it won't help if you start lying again." Hugo waited, but Drummond said nothing. "Her will, right?"

Drummond nodded.

"Where is it?" Hugo tapped the top of the metal table to get his attention. "Rob, you're not getting anything of hers—not her money, not her art, and not her flat. What happened to the will?"

"I tore it up and threw the pieces away. She had changed it. Recently. She felt bad about Josh, so she wanted the apartment sold and a third of the proceeds to go to him."

"I figured it was something like that." Hugo turned to Marchand. "Any questions you want me to ask for you?"

"No," Marchand said in English. "I think we have everything we need. I will have someone take him to his . . . *Comment ça s'appelle*? *Son cellule . . .*"

"His cell," Hugo said.

"Wait," Drummond said. "That *was* me in DC. I tried to run her over there."

"We know," Hugo said.

"Yes, but I'm admitting it. I should go to an American jail, right? For that?"

"Eventually, yes. For attempted murder."

"No, I mean now. Please, Mr. Marston, like you said, I don't want to go to prison here. I can't speak their language, I'll be alone and isolated. I'll die here."

"I'll do what I can," Hugo said. "You told us the truth, that will help."

"Tell them, the judge or whoever decides, that I didn't mean to kill her. It was the anger, the resentment, there was nothing I could do about it. And also . . ." He fell silent.

"And also what?" Hugo prompted.

"This sounds terrible," Drummond said in a whisper. "But I think part of the reason I was able to do it was because of my father."

"Your father? What do you mean?"

"I killed him, remember? And killing Alia . . ." He shrugged his big shoulders. "I don't know. It was easier the second time around, just like they say it is."

CHAPTER THIRTY-THREE

Hugo and Tom sat on a bench in the Luxembourg Gardens, both wearing long wool coats, hats, and fur-lined leather gloves. Their feet had left trails in the dusting of snow that covered the gravel pathway.

"Feel good to be alive?" Hugo asked after a while.

"Yeah. My ass is getting cold, but even that feels good." Tom shifted. "Hey, man. I need to say something."

"I'm listening."

"The Cofers are assholes who deserved to die. They killed my sister, so there's no doubt in my mind that they deserved to die. But the thing is . . ."

"Are you saying you regret shooting Cofer in Houston?"

"Fuck no!" Tom looked at Hugo, surprise on his face. "You think I feel bad about that?"

"It crossed my mind that you might recognize the extrajudicial nature that—"

"Shut up, Hugo, you sound like a lawyer. And let me be real fucking clear, I do not regret killing that bastard one little bit." The anger dropped from his voice. "What I'm trying to say is, I'm sorry for putting you in a position where you had to . . . compromise yourself. Back there and, eventually, here."

"I appreciate that, but I chose—"

"Dude, in Houston you had two choices, both shitty, and that was my fault. All my fault. I'd say nothing like that will ever happen again, but that's not a promise I can keep. I *can* promise that I'll do my best never to put you in that situation again."

"Good enough." Hugo felt the tips of his toes start to tingle with the cold, but Tom was right, it did feel good to be out there, with the crisp air and the laughter of a nearby group of kids trying to gather enough snow to make snowballs. He felt a stab of sadness that Alia and Ryan were gone for good, that he'd never see them again, but then he turned his mind back to the moment, the weak but warming sun and the knowledge that his best friend was alive, well, and not chasing a murderer.

"So, you're quite the knight in shining armor, I guess," Tom said.

"What do you mean?"

"Saving Claudia from the guillotine with the DNA trick."

"It wasn't a trick, Tom, is was solid, logical reasoning. And the guillotine, really?"

Tom chuckled and shook his head. "You're such an idiot."

"Why?"

"Many reasons, but this time it's because your adherence to logic and reason can be blinding."

"Well, I'm sorry if—"

"Not to me, to you."

"Not following," Hugo said.

"You need to think how other people think. I don't mean when you're off hunting killers—you manage to do it just fine then. Which, if you think about it, is pretty fucking creepy. But I'm talking about Claudia."

"I need to think like her?"

"You need to know how she's thinking. Dude, look. You think I'm being dramatic because I said you saved her from the guillotine, and you think that because they don't use it anymore. Well, congratulations for knowing what everyone else knows." Tom turned toward him. "What you need to understand is that Claudia feels exactly like you've saved her from losing her head. To you, it's a puzzle solved; you minimize the impact because . . . well, because you're Hugo. But you saved her. Maybe from a trial, maybe from a murder conviction. Maybe even from getting shivved in prison. But you did that, and even if you're going to be a dolt and not give yourself credit, you need to understand that she *is* giving you credit. And if you ever want to be with her, be with all of her all of the time, you need to stop holding back, to give up some of yourself and really start thinking like her, not just thinking *of* her."

Hugo sat quietly for a moment. "Getting shot by Rick Cofer turned you into quite the philosopher-cum-psychologist, huh?"

"Maybe it did." Tom blew out a breath, a puff that disappeared in a moment. "But you're not going to be here forever. You've had a good ride in Paris; but, who knows, one day maybe we'll get a moron of a president who doesn't believe in international relations and shuts down all our embassies to stop moochers like you from suckling off the government teat."

"The world will always need diplomats," Hugo said.

"Yeah, in theory. But what if you get fired, get moved on—or what if Claudia finds a man who'll commit?"

"Tom, come on. It's her not wanting to commit, not me!"

"You've had that conversation?"

"We've tried, yes."

"And I bet every time you've tried, someone's called your phone, or you've been summoned by Taylor, or . . . some damn thing has come up."

"Usually you," Hugo said.

"Yeah, well, you saved my life too, I guess, so now focus on her." Tom was quiet for a moment. "I'm sorry about Ryan, too."

"He was different, Tom. Too good for this sordid world we inhabit."

Tom smiled. "I'd never admit this in front of any other human being . . . but that's how I feel about you."

"Me?" Hugo was surprised. "No, Ryan was—"

"Look, don't compare yourself. And don't beat yourself up."

"I won't," Hugo said. "I expect I'll find a nice compartment for him, somewhere in the recesses of my mind, somewhere I can access from time to time to remember him."

"How many compartments do you think people like us have?"

"It's the only way we can keep going," Hugo said. "Without sorting them out, putting them away . . ."

"Oh, I know. Mine are not so much compartments as walled gardens, filled with monsters roaming around, gnashing their teeth."

"Sounds dangerous."

"It's only dangerous if they get out," Tom said, his voice quiet.

Hugo turned to him. "Speaking of dangerous, we never talked about the bullet you left in the .32 that Cofer went for."

"Nope, we sure didn't."

"Mind telling me what that was about?"

Tom held his eye for a moment. "Well, then. It occurred to me that you'd be in greater danger, from your delicate conscience, if you shot an unarmed man than you were from actually being beaten to the trigger by that asshole."

"Quite the risk you had me take."

"Nonsense. Fastest gun in the West, you are. Best shot in the academy and cool as a cucumber under pressure. I never had any doubt you'd fire first, and I knew you wouldn't miss. Especially at that range." Tom pushed himself to his feet with a groan. "Come on, Wyatt Earp, I'm cold."

"Were are you going?"

"To buy you a hot chocolate."

"You know, that sounds good. Really good."

"They serve it in bowls here," Tom said. "Did you know that?"

"No, Tom." He rolled his eyes, even though his friend had already started walking away. "I've been eating and drinking in Paris's cafés for five years; how would I possibly know something like that?"

"You don't have to be a sarcastic dick about it," Tom called over his shoulder.

Hugo smiled as he followed his friend along the pathway toward the park's exit, and he slipped off a glove so he could dial Claudia. He'd been planning on asking her to dinner, and still would.

But maybe she'd like some hot chocolate, first, he thought.

ACKNOWLEDGMENTS

To all the wonderful friends who allow/request/cajole me into using their names in the book, I hope you have as much fun with it as I do! Thanks for playing.

To my family, who, as always, puts up with my disappearances to the library and coffee shops to write, thank you for filling in the gaps and doing the chores I would otherwise love to do.

To the wonderful folks at my two favorite libraries. First, to Eric, Linda, Lyssa, and company at the Will Hampton Library at Oak Hill, who manage to show interest in whatever I'm working on while giving me the space to get on with it. And to my new friends at the Laura Bush Library in Bee Caves. You've created a haven for me, with peace, quiet, and beautiful views of the hill country. And you're open on Sundays, bless you for that!

My thanks as ever to the folks at Seventh Street Books: editor extraordinaire Dan Mayer, the wonderful Jill Maxick, fixer and font of all wisdom; editor-*cum*-genius Jade Zora Scibilia, publicist Jake Bonar, and the magnificent cover artist, Nicole Sommer-Lecht. And always a huge thank you to my agent, Ann Collette, who survived a move to Texas just to be closer to me and continue to guide my career . . . right?!

Finally, to a friend too-soon departed. My thanks to Philip Kerr, who was more of an inspiration than he knows, and a better friend than he realized. See you on the flip side, matey.

ABOUT THE AUTHOR

Mark Pryor is the author of *The Bookseller*, *The Crypt Thief*, *The Blood Promise*, *The Button Man*, *The Reluctant Matador*, *The Paris Librarian*, and *The Sorbonne Affair*—the first seven Hugo Marston novels—as well as *Hollow Man* and *Dominic: A Hollow Man Novel*. He has also published the true-crime book *As She Lay Sleeping*. A native of Hertfordshire, England, he is an assistant district attorney in Austin, Texas, where he lives with his wife and three children.